small cruelties

- stories -

jude davison

Also by Jude Davison

BOOKS

Cripples & Creeps – stories and a poem
Uncertain Heaven
Cybersoul
The Underwater Birds
A Writer's Prerogative

ALBUMS

Back to the Wonderful
Strange Fruit
Neurotic Erotica
God's Big Radio
Angels in the Slipstream
Blue Martian Dusk
Lizard Man
Highway Blues
Ordinary Dream
Bread & Bones
Circo de Teatro
Outskirts of Eden
Head Bone Gumbo
Cybersoul

small cruelties

- stories -

Copyright © 2024 Jude Davison

www.judedavison.co.uk

All rights reserved. This book is copyright material and must not be copied, reproduced, transferred, distributed. Leased, licensed or publicly performed or used in any way except as specifically permitted in writing by the publisher, as allowed under the terms and conditions under which it was purchased or as strictly permitted by applicable copyright law. Any unauthorized distribution or use of this text may be a direct infringement of the author's and publisher's rights, and those responsible may be liable in law accordingly.

ISBN: 9798332035319

Cover Design & Artwork: Jude Davison

Published by Pigeon Moods Music

www.judedavison.co.uk

For Thea, Claire & Nancy...

*'What if God was one of us
Just a slob like one of us'*

-   *Joan Osborne*

Forward

The majority of these stories were written between January and June 2024.

In 2023 I started writing a novel but found my writing to be disjointed and difficult. It was a very challenging year as it involved some significant life changes - namely, selling and buying a home; moving from the south to the north of England; the death of my mother; and finally, retirement from working for the NHS. However, there are three story lines that have been salvaged from the novel that appear as short stories here (*Root Canal, Body & Soul,* and *Shotgun Superstar*).

There are a few other pieces that date from previous times (*Ice, The River,* and *Curtain Call*), which I decided to include as I felt they fit in with the collection's overarching theme. It has been invigorating and fun to return, once again, to the artform and immediacy of the short story. I hope you enjoy this collection.

Contents

1.	Little Wing	1
2.	Beg Borrow or Steal	12
3.	The Brotherhood of the Beard	19
4.	First Foot	40
5.	A Bull Called Gringo	45
6.	The Unexpected Robin	66
7.	Root Canal	74
8.	Body & Soul	86
9.	Shotgun Superstar	114
10.	George and the Dragon	132
11.	Silloth Sunset	145
12.	Ice	150
13.	The Questionnaire	167
14.	The River	176
15.	Obituary	182
16.	A Wish	196
17.	Electric Chair	204
18.	Old Vinyl	215
19.	Lazarus Sky	218
20.	A Future Unwritten	225
21.	A Decent Rack of Balls	241
22.	Curtain Call	256
23.	Purgatory Street	294
24.	The Great Dawn of Perfection	311

Little Wing

Alex had his head down on the desk at the nursing station, just trying to grab a few moments of peace and quiet when Emily tapped him on the shoulder.

'You checked on Mr. McDonald yet?'

'Oh shit,' said Alex snapping back into reality, 'I'm on it,' he said, as he picked himself up, quickly strode down the corridor into room 210 and gently pulled back the curtain. The old man lying on the hospital bed slowly turned to look at this new intruder.

'Who the hell are you? Where's the nurse? Where's Emily?'

'It's okay,' said Alex, reassuringly, 'I'm a nurse too, just helping Emily out. How are you feeling tonight?'

'Feeling? I feel like crap – where's Emily, why isn't she here?'

'She's on a break. Listen, I need to take your vital signs, blood pressure and then your temperature, are you okay with a thermometer in your ear, otherwise we'll have to look at other options.'

'Other options? Like what?' said Tom, Alex gave him a knowing look.

'There are several different ways we can take your temperature.'

'Listen, I may be old and helpless, but you aren't going anywhere near my arse, not now, not never.'

'Okay, fair deal,' laughed Alex, 'so on a scale of one-to-ten, how's your pain this evening?'

'Ten,' said the patient, gruffly.

'Ten?' questioned Alex, 'that's pretty serious, you been feeling like that for long?' Tom nodded.

'You know, this dying thing, it doesn't really bother me none. I've lived my God damn life, but I sure as hell never expected this pain bullshit.'

'Well, we can help you with that,' said Alex, 'it's what we're here to do, keep everyone comfortable.' Alex looked over the patient chart and noted the PRN morphine prescribed.

'Looks like we might need to up your painkillers some, why don't I get that started.'

'You know,' said Tom, 'I always wondered about heroin. I was always curious. All the drugs them musicians did for fun back in the sixties. You ever heard of the sixties, kid? That was when music was worthy.'

'Well now, Tom, you certainly got my attention. Drugs? The sixties? Calling a forty-year-old, *kid*. So, tell me are you a Beatles or Stones fan?'

'Dumb question. The Stones had it in spades. Rock 'n roll ain't supposed to be about pretty songs, concept albums; it's about swagger and attitude. You ever done rebellion, kid?'

'Why sure,' smiled Alex, readying the IV port for another dose of morphine, 'I've cheated on my taxes and everything, but you seem to know quite a bit about this stuff are you a music aficionado, Tom?' The old man turned his head to get a better look at Alex.

'You know, I used to hang out with the likes of Keith and Mick, as it so happens.'

'Really? No kidding – you're full of surprises. How'd you manage to do that?'

'I was a booking agent. Worked the international scene, mostly. Bringing acts back and forth across the Atlantic. I don't suppose you ever heard of Motown. Berry Gordy?'

'Well, sure – who hasn't.'

'I booked all his acts on package tours of England. It was big business back in the day, a regular American invasion. The Beatles, Stones, Kinks, all them guys opened for the American acts up and down the country before they got famous. Jagger used to always be hitting on me for a few quid. He was a cheeky little imp, still owes me, too.' Tom grimaced a little as he tried to make himself comfortable.

'Well, who would have known?' smiled Alex, 'one of the things I love most about this job is all the interesting people you get to meet. You really were a player, huh?'

'So, you got any heroin?' asked Tom.

'You're serious – heroin.'

'Yeah, I'd say it's a step up from what you're drip feeding me now. And I figure it's the one thing I got left to do, if I want to understand Hendrix before I die.'

'I'd say there was a lot more to Hendrix than just the drugs he did,' mused Alex, 'he was tapping into something transcendent when he played, there was no precedent for where that music came from. My dad had all his records.'

'Mercurial. That's what my mate Steve Jeffery called him,' said Tom, 'he would have known too, he was road manager for the band. He said that managing Hendrix was like trying to bottle lightning,' Tom chuckled to himself as the extra morphine began to make its way into his bloodstream.

'Mercury,' mused Alex, 'the planet of fire.'

'Hendrix burnt bright then burned out,' said Tom, 'I'm sure that's why some of them musicians made friends with heroin. For the comfort and solace, it brought.'

'I'm from Glasgow originally,' said Alex, 'I've seen what heroin can do - it's nasty, a real scary drug.'

'Well, here's the thing, kid, it isn't scary if you ain't got nothing to lose. Not if you're already knocking on death's door.' Alex let Tom's words sink in.

'Look at me,' said Tom, a quiet resignation replacing his gruffness, 'I used to be quite a man in my day, just like you. Back then I never touched drugs. But now . . .' Toms' voice trailed off and he closed his eyes, 'now, I just want to have some say in how things go down at the finish line.'

'Hmm,' said Alex, 'I see your point, and if I'm being honest, I don't disagree. I've worked on palliative wards long enough to know everyone deserves a little dignity at the end of the road.'

'Well now, finally someone seeing things from my point of view – hallelujah.'

'Do you have family?' asked Alex. Tom shrugged.

'I did have, but you know I squandered all of that years ago, made the kind of regretful decisions many men make. I don't blame anyone but myself, but to answer your question – no, I don't think there will be anyone queuing up to make amends with me.'

'Well, here's something you should know,' said Alex, stepping closer and lowering his voice, 'we don't prescribe heroin these days, it's fentanyl - that does pretty much the same thing.'

'Will it rid me of this goddam pain, take me to nirvana to meet Hendrix?'

'With the right dose, I guarantee you'd never experience pain ever again – is that what you really want, Tom?' The old man closed his eyes and leaned back into his pillow.

'Satisfaction, simple as that – Jagger wanted some, and so do I. You know, I can still remember Keith playing that riff to me on the tour bus not long after he'd written it.'

Alex had a few days off and decided to drive to Brighton for a complete change of scene. He figured the sea air, the wide selection of pubs and lively nightlife would recharge his batteries, and help erase, for little while at least, some of the sadness that comes with nursing the dying. After a blustery stroll along the pebbled beaches and visit to the pier he opted for a bite to eat. Taking a seat in a quiet corner of the Queen's Arms Pub he ordered himself a pint and watched the flamboyant people as they came and went. Despite his best-efforts, and the strong ale, he couldn't stop thinking about Tom McDonald back in the Royal Infirmary, lying in that bed, wanting nothing more than to be done with his life. He pulled out his phone and dialled work. Emily answered.

'Hi Emily, it's me, Alex.'

'Oh, hi Al, I thought you were having a few days off, is everything okay?'

'Yeah, everything's fine, I'm just down here in Brighton. Listen, I was wondering about Tom McDonald, the patient in 210 – how's he doing? Is he still with us?'

'He sure is, still grumpy, still complaining, but otherwise still breathing. Why?'

'Oh, nothing really. I was just about to head to a record store, there's a few vintage vinyl shops here that are really great - see if they have any Jimi Hendrix.'

'Okay, you have fun now, anything you want me to pass on for you?'

'Nah, that's alright, I'll be back on Monday – thanks Em, have a good weekend – bye.'

On Monday Alex arrived for his shift at work and, after the usual morning handovers and drug rounds, headed to room 210.

'Morning Tom, still here I see. How are you doing today?' The weary patient looked over at Alex with a resignation that immediately registered.

'Shit, I feel like utter shit,' said Tom, 'I'm supposed to be dying, but the problem seems to be I ain't dead yet. Bit of an inconvenience, if you see what I mean?' Alex knew this process all too well, there were the people who came into end-of-life care and passed away effortlessly, quickly and without fanfare. Then there were the others whose bodies, constitutions, seemed to keep things going longer than the advertised shelf life. These were the tricky ones, the ones that gave Alex and the other nursing staff the sleepless nights. A month into his hospital stay and Tom McDonald's life had descended into a daily mixture of feeding tubes, enemas, IV meds, incontinence, blood tests and scans, and pain – constant, draining, pain.

'I brought this with me,' said Alex, pulling out a cassette tape of Jimi Hendrix's *Axis: Bold as Love* album from his pocket. 'Thought maybe you'd enjoy revisiting the good old days when music was worthy.' The old man craned his neck around to get a look at the familiar artwork.

'Most people think of *Purple Haze* when they think of Hendrix, but for me it's *Little Wing* –
now that is a real piece of sixties' artistry. Sure would love to hear that tune again.'

'Side one,' said Alex, waving the cassette, 'we have a little tape player we keep in the staff room, let me go grab it and we'll get that sorted.' When he returned Tom had closed his eyes, but he could see the fresh tracks of tears that had run down Tom's cheeks. Alex pulled up a chair, sat down and instinctively took hold of the old man's hand.

'Tom, you okay?' He opened his eyes.

'I never told anyone I was gay,' said Tom, quietly.

'What?'

Tom turned his head to face Alex. 'I never had the courage to live my life the way I wanted to. I never came out. That's my one big regret.'

'It's a hard thing – coming out. I get it. I've known lots of gay people who haven't done it for similar reasons.'

'I met him in Corfu,' said Tom, searching the ceiling for an image, 'he was a beautiful man, a beautiful human being. We spent a whole summer together. I was twenty-one and he was nineteen. I was on a break from university, miles away from my suburban life back in Surrey. We swam in the ocean; sunbathed naked together on sun-kissed rocks; bought fresh fish in the local markets; and cooked together, ate, and drank retsina. It was a marvellous time. I fell in love with a gorgeous Greek boy, but when I returned home, I couldn't tell a soul. I was ashamed of who I was - the feelings I couldn't control. For the rest of my life, I shut them all out.'

'That's quite the story,' said Alex, 'and a real

burden to carry all this time. Did you ever see each other again?'

'No. We wrote a few letters, exchanged photographs, then over time, we just kinda lost touch.'

'At least you have those memories,' said Alex.

'Sometimes I think I've squandered my entire life, because I never had the courage to be who I really am. Memories are nice, kid, but they don't keep you warm at night, do they?'

'I don't suppose they do,' said Alex.

'Now here I am, an old man, full of regrets, dying but not dead yet. Shit, I can't even seem to get that right and having to confess to my nurse . . . It's just pitiful.' Alex stroked Tom's hand.

'C'mon, let's get some Hendrix on. *Little Wing*, you say . . .'

Three days later and Alex was working the night shift. Once he'd checked all his other patients and assured himself that it was going to be a relatively quiet night, he stopped in to see how Tom was doing.

'Evening Tom, how are you tonight?'

'Well, if it isn't Saint Alex,' smiled Tom.

'Saint Alex? How so?'

'Well, I've decided you deserve a sainthood for listening to the confessions of an old man... that, and for recognising the divinity that is Jimi. That album is sublime.'

'Fair enough.' Alex stepped towards the bed, sat down and put his hand on Tom's arm.

'You know you were asking me about heroin? About finishing things on your own terms?' The old man turned his weary head to look Alex in the eyes.

'You got my attention, kid, go on.'

'I do need to ask you if you are sure, if you still would want to go through with things, if we could pull something like that off – the two of us.' Tom didn't even flinch.

'I haven't changed my mind one bit. Tonight is a good night to die.'

'Robbie Robertson?' said Alex. Tom nodded.

'One of the best damn guitarists of his time, he even made Dylan sound good,' smiled Tom.

'You like Dylan?'

'I like what he stood for more than the music he made. That and the fact that he turned the Beatles onto weed.'

'Thought you didn't like the Beatles?'

'I never said I didn't like them. I think I said I prefer the Stones. But after they discovered pot, the Beatles' music improved immeasurably. *Revolver* is a revelation.'

'You know Tom, reason I got into nursing in the first place was because of a good friend of mine. Sadly, he died of AIDs, it was tragic - a beautiful life cut short. Thing is, we all have our own path to walk in life. He had his, I have mine, and you . . .you've had quite a journey and what you are about to do, that's a mighty big path too. A big decision. Look, if you want to, we can pause right here, right now, and rethink this thing.

Maybe another night would be better? Maybe you got some things you want to reflect on?' Tom turned his head and looked at Alex.

'I've thought about things, long and hard, all my life. I'm finished with regrets, and this is my one chance to never have another. So, I think you should hurry along now and go and get that little tape player of yours, and if I could hear Jimi singing *Little Wing* just once more then, I think, maybe I could just fly away and never come back. Do we have ourselves a plan?' Alex gently squeezed Tom's hand, took the Hendrix cassette out from his pocket, and placed it on the bed next to him.

'I'll be right back.'

Beg Borrow or Steal

Wayne Cummings gently pulled at the corner of the tatty, sun-bleached curtains so that he could see outside into the busy lot where his vintage Chevy Malibu was parked. It was another typically hot night in LA and the Valley Motel 6 was booked solid with the usual travellers, businessmen and other miscreants, all keen to keep a low profile. The air con unit was rattling away as it worked overtime to keep the small space a liveable temperature, but the room still felt oppressive with the tireless heat and humidity.

'God-damn schmucks,' growled Wayne, 'don't even know how to park. That's a 70's classic, pal,' said Wayne, stabbing at the window, 'not a single scratch on that baby.' Then he pushed back the curtain in disgust and walked back to the bed.

'Oh honey, he didn't hit ya, did he?' said Deborah, 'why don't you relax, you're all on edge, it ain't good for your ticker, ya know.' The forty-something woman aimlessly flicked through the channels looking for something to relieve her boredom. 'I got a bottle of vodka in my bag, maybe you could use a drink?'

'The shopping channel, huh?' said Wayne, staring at the glossy images flickering across the TV as he lit up a cigarette, 'you like new things, do ya?'

'I like to see what's out there. A girl gotta be interested to be interesting.'

Wayne blew his smoke toward the window. 'Oh boy, you're gonna love Rosarito Beach, and its gonna love you. They got miles of shops, everything a girl could want, right along the ocean promenade. You can shop right in your swimsuit too – they don't care, they're used to it.'

'Sounds like a magical place.'

'Oh baby, I promise you it is,' laughed Wayne, 'there are sandy beaches for as far as the eye can see, and fancy food restaurants, too. I bet you like good food, huh? Once we get through Tijuana and dump this shipment, it's just a short drive down the coast. But the best thing is the sunsets - that's where the magic is. And, come tomorrow, all of it will be ours.'

'Light me a cigarette, will ya?' said Deborah, 'and while you're at it, why don't you tell me something about yourself. We never did get past the basics.'

'Oh yeah, like what?' said Wayne, as he pulled one from his pack, lit it from his own and passed it over.

'Like . . . what's the weirdest thing that ever happened to you?'

'Well, that's easy,' said Wayne, 'why just tonight, in fact, while I was waiting for your bus to arrive there was this guy who lurched in, couldn't tell if he was high, drunk or just plain crazy, but he sure made an impression.'

'So, what'd he do?'

'He had one of those swastika tattoos right there between his eyes, like he was one of Charles Manson's disciples or something. He had this old beaten-up gym bag with him, and he drops it on the floor and comes straight up into my face and yells – *beg, borrow or steal*? You know, like it's a question or something.'

'What'd you say?'

'Well, I had to think real quick, as I could see things could go south real easy. So, I just said the first thing that came to mind. Borrow.'

'I would have said beg,' laughed Deborah.

'Well, that's not the end of it,' said Wayne, 'next thing I know there's this dog barking, real loud and aggressive-like, round the corner somewhere. The guy dives into his bag and pulls out a gun and knife and just stares at them both like he's waiting for some sort of sign.'

'Jesus,' said Deborah.

'Then he drops the gun back in his bag and tells me to watch it for him. Like someone's gonna actually steal something off of this guy. Then he heads round the corner, and I swear it could have only been a minute or two before he returns. He's wiping blood off the blade onto his jeans. And the thing was, the barking had stopped.'

'Holy shit, that is weird,' said Deborah.

'He came right back up to me, squared off and said – *know what I just did, Tonto – I had to steal its soul*. I swear to God, them's the exact words. Then he just starts cackling like it's the funniest thing in the God-damn world.' Wayne stubbed out his cigarette and walked into the bathroom to fetch two water glasses.

'Think I will have that drink,' said Wayne, 'want some?'

'Sure,' said Deborah.

'Your turn. What about you?' said Wayne passing her a glass of vodka. Deborah took a sip and tilted her head back like she was really thinking hard.

'I had this dream once where I was part of a circus.'

'A circus? What were you, a clown or something?'

'I dunno, but there were these Siamese Twins – Lee and Kwan, joined at the chest. They did a little freak show act where they used to sing. But the thing was they had the purest voices, just like angels. Then this one night there was a bad fire, burnt the whole place down to the ground and one of the twins was hurt pretty bad. I was sort of taking care of them, well anyway, Lee died, and it was pretty clear that Kwan wasn't going to make it either.'

'Makes sense,' said Wayne, 'one Siamese twin dies, what effing chance does the other have?'

'So, as Kwan is losing consciousness, as he's dying, he starts seeing things. Flying things. I ask him if they're birds. He says yes, but thing is, they're flying under the water. What he described was so beautiful it made me wanna cry. I never actually cried in a dream before then.'

'Holy crap,' said Wayne, 'that's some dream alright, Debs.'

'You know, if you don't mind,' said Deborah taking another sip of her drink, 'I prefer Deborah. I don't like being called Debs, or Debbie even. I got those names back at school, and I hated it.'

'Is that right? See the thing is, as I get to know you better, I see you more as a Delores.'

'Delores?' shot back Deborah.

'Why sure, that's got real depth to it, just like you and your dream. Delores Westwood. Now that's a pretty high-kickin' name. Why, I can practically see it up there in lights – Delores Westwood, the latest greatest star of Hollywood.' Deborah laughed.

'You're funny, too,' said Deborah, 'I like guys who can make me laugh.'

'What would you call me, if I wasn't plain old Wayne Cummings?'

'Oh, I'm not good at that game – why don't you do it, you got a real knack for things.'

'Well, I always admired the name, Wyatt. Maybe I'd be Wyatt Legend.'

'Legend?' said Deborah, 'is that even a real name?'

'Who cares,' said Wayne, swallowing his drink and pouring another, 'Delores Westwood and Wyatt Legend – a table for two, with an unobstructed ocean view. Honey, we need new names because soon you and me are gonna be living the high life in Rosarito, Mexico. I can see we got a real future ahead of us.'

'You know what I'd like?' said Deborah, 'some mixer and ice for this drink. You got me all fired up suddenly and in a festive mood.'

'Okay, honey, what will it be?'

'Orange juice sounds nice. It goes with vodka, right?'

'Like they were made for one another. It even has a name,' smiled Wayne, 'they call it a screwdriver. Hey, maybe that's like us, huh? – the fugitive screwdrivers.' Deborah laughed again.

'There's a Seven-Eleven just down the street. Why don't you get comfortable, and I'll be right back with the party.'

It had gone forty-five minutes before Deborah heard the key turn in the lock, and by then she was pretty beside herself with worry - who takes forty-five minutes to walk a block and back? In stumbled Wayne clutching at his chest. She could see straight away that he was bleeding badly.

'My God, what happened?'

'I was jumped. They got the entire shipment. Stole the car and everything.'

'You're hurt!'

'They shot me, to make sure I wouldn't follow 'em.'

'Jesus, where are you hit? Lemme take a look.'
Wayne staggered into the bathroom and pulled up his shirt.

'It looks pretty bad. We gotta get you someplace, maybe get a doctor or something - look at all the blood you're losing,' stammered Deborah.

'We can't,' said Wayne, 'too risky. Grab me a couple of towels will ya and bring me the vodka.' Within half an hour Wayne and Deborah had patched him up as best they could, using some vodka to sterilise the wound and strips of towels as make-do bandages. Now Wayne was propped up on the bed trying not to move too much. Even in a room that was only lit by the flickering light from the TV Deborah could still see that Wayne was getting paler and smaller.

'Why don't you let me call a cab, get you to ER?'

'Shhh,' said Wayne, taking hold of her hand, 'find the shopping channel for me. I wanna see what you're gonna wear when we stroll down the ocean promenade together.' Deborah did as Wayne said and then nestled herself under his good arm.

'Don't fall asleep Wayne, promise me you won't.' Wayne smiled quietly as his eyelids began to grow heavy.

'Why don't you call me Wyatt,' said Wayne dreamily, 'I'm getting a liking for it.'

The Brotherhood of the Beard

It happened accidently. I mean, it's not as if I set out to grow a beard, as some men do. It was really the incapacitation that did it. I was laid up for longer than expected, knocked out in a hospital bed suffering from a bout of glandular fever - mono. But mine was worse than just that. No, what made my hospital stay stretch from a week into months was the severe anaemia. A reduction of red blood cells, the body not working properly, an unexpected complication of the mono. But the thing they don't tell you about hospitals is they're not really good for your health. All them sick people, breathing in and out, coughing, sneezing, spewing their viral infection onto the wind of recycled air. Patients, too ill to get themselves up, lying in their own sweat, prostrate for days on end, eating lukewarm slop that passes for meals, while watching mind-numbing repeats of daytime soaps on rent-by-the-day television sets. None of it good for your mental or physical health, and in my case, likely what led to my secondary infection –

pneumonia. All of which meant, if not treated properly, I was straddling a real precipice between making it to thirty or becoming another grisly statistic. People in their twenties aren't supposed to die from stuff like mono. It's not uncommon for a young person to catch it, but the chances of complications are in the lower percentile, while the fraction who get a secondary infection on top of the first one is even slighter. But that's me, always playing the odds. Point is, with all that life and death stuff going on, and a longer than anticipated stay in hospital room 306, the last thing on my mind was personal hygiene, grooming, or my appearance. And so it was, during my hospital stay, I accidently grew a beard.

I'd never been much of a facial hair aficionado before to be honest, never really gave it a second thought. You usually learn how to shave around the age of fourteen, when those initial spotty sprouts of beardy growth and that slightest layer of fluff on your upper lip starts to resemble a moustache of sorts instead of a shadow of one. Besides your very first-time ejaculating, which is arguably the biggest shocking revelation to happen during a boy's puberty, shaving provides one of your first initiations into the world of masculine life. Letting you know for certain that you've somehow now transcended from boy to man A condom and a razor – the very essence of manhood. The first time I shot my wad I must have been all of thirteen and I was swept away on a feeling of euphoria. Not from the orgasm per se, but because in my mind it confirmed that I could take my place with the rest of half the genus of humanity to do my bit for the procreation of the species. In other words, I could father a child. Big, revelatory stuff. But my first time needing to shave, well that was just pure John Wayne machismo.

'I'm a man now, pilgrim. Draw when you're ready.' For my first shave, I borrowed my dad's old-school brush and soap dish creating a proper lather job all over my pimply face, and then with only several nicks, ran the blade down that virginal chin and cheeks leaving me fresher and closer than the day I was born. But after the initial cowboy thrill had worn off then it just became a habit. You just keep on shaving, if not daily, then every other day or so without even giving things a second thought. I never once considered a beard as something I'd have to attend to, cultivate or care for. It wasn't even a fleeting notion, but here I was, twenty-five years of age, newly discharged from hospital, a few pounds lighter to be sure, with a beard that was full and shaggy.

Just before catching mono and doing my time in the infirmary, I'd been dating this girl, Gail. She was alright, not a real stunner, but she liked to smoke weed, didn't mind listening to my death metal CDs and she put up with Truffle, my pet rabbit. It wasn't the fact I had a rabbit that put most people off, it was the fact she was a proper roam-around-the-house pet that usually threw them. Truffle had the run of the place and as such would sometimes pop out and dive at your feet when you least expected it. But mostly, I think, it was the ubiquitous rabbit droppings that really unsettled folk. What can I say – rabbits eat and shit a lot. I'd clean things up best I could, but Truffle had reign over the entire place and those little lost turds would get everywhere. Not so pleasant when you were stepping barefoot from the shower blindly looking for your slippers. Luckily, this didn't seem to faze Gail in the slightest. She had ugly feet - her assessment, not mine - and so she never went barefoot anywhere. I never once saw her stubby toes, or those weak arches that apparently dipped awkwardly inward. Even when we had sex, she would keep her socks on. Occasionally she'd scrape off a little Truffle surprise from her Chuck Taylors with a nail file and announce to me another finding.

'Truffle shat in the kitchen again, Gavin.' Then I'd race around with my little brush and broom scooping it up, making, what I thought was a real show of my domesticity. I think I'd read somewhere that women find men attractive who are handy around the house and who share in the chores. I wasn't too sure if Gail and I were destined for longevity, but I figured getting some practice in couldn't hurt.

Gail worked for an agency that specialised in office temps, so she never knew where, or for how long, she'd be working. Sometimes for the local council, sometimes at a fertilisation clinic or garden centre doing their books. Usually, I'd get a text saying she was on her way over then once she'd arrived, we'd smoke a joint and fire up the stereo with some Morbid Angel or Napalm Death Babies at full blast to wash away the malaise of the day. Then we'd progress onto a dinner of sorts, usually something simple like a frozen pizza from Tesco, or occasionally when the bank balance was flush, we'd get a takeaway order of fish and chips from Sunny's with a deep-fried Mars Bar for dessert. Then relish in the sheer joy of all that salt, fat and sugar as the meal slipped down as easy as ice cream. Sometimes Gail would stay overnight, but other times she'd make a retreat back to hers, especially if she knew she had work in the morning. She was a stickler for personal hygiene and always wanted a fresh pair of knickers and socks after a reviving post-coital shower before heading to work. She had a thing about body odour too and always made a point of making sure she had on enough deodorant - never anti-perspirant, as this she deemed to be a health risk, studies ensuring it to be cancer causing. Whatever the case, she'd apply enough deodorant to guarantee she'd never be caught smelling gamey at work. And so it was, Gail, with her poor feet and propensity towards cleanliness, that I entrusted to take care of Truffles once I was admitted to hospital. Initially, Gail didn't seem to mind, the texts and occasional pic coming in daily to tell me about how things were back at mine. The scorecard of rabbit droppings increasing daily along with the unopened post that was starting to pile up, all noted and annotated in her text entries. Then once my malaise started to become more serious and it became obvious that my hospital stay was going to last far longer than originally anticipated, there was a shift in our relationship, or at very least, in Gail's attitude towards me. As is the modern way, I received a text one day that stated matter-of-factly that Gail and I were through. As for Truffle, she'd already arranged for an adoption agency to find her a new home. If I had been more lucid, I would have been devastated. As I was incapacitated and barely hanging onto life itself, what choice did I really have in the matter? Fact was, Gail was breaking it off, so how could I expect her to tend to my belongings or Truffle as I either recuperated, or worst-case scenario, died. Still, I have to admit, being dumped by text message stung a little.

And so it was, I left hospital, one beard greater but without a girlfriend or pet rabbit. When I got home there were still rabbit droppings all over the place, but with the passing of several months they had now hardened and were much easier to pick up. As for the facial hair, I decided to keep it for a while. Having gotten out of the habit of shaving while in hospital it made the morning routine much simpler and guaranteed at least ten extra minutes of duvet time each day. I stopped by the local Turkish barbers for a freshen-up, though, before returning to work and Dimitri shaped and sculpted my flowing facial growth into what I can only assume was a tidier version. I'd always admired ZZ Top, not only for their rip-roaring Texas Blues Boogie, but for their unabashed devotion to letting those beards hang down low. One thing about beards that I wasn't aware of is there seems to be a collective that you are automatically accepted into once your whiskers reaches a certain length. The brotherhood of beards. Not an official thing, but for those accepted into the alliance, definitely a secret handshake and nod kind-of-thing. Not everyone with facial hair gets to automatically join. Those with mere stubble are considered light weights and don't get an invitation. Those with fussy manicured face-sculpting are definitely not invited. The brotherhood seems quite specific in its acceptance criteria - the beard must be of acceptable length and sport a certain unkempt attitude to allow membership into this most hirsute of clubs. Now, I've known about other automatic affiliations to various fellowships over the years. First one that springs to mind is the motorcycle allegiance.

A few years ago, I bought a second-hand scooter, not a Vespa but one of those Japanese knockoffs made for the UK market, a Honda Jazz, made in the image of an Italian classic. It was fun to ride, cheap on petrol, and provided all the thrills of the real deal. Strangest thing was, whenever I passed an oncoming motorcyclist, especially one of them Harley-riding biker-types, I would get the hand salute, a clear indication that I was a fully participating member of the club. A free spirit, just like them. Sharing that Easy Rider ethos, that love of the open road on a machine that defied conservatism. A true rebel. Truth be told I didn't feel like a renegade anything riding a Honda Jazz, the thing wouldn't go above thirty-seven miles an hour when completely wound out, and at top speed it sounded more like an over-worked sewing machine, but I suppose it was still a motorised two-wheel escape to that wind-in-your-hair feeling of the open road. Welcome to the club, indeed.

Having a beard of a certain length had a similar effect. I was automatically accepted into the brotherhood. This place was retro, masculine, and above all, the new sexy. Suddenly, men with long beards were in a class all by themselves. Neither old fashioned nor twee modern, they were like Scottish warriors of old yet with an added dash of New York trendiness that belied what it meant to be the new modern man. Women loved them and were drawn to them like moths to a flame. I really hadn't clocked the additional attraction that my facial hair provided; I must admit I was always a little slow on the communiqué uptake to notice all the cute women who were obviously ogling me. Trendy - is that a thing? Then I guess, unwittingly, I embodied it. All down to the beard. Whatever the case, one evening I found myself at an art gallery opening, another ingenue artist showing their impenetrable genius to all those who deemed themselves patrons of the arts, purveyors of taste – the whole artistic nine yards. Why was I there? Only to make sure the IT worked. That was my gig. I had worked as a freelance computer nerd for years. A good fit for someone like me - systems, computers, an order, a symmetry. Death metal was my release valve, petting rabbits my sanctuary, but it was IT that paid the rent. So, there I was, wearing an ill-fitting suit, my trusty doc martins, and sporting that unwittingly trendsetting facial hair. I could feel the stares, the women tingling in their own skin, the men frothing with jealously. Then I couldn't believe my eyes, this absolutely out-of-my-league gorgeous woman across the room was staring at me. I tried to play it cool, nodded hello then nervously ran my hand over my beard. That must have done it. Touching the thing. She made a beeline for me, champagne glass in hand, her glorious figure, sashaying from side-to-side, focused on one thing only – me.

'Hi, I'm Stephanie, but you can call me Steph,' she said, draping her arm over my shoulder like we'd been lovers forever.

'Gavin,' I replied.

'Is that Scottish?' she said, hopefully.

'Not sure,' I answered, 'maybe more Milton Keynes?' Stephanie laughed and stroked her hand across the lapels of my jacket.

'I have a suggestion.'

'You do?'

'There is a fabulous restaurant I know that does the best steak tartare this side of Paris. Are you hungry for anything, Gavin? Food, or lust, perhaps?' Stephanie's comment threw me completely, not only for its brazen honesty, but for its directness.

'Food *and* lust, I guess,' I stammered.

'Perfect. Shall we get out of here?' said Stephanie, picking up her phone and direct dialling for a reservation.

I had never expected to end up a love slave to a beautiful woman, but after our dinner at L'Petit Auberge, my life changed dramatically. Stephanie and I became inseparable. She worked for a modelling agency based in the heart of London, providing exquisite looking young women and men for all manner of jobs. Fashion shoots, catwalks, magazines covers, you name it. She coordinated the whole deal, from booking the talent, facilitating the venues, catering the events, and all the other details that made these happenings the talk of the town. She knew all the movers and shakers of the fashion industry and was slowly, but surely, climbing her way up the ladder of success. So here I was, a mostly gormless bearded bloke with an unimpressive IT qualification and a penchant for bunnies and heavy metal attached to the arm of this gorgeous woman stepping out at all these prestigious affairs. My social standing had improved by leaps and bounds as I walked the floorboards with Steph. Did I feel a little out of my depth? Of course, and to be honest, and this is likely in direct relationship to my complete lack of social perceptions, at the time I never once clocked what it was that was drawing all the attention.

There was a young woman, called Jane, who worked for Stephanie's agency. She was a PA, really a dog's body of sorts, who was at the beck and call of the various higher-ups that needed all manner of things attending to: dry cleaning; hotel bookings; manicures and pedicures arranged; lunch and dinner sorted; and she was also expected to be the front face of the office – answering the phone, sending emails, and attending to the post. One evening while Steph and I were at another opening night party, I found myself, glass of champagne in hand, alone with Jane as Steph worked the room solo. She had me clocked straight away as an ordinary bloke who had haplessly fallen into this.

'So, you're Stephanie's latest boyfriend?'

'I guess so. Latest? Have there been many more?'

'A few,' quipped Jane, 'she usually changes her dates to go with the seasons. An Italian boy for summer wear, something more rustic for the autumn lines.'

'Geez, what does that make me?'

'You're the new new.' I scratched my head. 'Don't sweat it,' she assured, 'I think you might have more staying power - what do you think of the champagne? Too dry? I'm never too sure about these things.' I tried to stare wistfully into the bottom of my skinny glass.

'I'm not much of a champagne drinker to be fair. I'm more of a beer drinker.'

'Me too,' said Jane, crinkling her brow.

'So, Steph's your boss?' I asked.

'Yup, I report to her and few others.'

'You have more than one boss? That's gotta be tough.'

'It's a living, but most days I keep up. How about you?'

'One boss, thank you very much. Mostly they leave me alone, so long as you keep your head down, and can fix the endless tech issues.'

'You know, there are some Heinekens in the fridge if you fancy one,' said Jane 'I made sure I had some stocked in case there were some beer drinkers here tonight.'

'I'd love one,' I said.

'I'll grab us a couple.' Jane returned with a pair of cold ones, and I was glad to put down my fussy flute glass in favour of the slender cold grip of a beer bottle.

'Have you always had a beard?' asked Jane.

'Oh, this thing,' I said, stroking my chin mane, 'only really since I was in hospital – maybe six months at the most, I never had facial hair before that. It's a bit of a beast to tell the truth, got an unruly mind all of its own.'

'I think it gives you a barbarian look, but in a good way,' chuckled Jane.

'I may do away with it soon,' I said, which made Jane's eyebrows raise involuntarily.

'Oh, I think facial hair on a man is so now. Very masculine,' said Jane, taking a long swig of her Heinie.

'Well, I have a job interview next week, it's for a supervisory position, a step up for me. I think I might stand a better chance if I don't look quite so barbarian.' Jane shrugged, and then Stephanie appeared and popped her arm through mine.

'Some real influencers here tonight,' she said, tipping back the last of her champers, 'Gavin, I'd like to introduce you to some people who are dying to meet a real man.' Steph handed Jane a business card, 'can you set up a meeting for some time next week, my office, for me and the entire team of Stitch-U-Up and make sure to have some canapes and drinks on hand. Nothing too expensive, but showy none-the-less.' Jane took the card and nodded.

'C'mon darling, let's you and I work this room.' Stephanie linked arms with me and soon we were gilding across the floor as if on air. After half an hour eavesdropping on some conversations I didn't really understand, I came across an errant bottle of Scotch, Glen-something-or-other, on a bureau in one of the nearby offices. I figured if I looked like a barbarian then I might as well drink like one. Besides, whenever else would I be able to afford unlimited access to fifteen-year-old single malt whiskey in all its peaty goodness. I raised my glass and shouted, *Och aye the noo*! as the whiskey went down as easy as a midnight kiss at Hogmanay. I could literally feel my fierce inner Scot starting to strap on a kilt and sporran as everything in my brain started to swirl and eddy like a gentle whirl-pool in the Clyde. It wasn't long before I found myself on the wrong side of inebriated. I listened to people I didn't know, pontificate about their latest conquests, their plans for future fashion lines, all of which started to blur into one big noise of ostentatious shemozzle. None of it sounded real and all of it clanged of boastful ludicrousness. But the Scotch smoothed everything over and I watched Steph cluck and caw with the best of them, laughing loudly at their jokes and working the seam like the pro she was. As the evening drew to a close, Stephanie hailed us a cab home and soon we left the party and were flying across London to her love nest. Once inside her flat, all I could think of was how good it would be to plunge head long into that soft duvet and sleep, but Stephanie had other plans.

'Gavin, can you please undo me.' I managed to stagger over to where she was standing next to the king size bed, then with fingers that felt like tree stumps I clumsily unhooked her bra. Stephanie had a healthy sized bosom, not too large, but definitely what one might term as pendulous. Now normally, being somewhat of a tit man, I would have taken this opportunity to gently cup her breasts from behind and begin my best arousal techniques in earnest, but to be honest, everything was blurring rather badly, and I could feel my eyelids descending like blinds.

'Thank you darling, and by the way, you were magnificent tonight, even my tiresome gay friends were impressed.'

Steph turned and kissed me before padded off to the ensuite to do whatever women do before bed.

'I won't be long . . .why don't you get yourself naked . . .tiger!' I sat down on the bed and attempted to reach for my shoes but before I knew it, I was floating backwards, faintly aware of my head hitting the pillow with a gently thud.

When I awoke there was no sign of Steph, the flat was quiet and from the bright light that was reaching around the blinds I had the distinct feeling I'd overslept. As I gingerly sat up, I became acutely aware of the heavy metal drumbeat pounding in my temples. Then the dryness in my throat, in fact, as I started to survey the hangover damage report my entire mouth had a weird taste almost as if I'd gargled with several of Truffle's turds and washed it down with pure peat. Damn, that Scotch - I just knew this hangover was going to be bad. I looked for my phone and switched it on – 10.30 a.m. Shit – I was so late for work! Nothing that could be done now, except to call in sick. I dialled the number and got Steve on the line. It was a slow day – I was in luck. My twenty-four-hour stomach-bug-could-be-food-poisoning-excuse was duly noted in my burgeoning personal file, but other than that – pure relief! Then I remembered I'd made an appointment at Constantine Cuts – my favourite Turkish barbers, to have my beard shaven off in readiness for my interview later in the week. What time was that at again? I checked my diary - 4.00 p.m. Brilliant, loads of time. All that was left to do now was have a leisurely day of non-work, replenish some bodily fluids to nurse my hangover and all would be right with the world. As I happily sauntered to the kitchen to find coffee and water, I noticed the note from Steph.

Have a good day, sleepy head.
You were a stallion last night!
Don't forget its cocktails tonight,
7.00 p.m. – The Black Stag Inn
See you later - Stud! xo

Stallion? Stud? How was that possible? All I could remember was . . .well, nothing. I couldn't recall how the evening had ended at all. But if Mr. Upright had been upright and Steph had been able to ride the wild wind without me, then everything was doubly right with the world. I had the feeling that I was hitting my lucky streak . . . what could possibly go wrong?

I spent the rest of the day having an unhurried bath in Steph's opulent tub then taking the tube back across town to mine to freshen up my clothes in readiness for another evening soiree. I wasn't sure how it had happened, but within the last six months I'd gone from my literal death bed and losing my girlfriend and rabbit to finding the woman of my dreams, one who thought I was a thoroughbred in the sack. I had a feeling I was about to get a deserving promotion at work too. Amazing how your luck can change, just like that. And what a great way to finish an otherwise tumultuous year and head towards the Christmas holiday season. Parties, parties, parties. I arrived at Constantine Cuts at 3.45 p.m. with two Costa gingerbread lattes in my hands.

'Afternoon Dimitri, can I interest you in a seasonal latte – my treat?'

'Well, look at you Gavin, a big shot spender now, what happened, you win the lottery or something?'

'Life's lotto, Dimitri. Plain and simple. When things start going right, you just gotta roll with it.'

'If you say so my friend. So, what are we doing today? Short back and sides? Beard shampoo and trim?'

'I have an interview this week, got my eye on a nice promotion at work. So, if you don't mind, it's off with the beard.'

'All of it?'

'Yeah, it's been fun while it lasted, but I think it's time to see my face again, say goodbye to Gavin from the Dark Isles. Dimitri, you have permission to shave it all off!'

And that, as they would say, was that.

Cleanly shaven and shining like a new dime on my way to the Black Stag, I decided to pick-up a bunch of roses for Steph. I was riding high and figured, what the hell, I could be a stud and a sensitive man all rolled into one. How could she possibly resist that? When I entered the pub, I could see her with Jane and a group of her work colleagues over in the corner chatting, drinks in hand. Steph had her back to me, so I figured I could sneak up and surprise her with the flowers. Perfect. Standing behind her, I gently put my hands over her eyes.

'Okay Gorgeous,' I said, 'I have a real surprise for you . . .' Steph turned around and she and the entire table collectively gasped.

'Ta dah!' I smiled, holding out the roses, 'for last night, for you.'

Rumpelstiltskin, Rambo, and Bubbles were all waiting anxiously for the weekly clean of their cages and each one seemed to be giving me the hairy eyeball, as clearly, I was running half-an-hour late. How these rabbits remembered, or anticipated, a timetable for feedings, cleaning and exercising, was beyond me, as Truffle always seemed oblivious about such things. But so it was at Pet Village, the rabbits awaiting to become pets seemed to possess an inordinate sense for timings. I'd been in post for three months already and during that time had quickly discovered that the title of Assistant Store Manager didn't really amount to much more than a Store Clerk, as there was only myself, Stuart (who worked Saturdays), and Brian (who was the actual Store Manager), who worked there. Admittedly, an assistant manager cred on my CV was better than clerk, but in reality, I think I only had that title so that Brian could finish early most days, leaving me to close-down and lock up the store. Clearly, a task that was deemed to be part of an Assistant Manager's job description, not a lowly clerk. Besides that, the position paid poorly, didn't really have any prospects for advancement, with the only rudimentary reward being that I had rabbits in my life again. I didn't get the promotion at InterTech Systems, and in fact, was let go due to what they claimed were excessive episodes of sickness. Apparently, my extended hospital stay had racked up most of my sick leave credits and the several times I needed to call in sick due to hangovers or late mornings with Steph seemed to make me an unreliable employee. Who knew? Once I made the ill-fated decision to shave off my beard, Stephanie ditched me like a haggis hurled at the Braemar Highland Games. Well, I admit that I did go from a trendy barbarian thirty-five-year-old to a milk-soppy sixteen-year-old weakling look, within a heartbeat. The brotherhood? Over as well. I was out the door, banned for life, branded as a hirsute charlatan. Well, Warhol once mused that each of us would get fifteen minutes of fame, but I think the very same could be said for a lucky streak. Mine seemed to last for mere fragments of time. I was on top of the world one moment and then next thing I knew I was getting condemning looks from cage-dwelling animals. Hero to zero in less time than it takes to shovel rabbit shit.

Despite knowing I could never really recover my premium trend status again, I figured the least I could do was regain some much-needed self-esteem, so I decided to grow back the fuzz. I was barely a month in, but the stubble was progressing nicely, it would take months, however, until I had respectable whiskers. I heard the shop door swing open and I could hardly believe my eyes, as in walked Gail with some shaven-headed bloke on her arm.

'Gavin, what are you doing here?' said Gail. I swallowed hard.

'I work here,' I managed, 'Assistant Manager.' She nudged the bald guy next to her in the ribs.

'This is Mitch,' she said, 'he works for the council. He drives lorries.'

'Oh,' I smiled and reached out for a handshake, 'nice to meet you, Mitch. Big lorries?' Mitch nodded.

'I heard you were on the mend,' said Gail, 'they said you almost died.'

'Yes, it was touch and go for a while,' I said, wearing my best, show-me-sympathy, look.

'So, when did you decide on the career change?'

'Oh, you know,' I sidestepped, 'they said the underlying cause of my illness was due to too much stress. IT can be so complicated, you know, so I figured working with animals would be a better fit. Me and rabbits – that just shouts therapeutic. What about you?'

'We're shopping for turtles,' said Gail, 'Mitch inherited a terrarium from his uncle.'

'Turtles? Well, you've come to the right place, all our reptiles are over in the back corner, let me show you.' I led Gail and lorry-driving Mitch over to where we had some turtles, assorted grass snakes, and one baby crocodile called Spenser.

'There you go,' I said, 'all the turtles are £50 which includes a complimentary carry-home container. Let me know if you need any further help.' I sauntered back to the counter and waited for Gail to peruse the reptiles with her new squeeze. A couple of minutes later they appeared in front of me.

'So, did you find the perfect match?' I said, with just the smallest hint of sarcasm.

'No, nothing there that took our fancy,' shrugged Gail.

'We may have some more in next week,' I said, genuinely aiming to be helpful.

'Maybe, yeah,' said Gail, 'we might drop back. C'mon Mitch, let's see what's on the high street.' As the two walked to the door I unconsciously blurted out.

'Well, it was good to see you again, Gail.' She spun around on her heel, and I swear I could hear her stubby toes painfully scrunching against the inside of her, obviously new, Doc Martens.

'Yeah, you too,' she said, 'by the way Gav, bit of free advice - I'd ditch the beard if I was you, it doesn't really work with your face, does it?'

First Foot

I tentatively knocked on the front door. What had it been - fifty-two years since I was eight years old and knocking on the same door? At that time, it was home to my Nan, a fiery Scot who was as superstitious as she was thrifty. The characteristics of a typical Scot, or so I'm told. My mother had sent me early on New Year's morning to be my Nan's first foot. A dark-haired man was what was needed, but in my case, a dark-haired kid would have to do as my father was bald, and my brother was fair, so I was nearest as anyone to fitting the brief.

The door opened and stood before me was a young woman holding a baby.

'Hello,' she said, 'how can I help you?'

'Really sorry to intrude but this used to be my nan's house, years ago, back during the Second World War actually, she lived here all the way through to the late seventies. Well, you see I haven't been back here in years so I was just wondering if it would be possible to have a little look around inside? I have some real memories of this place.'

The woman looked me over.

'Who was your nan?'

'Collins was her married name, Gaskarth was her maiden name, Elizabeth Collins or Elizabeth Gaskarth, she would have been known by.'

'There are a family of Gaskarths a few streets over,' she said, 'but I don't know of anyone by the name of Collins. Derek and I bought the place three years ago but there must have been a few owners over the years. Sure, why don't you come in. Don't mind the mess.'

'That's very kind of you.' I followed her into the small front room and was immediately overtaken by nostalgia. The décor was different, modernised, but the room was still similar. The old coal fireplace where we used to toast bread on frosty winter mornings was gone, replaced by a modern heater, and the old sideboard that housed all sorts of nicknacks that Nan would share with us was now home to a computer desk, but otherwise the place hadn't changed.

'Well, good morning,' said my nan, 'looks like my first foot has arrived. Happy New Year to you, deary.' And she swept me up in her arms and smothered me in a big hug.

'Come on inside before you catch your death.' There was a cheery fire already going in the grate and the room smelled of fresh baking.

'Have ye had yer breakfast?'

I nodded, 'a Weetabix.'

'Aye, well that's not enough for a growing lad. Sit yerself doon and I'll fix ye a wee bit of toast. The breads no long oot the oven.' I sat down on the little couch in front of the fire and could feel the warmth dancing on my legs. Nan returned and handed me a small plate with a piece of fruit cake and a small glass of something.

'There ye go. You need to drink a glass o' sherry to be a proper first foot. On wi' ya. The toast is just coming.' I looked at the fruitcake – I didn't like currents and raisins, but I knew I couldn't say no, so I took a drink of the sherry first - it was strong and sweet and almost made me cough. Then I took a bite of the cake and quickly swallowed. Almost immediately a funny sensation come over me. Something I'd not felt before – hard to describe, but pleasant. Nan soon returned with a couple of pieces of toast slathered with butter and golden syrup.

'There ye go. That'll make a footballer of ye. Ye still playing at school?' I nodded.

'Aye, I can see, you've got footballer's legs.'

'Have I?' I said, peering down at my skinny little legs.

'Aye, ye have.'

Pleased, I took a bite of toast, the bread was warm and delicious, and the butter and syrup mingling together, was pure heaven.

'Would you like a cup of tea?' said the young woman. I snapped back into focus.

'Tea? That would be lovely,' I said. 'Three years, you've owned this place, you say?'

'Yes, it's just the right size for us now' said the woman, returning and handing me a mug of tea, 'but we might want another little one in a few years' time, then I think we'll outgrow this place.' I thought back to when this was my nan's house, a small terrace, two up-two down, when it still had an outside loo. The place housed all four of them, my grandparents and their two daughters right up until my mom and her sister got married and left home. They made do. A different era, I guess. My mom used to tell stories of having a bath on Sunday nights in an old tin tub set up in the kitchen that they filled with boiling water from the stove.

'Gaskarth, that sounds Scottish?' said the young woman.

'Yes, my gran was a typical Scot. Very superstitious. I have a vivid memory of being sent to be her first foot. In this very house.'

'First foot,' said the woman, 'what's that?'

'Oh, just something they did back in the day,' I said, 'something meant to bring you good luck.'

'Oh,' she shrugged, 'I guess we all could use a little of that.'

I nodded. 'Well, I've taken up enough of your time, thanks for the tea,' I said, 'I do appreciate you letting me look around again.'

'I hope you found what you were looking for.'

I stood across the street, phone in hand, for a

moment or two contemplating taking a picture of the old house. I slipped the device back into my pocket, wanting instead, to remember my nan and this house in my own way, just as it had been back in 1970 - outdoor loo, first footers, and all.

A Bull Called Gringo

The drive from the Puerto Vallarta airport to the resort was straightforward enough and the excitement amongst the slightly drunk vacationers for their imminent holiday was palpable. All the hotels had their own air-conditioned vans that met the flights that landed full of tourists eager to get their winter sun break started. Luggage collected, passports stamped, welcoming smiles with *Bienvenido a Mexico*, then everyone was quickly and efficiently whisked off towards their various holiday destinations. Along the route the wide-eyed tourists would drink in the exotic landscapes - scrabbly mountainside vistas, flowering jacarandas, spiky cactus, and palm trees that danced gently on the Mexican breeze, and then a collective breath once the shimmering sea panorama came into full view for the first time. It was, of course, why they had all come here in the first place - the sun-drenched Pacific Ocean. A world away from the frozen snow-covered streets in the northern towns of Saint Catherines, Mississauga, Thunder Bay, or wherever it was in Canada they'd left behind.

Tammi and Stu had been looking forward to this winter break for ages. How great it was going to be to escape from their ordinary lives in suburban Toronto, so once in their room, they took no time in getting ready to take advantage of all that cheap booze, swimming pool action, and the endless sun and expansive beaches that Puerto Vallarta was famous for.

'Did you bring the sunscreen?' said Stu, piling his ample girth into last year's swimming shorts.

'I thought I asked you?' said Tammi, who was busy in the bathroom, giving herself a last-minute Brazilian Shave before pulling on the brand new two piece she'd bought specifically for the trip.

'I didn't pack any,' said Stu, 'sunscreen is your shit.'

'Well, I'm sure they sell some in the foyer or gift shop. We can ask at the front desk, or why don't you call down?' Stu ignored her as usual, fiddling, instead with the ties on the front of his shorts.

'You want to hit the bar first or go straight to the pool?' asked Stu, checking himself in the mirror then opting to pull a Toronto Bluejays t-shirt over his ample beer belly. Tammi appeared in the room wearing her bikini and full makeup.

'Don't you remember the brochure, Stu? There is a bar *in* the swimming pool. We can get pissed while we tan. Maybe we should get something to eat though, huh? You already downed quite a few on the flight.'

'I'm on effing vacation,' retorted Stu, 'off the leash for an entire fortnight. Plus, this is the land of tequila - bring on the margaritas. C'mon, you ready to roll or what?' The two grabbed their towels, sunglasses, slid on flip flops and shuffled their way to the elevator. Once down in the lobby, they were pulled in various directions – should they opt for the bar with its expansive outdoor palm tree-filled patio that looked out invitingly onto the ocean, or the pool, which seemed, at that moment, to be teeming with kids splashing around making all kind of annoyingly gleeful noises. Stu gave Tammi a knowing look, 'I vote for drinks on the patio before we do anything else, besides we can order a few appies to make sure we got a good base for the night ahead. Tammi nodded her approval.

The two sat at a table as near as they could get to the expansive sea views, ordered nachos and a pitcher of margaritas.

'Hey amigo,' said Stu, eyeing the waiter with suspicion, 'is this water safe to drink?'

'*Si señor*, of course.'

'We don't want to get any of that Montezuma's revenge ruining our vacation,' said Stu.

'I assure you, all our water is bottled,' said the waiter, 'even the ice cubes.'

'Good,' said Stu, dropping a meagre twenty pesos tip onto the waiter's tray, 'what's your name pal?'

'Javier, señor.'

'In which case, Javier, why don't you grab us

another round - keep the margaritas flowing.'

'*Gracias*,' said Javier, surveying the money then bowing slightly and moving away from the table.

'You didn't tip him very much,' said Tammi.

'Relax, they're Mexicans, that's big bucks to them.' Stu pulled out his phone and dialled in the hotel's Wi-Fi code.

'You wanna know what the temperature is back in TO right now?' said Stu, inspecting his weather app. He didn't wait for an answer, 'effing minus fifteen with a windchill that would freeze your nuts off.' Tammi slid the sunglasses down onto her face and sighed deeply.

'Cheers then, babe,' she said, clinking glasses, 'here's to all the sand you can get stuck in the crack of your ass instead of shovelling snow.' Stu almost snorted out a nose full of margarita on that one and slapped his knee.

'No shit, right? This is gonna be the best effing winter vacation ever.'

After Javier cleared away the appetisers and another jug of margaritas appeared, a middle-aged couple sat down at the table next to them. After a minute or two the man leaned over and spoke to them.

'Canadians, right?'

'Sorry?' said Stu, giving him the once over.

'You're from Canada. I mean, the Blue Jays shirt is a dead giveaway, but you just look like the types. Am I right, or am I right?' The woman sitting next to the man, leaned her elbow nonchalantly on the table and blew the cigarette smoke out of the side of her mouth.

'Dwayne has an uncanny sense about these things. He's rarely wrong – I bet Toronto?' Tammi uncrossed her legs.

'Scarborough – right in the beating heart of suburbia.'

'Bingo,' said Dwayne, 'I knew it.'

'Us too,' said the woman, 'geez, where are my manners, I'm Barbara – but most people call me Babs, and this is Dwayne, we got a nice townhouse on Finch Avenue, right close to Markham, where are you guys from?'

'We live really close to Steeles Avenue but nearer to Kennedy, just a one bed apartment, but we have an awesome view,' said Tammi. 'What a coincidence, it's nice to meet some other Canucks here.'

'Honey, this place is crawling with Canadians and Americas.' Tammi smiled and nodded.

'Did you guys just arrive, too?'

'No, we're into our second week' said Babs, 'we come here every year, same hotel, same two weeks every time, ain't that right, babe?' Dwayne poked a toothpick into a ring of calamari, held it up to admire it before popping the entire thing in his mouth.

'Endless seafood,' said Dwayne, crunching through a mouthful of battered goodness, 'and the Mexican culture, that's what we love.'

'Culture?' said Stu, slurping back the rest of his margarita, 'Kahlúa and tequila – tell me, am I missing something here?'

'Well, the Mariachi music,' said Babs, 'it's all those authentic little outfits the musicians wear when they play, it makes everything so much more festive.'

'And bullfights,' added Dwayne, 'you ever seen one?'

Stu looked over at Tammi, 'No, I can't say I ever have – you, babe?' Tammi shook her head.

'I thought bull fighting was only in Spain?' said Stu, 'that's where they do the running of the bulls, isn't it?'

'City of Pamplona, every July,' said Dwayne, authoritatively, 'well, it just so happens Puerto Vallarta has some of the finest *corrida de toros* in all of Mexico.' He winked at them both, 'if you want real Mexican culture, I highly recommend it.'

'You mean like those big red capes those matadors hold while they strike poses and yell *olé*?' said Stu, laughing. Babs lit herself another cigarette.

'Oh, I think you'll find it's much more of a sport than you imagine, ain't that right, Dwayne?'

'Hell yeah. Hey,' said Dwayne turning to look at his wife, 'ain't we got a couple of tickets for Friday night we ain't gonna use?' Dwayne turned back to Stu and Tammi.

'Thing is, we're having to head back a day early this year. Bab's mom, well she's just been diagnosed . . .well, long story short and a bit of an inconvenience, but fact is we won't be needing the tickets. You seem like nice kids, and it would be a shame to waste them – would you like 'em?' Stu looked over at Tammi and shrugged.

'Sure, a real bullfight sounds rad, can you buy beers there?' Dwayne laughed out loud and waved at the waitress across the room.

'*Señorita*! - four *tragos de tequilas por favor*. And make it four cervezas too' The waitress nodded her understanding and began to prepare the tequila shots.

'Ya gotta do beers with tequila shooters,' said Dwayne, pulling out two tickets from his wallet and sliding them across the table to the pair.

'Don't say I didn't warn ya,' winked Dwayne.

Within only a few days Stu had managed to badly sunburn himself as he usually spent most mornings passed out by the pool sleeping off one hangover after another. Today he was desperately seeking shade and looking for something to dull the pain.

'She looked at me like I was a moron,' said Stu, 'I just kept repeating, Tylenol por favor, sunburn ya know? I couldn't believe it, she just stared right through me, don't these local-shmocals learn how to speak English?'

'So, did you get anything?' said Tammi.

'Hold on,' said Stu, 'I ain't finished my story, so finally I say aspirin, you got any aspirin. Then you know what she did?' Tammi shook her head.

'No, what?'

'It was like the God-damn effing light bulb went on – 'oh *aspirinas*' she said! Like my pronunciation wasn't even close – geez Louise.'

'You should have put on more sunscreen, I told you so,' said Tammi as she went back to perusing her lunch menu, 'now you're all burnt.'

'Point is, we're practically paying their God-damn wages here, is it too much to expect them to make an effort with English?'

'Oh, stop being Mr. Crabby,' said Tammi, narrowing down her choice for lunch.

'It's too effing hot here. I had the God-damn shits last night and I ain't sleeping good to boot,' said Stu, stabbing his stubby finger at the page, 'I think I'm gonna go with a burger, I'm getting a little sick of fish and avocados.' Tammi rolled her eyes.

'Suit yourself, but I love the guacamole.' Soon Javier appeared with their drinks.

'Here we go *amigos*, dos cervezas. And how is your vacation going so far?'

'Great,' said Tammi. Stu wrinkled his nose.

'I thought you said the water here was all bottled?'

'But I assure you it is,' said Javier, smiling, 'perhaps you should stick with the beers, amigo?'

'Oh, he is,' said Tammi, 'he is.'

'Hey,' said Stu, ignoring her, 'how do you say Tylenol in Mexican? You know the thing you take for headaches.'

'Si señor, I believe I know what it is you speak of. In Spanish you would say *el acetaminofeno*. I hope you are not suffering from something bad?'

'It's his own fault,' said Tammi, 'he's sunburnt. He overdoes everything, don't you babe?' Stu shot her a look.

'Anyhow Javier,' said Tammi, handing him her menu, 'I'm gonna have the fish tacos and Stu is having the burger. Better make it well done.'

'Gracias,' said Javier, as he put the menus under his arm and sauntered off towards the kitchen.

'What do you wanna do today?' said Stu, 'we've already shopped 'til we dropped, my Visa is through the roof.'

'I dunno, you said you wanted to try parasailing. They have that right on the beach. That looks like fun.' Stu scrunched up his nose.

'Not with this burn,' he said, touching his shoulder, 'you seen the harnesses they make you wear? Ouch.'

'What about a fishing trip, then?'

'No way José, they want a hundred pesos for an effing hour, I already checked, that's Mexican robbery, besides, I think I gotta stay in the shade for a bit.' Tammi stared off into space.

'Hey, I know,' said Stu, brightening up, 'it's Friday and ain't we got ourselves freebies to see the bullfight. That's gotta be good for a hoot.'

'When's it at again?' asked Tammi. Stu pulled out the tickets.

'Five o'clock. That's perfect. We got plenty of time for a few more bevvies before we soak up some culture. Olé!' yelled Stu, flapping a napkin past Tammi's face.

'Okay,' said Tammi, pushing his arm away, 'keep it in your pants, Pepe. I'll go as long as you don't embarrass me.'

It was just turning quarter-to-five when Stu and Tammi stepped out of the taxi in front of the *Plaza de Toros* and Stu was already a little unsteady on his feet. They hadn't left the restaurant since they'd finished lunch, instead Javier kept a steady flow of beers and tequila shooters coming to the table all afternoon – Stu's orders. The sun was still high in the sky, and the sheer brightness along with the oppressive heat made them both squint and feel a little queasy after all that booze. The stadium was surprisingly plain and smaller than they'd imagined it to be, and, as with most things that were off the tourist grid in Mexico, it seemed a little on the rundown side. The walls were whitewashed but flaking, the seats were simply hard wooden benches and the big sign out front advertising 'Plaza de Toros', looked like it was in need of some basic repair. The pair gingerly made their way to the nearest entrance, shading their eyes from the sun, showed their tickets and then Stu immediately felt the overbearing urge to urinate.

'Wait here, Tam. I really gotta take a wizz.'

'Hurry up,' said Tammi, looking around and correctly sensing she was the only female in the vicinity. As she stood by a wall waiting, she began to notice there were no other tourists here, at least none that she could see in this part of the building, instead, she became aware of the stares of dark eyes piercing into her as the local men walked past, beers in hand, sizing her up, comfortable on their own turf. Tammi was glad when Stu returned.

'Where are our seats?' asked Tammi. Stu checked the tickets.

'It just says, *admisión general*. Why don't they write things in God-damn English? But I'm guessing that means there isn't reserved seating, but how about over there?' said Stu, pointing to where there seemed to be a little bit of shade. They settled themselves onto a bench, glad to be out of the direct sun for a while.

'I'm gonna see if they got any cold brewskies,' said Stu, 'you want one?' Tammi shook her head.

'Hurry back, will ya Stu, this place makes me nervous.'

'Nervous? What for?'

'I dunno,' said Tammi, reducing her voice to a whisper, 'but I don't see too many other white faces.'

'Relax,' said Stu, 'this is Mexico, where tourists are king, they love us here.' When Stu got back, a cerveza in each hand, it seemed like the show was about to begin. Down in the ring an older Mexican gent was walking around the perimeter holding a big white cardboard sign for everyone to read. On it was painted: *Toro número uno – 'Gringo'*.

'What's that about?' said Stu.

'I think they're introducing the first bull.'

'Gringo – what the hell does that mean?' said Stu.

'Pretty sure it means white man,' said Tammi, pointing, 'look, here comes the bull, I think it's about to start.'

'Wicked,' said Stu, pulling on one of his beers, 'we're finally about to see some effing bullfight action.' Stu raised his beer into the air and yelled, 'come on, Gringo!' A few brown faces turned to give him a hard stare, and Tammi tugged on his shirt for him to sit down and be quiet. Then the gate flew open and in charged the bull. It looked a lot bigger and scarier in real life and already seemed angry and ready for a fight. Cheers rang out from around the stadium and the man with the sign quickly made a dash for one of the exits. The bull circled around the ring swinging its heavy neck up and down, stamping its hoof against the ground and steam was blowing out of its nostrils which made clouds of dust appear in the languid evening air.

'Whooee,' said Stu, 'look at that thing, it's massive, I'm voting for the bull.' A second gate opened and in strode two horses and riders, both of which were wearing some sort of heavy protective armour. The bull looked from one to the other as they began to circle, purposefully aiming to confuse it. In the riders' hands were spears and as they rode past the unsuspecting creature, they forcefully plunged the lances into its back and shoulders, leaving them inserted deep within the beast. The bull snorted, violently flipped its head from side to side and started to stagger after them, pursuing them around the ring. With every step it made, blood began to spurt out of its wounds like an erupting geyser on its back. Seeing the blood, the crowd cheered its approval. The riders retrieved more spears and swords and circled the bull again, plunging their blades deeper and deeper into its body. Blood now began to froth from its nostrils as it tried, unsuccessfully, to chase and swing its horns at the well protected horses and riders. Blood was now literally spraying out of the animal with every move it made and the sand on the bull ring floor began to be patterned with the lifeblood of the bewildered creature. Then the loudspeaker crackled to life and on came an announcement in Spanish introducing the matador for today's fight, Alejandro Perez. Suddenly there he was, in all his pageantry splendour. He was a rather diminutive man, thin waisted, but wearing a rather fine exquisite *traje de lucas* - matching embroidered trousers, waistcoat and jacket, and he was sporting the traditional *montera* on his head. He bowed in all directions to the audience, acknowledging everyone. Then he bowed in the direction of the bull and showed it his long sabre. The crowd was now on its feet, cheering and whistling their approval as the barbaric show was about to get even more grisly and merciless. Alejandro then faced off against the beast. He hid his blade behind his cape and yelled at the bull and offered the robe to the animal's line of sight. The bull, seeing the swaying bright red, made a slow staggered jog towards the matador. Alejandro, waiting until the last possible moment, deftly stepped aside, and as the bull moved past, stuck his long blade right up to its hilt, deep into

the animal's neck. Cheers rang out from the crowd. The
bull was now more or less covered in blood and sweat
and looked completely disorientated and waning. Froth
and steam and spit and more blood ran from its mouth,
where its tongue was spastically protruding, while its
eyes bulged out in confusion and exasperation.

The beast staggered over to one side of the ring,
seemed to look around at all the faces that were jeering
at it, then slumped down as its hind legs gave way. Like
a conquering hero, Alejandro strode up to stand before
the beast and raised a dagger high into the air. The
Mexicans around the stadium were yelling their
approval. In one swift, powerful and celebratory move,
Alejandro plunged the blade into the space behind the
skull and with great force pushed it in as deep as it
would go. The beast let out one final bloody snort before
completely slumping to the ground. Cheers ran out, this
time in victory. The matador removed his dagger and
quickly proceeded to hack off one of its ears. Once he
had the leathery item in his hand, he raised it high into
the air and paraded around the ring receiving a
conquering hero's applause.

Tammi had sat frozen in her seat, shell-shocked,
right after the first spear was stuck into the bull and
she'd witnessed the first sight of blood. Stu, who hadn't
touched his beer the entire time was as white as a sheet
as he finally turned around to face Tammi.

'Jesus Christ, that was effing brutal, what'd you think?' The horrified look on Tammi's face said it all.

'You don't look too good, you alright?'

'I think I'm going to throw up.' And with that, she turned her head just as a stream of vomit erupted from her mouth and sprayed onto the concrete steps. Several faces turned to share their annoyance.

'Jesus, Tam,' said Stu, not knowing whether to rub her back or hold her head. Finally, she sat up, wiped her mouth with the back of her hand and turned to Stu.

'I wanna go.' Stu nodded and did his best to help her to her feet and the two staggered down the steps and toward the exits. All the way they could feel the hostile stares of the locals burning into them. Two gringos on the wrong side of the tourist tracks. Just as the pair were nearing the gate they had to stop for a moment as the ring door flew open in front of them to let a pickup truck drive out dragging the bull's carcass behind it. Tammi, had to avert her eyes and cover her mouth so she didn't throw up again and as she turned her head, she could see that inside the ring the next sign was being paraded, this one read: *Toro número duo: 'Tourista'*.

The pair finally made it out into the street and Tammi leaned forward, hands on her knees, and tried to take some deep breaths.

'That was bizarre,' said Stu, 'no idea what Dwayne and Babs see in it.'

'That's not a sport; that should be against the law,' stammered Tammi, 'I want to go back to the hotel and never leave the pool again.' Stu looked around, but as the bullfight was still in progress the street was empty, and there wasn't a single taxi in sight. The sun was now setting, and the air was rapidly cooling as twilight descended. Stu looked back over at the exit gate where a couple of attendants were smoking and laughing, and he could have sworn they were talking about the two of them. Suddenly Stu didn't feel comfortable asking one of the locals for help or directions, recognising his total lack of Spanish wouldn't buy him any favours.

'I think we're gonna have to walk,' said Stu, 'there's no taxis here. It can't be too far, are you gonna be okay?' Tammi nodded.

'Which way is the hotel?'

'This way, I think,' said Stu, desperately trying to recall anything familiar from the drive in.

'C'mon, I'm pretty sure this is the way.'

Tammi and Stu soon found themselves lost and far from the streets and restaurant-strewn boulevards that lined the tourist part of town. Instead, they were meandering through shanty neighbourhoods that were unfamiliar, residential, and poor - the lower east side of Puerto Vallarta were the locals lived. The signs of extreme poverty were everywhere. Scrawny chickens scratched in the dirt looking for anything to eat in the stubbly front yards of the lean twos that were no more than the size of postage stamps. Tim roofed shacks leaned against one another and filthy faced youngsters looked up from their simple games as the two gringos stumbled by. Tammi clung tightly onto Stu's arm, still feeling ill from the horror and gore they'd witnessed, and now feeling apprehensive to be so far away from their hotel. Meanwhile, Stu frantically tried to find something - a street sign, a building, a store, anything, that would help him navigate their way back to a hospitable part of town, but so far, there had been nothing recognisable. It was now getting quite dark and there were no streetlights in this part of town, which made their situation worse. For forty-five minutes they wandered, perhaps heading in the right direction, perhaps not, perhaps only in circles – who could be sure?

'I think this is the way,' said Stu.

'That's what you've been saying all along. How do you know?' said Tammi, barely holding back tears. Stu shrugged his shoulders.

'There's a light,' he said, pointing. They turned the corner and found themselves entering a small courtyard. Across the square a few men stood in the shadows, leaning against a wall smoking cigarettes and passing around what looked like a bottle of tequila. Off to one side, sitting around an overturned wooden crate, another group of men were playing cards and drinking beers. There was Mexican rap music coming from inside one of the dimly lit rooms and the stale smell of cooking, grease and smoke hung thick in the air. Stu stopped for a moment, unsure what to do - turn back around or walk through the courtyard? He didn't feel comfortable with either option. But it was a little too late for decision making as right then all the eyes descended upon them – the two unfortunate gringos.

'Excuse me, amigos,' said Stu, 'we seem to have gotten a little lost.' Stu turned to Tammi, 'how do you say lost in Mexican?'

'*Perdido*, I think.'

'Perdido,' said Stu, towards the men, 'perido. Can you point us in the direction of the hotels? Dos tourista hotels . . .' For a moment all went silent, then a man stood up from the card game and walked over to them. He stood in front of Stu so that his unshaven face was nose to nose with him. Stu could smell his sweat and, on his breath, the stink of cigarettes and booze. The man took his hand and slowly tilted back his baseball cap.

'Si señor, you are indeed not where you should be.'

'Thank God – you speak English.'

'Many of us speak *Inglese* so we can work in *la industria turística*.' The man laughed, 'you are turistas, no?'

'Sure amigo, all the way from Toronto Canada,' said Stu, happy to have been able to communicate. The man dropped his cigarette onto the floor and put it out with the grind of his heel.

'One thing señor, we are not your amigos,' and he poked Stu in the chest with his finger, 'Gringo turistas.' The men around the courtyard all laughed. Stu could feel the blood draining from his cheeks and Tammi tightened her grip on his arm. A man from the shadows began to hobble across the courtyard towards them. His left leg, clearly shorter than the other, made a dragging sound as he pulled it along behind him. He was agitated and spoke very quickly and loudly to the other man in Spanish.

'*Por qué no le corto el cuello?*' Then he pulled a knife out of his jacket and held it up. The first man reached into his pocket for another cigarette and slowly began to light it. He inhaled long and hard then blew the smoke into Stu's face.

'He says he would like to slit your throat, señor.'

'What?' said Stu, 'he can't do that, we're tourists, Canadians, fuck . . .' The courtyard erupted in laughter again. The man turned to look at his friend.

'Diego is, how you say, a crazy man. An angry one, too. Once he sets his mind to something, we have little control.'

'Oh my God,' said Tammi, 'please let us go. We have money, we can give you money. What do you want?' The man turned to look at Tammi.

'Not everything is about *mucho dinero*, señorita. Sometimes victory is about something else. Something more worthy, like you might see in one of our bullfights.' Tammi put her hand over her mouth.

'Please,' she gasped. Just then Stu felt a hand land on his shoulder and a familiar voice began to speak.

'*Déjalos en paz Juan, se quedan en mi hotel.*' The smoking man shrugged and took a step back. Stu turned his head, and to his relief behind him was none other than Javier, the waiter from their hotel.

It was Sunday, 15th February, just gone noon, and Tammi and Stu had packed up their belongings, stuffed their souvenirs into their carry-on luggage and were waiting patiently with the others in the hotel lobby for the shuttle bus to arrive. Stu dialled into the Wi-Fi and checked the weather back home.

'Shit,' said Stu, turning to Tammi, 'it's like plus two right now in Toronto, all the snow is melting.'

'I thought you hated the snow?'

'When did I ever say that? Tell you what though, I will be glad to be back to normal temperatures again.'

'I'll just be glad to be home, in my own bed, under my duvet,' said Tammi.

'I can't wait to have a McDonalds, that's the first place we're going when we get back.' Tammi looked up and smiled.

'Okay.' Just then they heard the sound of the shuttle bus arriving out front and within a few minutes the lobby was teeming with fresh-faced vacationers, Canadians and Americans, all looking excited to be starting their own winter vacation.

'Wait a second,' said Tammi, pointing, 'isn't that your friend Doug, from work?' Stu squinted his eyes.

'Well, so it is, I'm gonna go say hi.'

'Make it quick, the buses are here, we'll be leaving in a minute or so.'

On the ride to the airport the atmosphere inside the vehicle was rather subdued. Perhaps everyone was all partied-out, or sad to be leaving, or as in Stu and

Tammi's case, glad to be heading home. As the bus rolled down the highway, the impact of the last two decades of tourism in Puerto Vallarta showed; there were buildings stretching from the seacoast to the foot of the mountains and some encroaching further up the mountainsides.

'So, what did you say to Doug?' said Tammi.

'Oh, I just said hi and gave him a few pointers about the place.'

'Such as?'

'Don't drink the water and I told him they have bull fights here.'

'You didn't recommend to your own friend that he goes, did you?'

'C'mon, Doug is no real friend of mine - he got my promotion, remember? Besides, what do you effing think I'd say? Geez Louise.'

The Unexpected Robin

'I'm going for a walk,' announced John, as he finished lacing up his old leather boots. No reply. Cathy must still be sleeping, he thought to himself.

'I need some air, clear my head. I've been up since five,' he muttered to himself as he sighed heavily, 'when will I ever be able to sleep like a normal human again?'

The sound of key turning lock did nothing to rouse his sleeping wife and John was soon outside looking up and down the quiet street for any other signs of life. The road was bereft of traffic or people; he was all alone. He turned, pointing himself southbound, made his usual shortcut down through the church yard and cemetery, over the bridge which arched the train tracks, and soon found himself walking along the muddy path that traced the river Eden's sludgy meander. The early winter morning light was hazy, quite dream-like. There was a light frost, the air was sharp, and the morning mist hung above the ground like a shroud covering the entire landscape. The river gently splashed and whispered as it snaked and eddied its way through the Cumbrian countryside. No one else was around, not even dog walkers. The daylight of this dead-of-winter day was slow to reveal itself, possibly reluctant to be seen in the starkness of dawn. The natural beauty gone missing perhaps, or just temporarily forgotten. The wet, blackened bark frostily glistened on the lofty oaks and willows, naked now, grieving their summer glories. The trees watched in silence, their gnarled fingertips pointing towards the ground. Dead, but not dead. Just dormant until Spring.

John took a sharp in-breath of freezing air and then as his boots squelched in mud he began to walk in the direction of the eddying river. It had been a hard few months, life dealing out its inevitable changes, sudden and shocking, commonplace and unkind. The unavoidable happening right before his eyes. A phone call, out of the blue, but not unexpected. His mother. Gone. Then the tidal wave of grief and sorrow. The practicalities, necessary arrangements, all knocking at the door at the exact same time the deep sadness arrived. How to process both? An emotional and logistical juggling act. Since then, his sleeping pattern had been seriously interrupted and he felt like a panic attack might strike at any moment. This is what often prompted him to step out early into the great outdoors for some fresh air and a much-needed chance to walk it off. Today was no different. He'd been awake since half four, had already had three cups of tea, read his emails, checked the weather and news before the dead weight of sorrow smothered him again. His mother had been dead for over two months, yet it still felt like it was only yesterday. It had been six months since he'd last seen her, talked to her, held her hand, and told her how much she meant to him. That he loved her. Had she understood that? Had her confused mind been able to take in any of it?

As he rounded a bend in the river, he stopped at a bush – he noticed a pair of beady eyes that appeared to be watching him.

'Hello there,' said John, and the little bird twitched its head in response to the sound of his voice.

'Well, aren't you a brave soul. Not going to fly off, then?' The robin jerked its head again and jumped a few twigs closer. John was now just a foot or so away from the tiny inquisitive creature. It definitely was looking straight at him, and he could distinctly hear the little warbling sounds it was making, unfamiliar and delicate.

'Well, you have quite a lot to say, don't you?' The bird kept turning its head to the side and, chirping, tutting, quietly communicating in its own ethereal way. John didn't quite know what to make of this strange, but charming encounter, so he just stood there watching and listening. After what felt like ages, but was likely only a minute or two, John decided it was time to continue his walk.

'It was delightful to meet you. If you're here tomorrow, same time same place, we can cross paths again if you like?' The robin released a series of distinctive tutting sounds as if it were chirping farewell, which made John laugh.

'Okay, bye-bye, little bird, sounds like we have a plan.' With that John pulled the scarf tighter around his neck, stepped back onto the path, and for the first time in a long while, had a big smile across his face.

The Fair Oaks Nursing Home was a typical elderly care residence, more like a hospital ward than a place to reside. But typical of the places our loved ones live in once they reach that inevitable age or incapacity where they require constant round-the-clock care.

'Would you like some more milk, Mom?' Joan stared off into the void. Some days there would be a glimmer of recognition, a hint of remembrance, even a few words spoken and shared, but mostly there was little acknowledgement. Today was much like the other days John had planned to spend with her. It was a long trip to make, across the ocean and back, but worth it, to see her one more time. It was clear even then that she didn't have much time left. But who really knew? She had all but given up eating and all she really did now was drink the milk that singularly seemed to keep her going. Today, however, she had looked at him as if to acknowledge his presence, say hello, before drifting off again, back into darkness of her mind. Had she already gone, disappeared? One foot here and one foot beyond? John took hold of his mother's hand and stroked it gently.

'Do you remember when we used to go on holiday to the Lakes, Mom? We'd go swimming even if it rained, especially if it rained - that was actually more fun. And you'd let us stay up late to watch the stage shows. What was I then, seven or eight? Such good family memories – do you remember those times?'

Joan sipped at her cup of milk then lightly banged it on the counter in time with the nursery rhyme that often was the thing that seemed to play on repeat through her mind.

'Sailing round the water, like a cup and saucer . . . milk. I want some more milk,' said Joan suddenly, in a cracked, agitated voice.

'I'll go and see what I can find,' said John, taking the cup and leaving her room in search of a support worker. When he got back, Joan was asleep. She slept a good portion of any given day. Same as the other residents. Lunch times were sadly comical. A table of old ladies nodding off in their wheelchairs while plates of lukewarm food were placed in front of them as the handful of care assistants tried their best to get a mouthful swallowed. Most of it ended up in the bin. Yet every day would see the same fruitless charade, thrice daily, meals prepared but rarely eaten. At three o'clock the rounds were made again, this time a cup of tea and a small muffin appeared. The care worker put the food on the tray in front of Joan.

'Are you enjoying seeing your mom?' asked the assistant.

'Yes, it's been lovely. I wasn't sure I would see her again, with the pandemic and all.'

'But you made it. We all love your mom. She keeps us all on our toes,' laughed Serita.

'That's really nice to hear . . .and, thank you . . . for all you do for her.'

'You're welcome,' smiled Serita.

'I'll wake her up,' said John, 'and make sure she has some of this.' After Serita left the room John stroked his mother's hand and she slowly opened her eyes. She didn't say anything, but the smile was unmistakable. She was back again.

'I have to go home tomorrow, Mom, back home to Carlisle. It's been really nice to spend all this time with you.' Joan looked up at her son and for a moment she seemed lucid.

'I like your hat. It's red,' said Joan.

'Yes, it is, isn't it? Here, do you want to try it on? I'll get a picture of us together.' John put the baseball cap on his mother's head. It swamped her, she'd lost so much weight in the past year, she was just skin and bones.

'Smile, Mom!'

John didn't check his phone or look at the picture until he'd arrived home. Mom in the oversize red cap, fidgeting with her night gown, as had become her anxious habit. John smiling down the selfie lens. What a whirlwind trip it had been. So emotional. It all felt so final. Then a few months later his brother called. John didn't need to hear the details; he knew as soon as his phone rang at that irregular hour what the news would be. And so, it was. The end of her life. A few weeks later a package arrived in the post from his brother. He knew it would be a small urn with his share of the ashes along with a few other mementos salvaged and shared from the few belongings she had left. He left the package unopened, lacking the strength or resilience, to open it and deal with his mother's remains.

John left the house, heading out for his usual morning walk. It was another cold morning and he'd made sure to dress warmly. As he trundled along his mind drifted off onto the many things he needed to do. Work mostly; and Cathy's upcoming birthday present he needed to buy. Then he heard it. That same sweet little tut-tutting sound. He looked up from the path and there, once again, was the little robin.

'Well, hello again. Are we making a regular thing of this?' The bird hopped forward, sitting on a branch that was almost at eye level with John.

'You are a pretty one, aren't you?' Although it was just a bird, indistinct really from any other, John just knew it was the same robin. There was something about the way it came so very close to him, didn't seem frightened at all, and in fact, he was almost sure it seemed to be chirping and speaking directly to him; that sent a warm tingle through him. When he got home, he made a cup of tea, sat down at his desk and noticed once again

the unopened package from his brother. He picked it up
and felt it. It had some real weight to it; he'd read somewhere that ashes were dense and heavy. He picked at the
wrapping and began to tear it open. The first thing he
found was a note from his brother.

*Hi John, I've divided up Mom's ashes as we dis-
cussed. Sarah and I are putting some of ours down at the
beach where Mom liked to sit sometimes. Hope you find
somewhere you think will be appropriate for you. Oh,
and here are a few things she had on the shelf in her
room. I'm pretty sure you gave her these, so thought you
might like to have them back. Love, Greg.*

When John opened the package further, he found the
heavy urn inscribed with her name and to his surprise
was something he'd forgotten he'd given his mom. He
turned it over in his hand to get a good look. On the
bottom in his own handwriting, it said: Merry Christmas
1993 – love John. He'd always thought it was a good
likeness of the real thing, and something he knew his
mother would cherish. He placed it on the shelf in front
of him – and there it stood, as if staring back, a little
porcelain statue of a red-breasted robin sitting on a small
twig.

Root Canal

'Suction please.'

Francis Grace, dentist to the rich and famous, had his surgical gloved hand deep in the mouth of another squeamish and vain actor. For once, he wasn't providing one of his custom Hollywood smiles, teeth which had a counterfeit sheen and glamour about them - whiteness that was off the charts. A customary dental repertoire which included, at considerable extra cost, a particular shade that was called White Angel, suggestive of the heavenly bodies that inspired it. This particular client had already had that procedure done some years back so instead of beautification, today Francis was halfway through a root canal and had already drilled out the inner cavity of the affected tooth and was just working on cleaning out the infected pulp and nerve at the root, all part of an expensive endodontic treatment plan. Save another tooth from extraction. Another seventy-five bucks in the bank. Bread and butter money for Francis and about twenty-five percent above the asking price that other dentists charged for a similar procedure. Dr. Grace pulled back a moment from his work.

'Could you suction that up around the gum, please, Brenda.'

'Of course, Dr. Grace.' The assistant leaned in over the patient and ran her suction tool along the patient's gum line. Francis watched her work and couldn't help but notice how tight her scrubs fit, especially across her shapely buttocks.

'You know Brenda, you really must share with me your jogging route, I'm keen to get into as good as shape as you.'

'Why thank you. I find that running allows me to be so much more flexible.' Francis Grace immediately imagined Brenda, scrubs down around her ankles, flexibly bending over the orthodontic chair waiting for him to mount her.

'All done, Dr. Grace.'

'What?' said Francis, snapping back into focus.

'The suctioning. It's all done. All sucked dry and ready for you.' Francis couldn't really tell behind her masked smile if Brenda was flirting with him or not.

'Why, thank you Brenda.' Francis fired up his drill again and moved towards the gaping mouth of his patient. The man opened his eyes momentarily and looked up at the dentist and attempted to unintelligibly mumble a plea.

'Everything is in order, Mr. Stone. Now why don't you just focus on the relaxing sounds of Debussy, and we'll have you sorted in no time.'

Truth was that Dr. Grace offered something much more than mere basic dental procedures. A visit to the *Teeth by Grace* dental clinic was a total aesthetic experience. From the comfortable spa-like atmosphere of the waiting room with its piped-in soothing music; scents of jasmine and eucalyptus; array of the latest art and décor magazines; and complimentary water, the clinic also boasted the latest high-tech equipment that money could buy. If there was a new gadget or item of dental technology that Francis could boast about to his patients, he had to have one. The thespian patient, one Rudyard Stone, settled back on the ergonomic chair - a chair of utmost comfort, design and usability, and, having already braved himself half-way through his root canal ordeal, tightly gripped the armrests with sweating hands, praying for this thing to be soon over. Stone shut his eyes tight, neither wanting to see the sharp instruments coming towards his mouth or view anything pulled from his gaping cavity when, Susan, the clinic receptionist, interrupted the procedure.

'Excuse me, Dr. Grace.' Francis released his finger on the drill and turned his head to look at the flustered young woman.

'Susan. What is it?'

'The hospital. Your wife, Sir. On the telephone.'

'My wife is on the phone. Can you take a message please.'

'Well, no. I mean it's the hospital calling – they said the baby is coming.'

'The baby! What, now?' said Francis, the sudden

realisation that his wife had likely gone into labour.

'Are you sure? Is Nina on the phone?'

'No Sir. They hung up. They said they just wanted to let you know. She called for an ambulance herself, your wife is already at the hospital, on the maternity ward, they said her contractions are strong and increasing.'

'Great Scott,' said Francis, quickly extracting his hand again from Stone's gapping mouth and smearing bloody tooth pulp across his forehead as he wiped at his brow. The patient opened his eyes again and looked up expectedly at the dentist – a father-to-be who was desperately trying to figure out his next move. Francis pulled off his mask and turned to his assistant.

'Brenda, we're going to need some sedative filling – ready some eugenol antibacterial paste, two milligrams should do just fine.' The young dental assistant's eyes flashed in slight disbelief and looked over at the dentist.

'Filling? But the canal, aren't you going to...' Francis cut her off.

'I haven't time for this now, I promised Nina I'd be there. Elijah or Rosalind, whichever sex it turns out to be, are on their way. I'm about to be a father!' shouted Francis.

'That's wonderful Dr. Grace, but shouldn't we finish this up first?' Rudyard Stone turned his head slightly and grimaced at the dentist. Half of him wanted this done now, the other half was happy for the sudden reprieve.

'Re-book Mr. Stone for a follow-up appointment. Next week will be fine. I'll prescribe him some antibiotics to tide him over. We can finish the canal then.' Francis stood up, a look of resolve spread across his face as he peeled his surgical gloves off and tossed them into the clinical waste bin.

'But Dr. Grace, aren't you going to at least do the filling?'

'Brenda, you've watched me do this procedure a thousand times – today you get to move up the ladder. Succession planning in action. I'm sure you can give Mr. Stone a lovely temp, he will be in your capable hands.' Francis Grace stood up, pulled off his apron and turned towards the door.

'And Brenda . . .' The assistant looked expectedly at Dr. Grace, hoping perhaps, he'd changed his mind.

'Yes, Sir.'

'Offer Mr. Stone a twenty percent discount on his next visit and cancel the rest of today's appointments. Leaping lizards, I'm gonna be a father!' With that, Francis Grace disappeared out of the surgery.

The dentist pushed open the door of his midtown office building and stepped out onto the snowy streets of Manhattan. His comfort-comes-first work shoes quickly found themselves covered in snow and as he looked around, he was a little taken aback by the amount that had gathered since he'd left home that morning. Not to mention, the amount that was still falling. The second thing he noticed was an eerie quiet, something quite out of place for this pre-rush-hour time in Midtown. It was as if all that snow was absorbing the usual sounds of life, never mind putting a stop to the flow of traffic that usually ran up 5th Avenue at this time of day. Grace looked left then looked right, hoping to flag a cab, but there wasn't a single vehicle in sight. Fact was, there wasn't a single car, bus or taxi moving at all. The city, it would seem, had ground to a stand still. Francis checked his watch – 3.30 p.m. Mount Sinai Hospital was located far uptown, just across from Central Park, un-walkable, especially in this weather. His choices were few and his mind landed on his only, yet detestable, option. It had been many years since Francis had ventured under ground. The subway system most certainly wasn't his thing, and in fact, made him terribly anxious to be burrowed that far underground travelling on a speeding-bullet of a train. With the mere thought of traversing the many steps down into the subterranean abyss, he could feel his chest tighten, and stomach start to churn as a wave of uncontrollable claustrophobia swept over him.

'Damn it,' he said, immediately regretting cussing out loud, 'this is less than ideal.' Still, having no other options and fearing he was going to miss the birth, he started trudging northward towards the nearest subway station. The going was hard as the snow made walking treacherous and slowed him down considerably. He couldn't run for the fear that every step he took in his smooth-bottomed shoes could result in a slip – something he firmly believed was just an accident waiting to happen. Two years earlier he'd suffered a ruptured disc from a bad fall he took after stumbling on a sidewalk that was wet from a window cleaner's soapy spills. Surgery, a longish stay in hospital, and many months of painful rehabilitation, was a memory he couldn't erase – or risk again. He'd had to temporarily close up his practice losing considerable income, not to mention the loss of a few key staff and well-paying clients. Once he was well enough to return to work it was almost like starting over again, building his brand and clientele up from scratch. Since that time, he had insisted that all his office furniture should be ergonomic, comfortable for both patients and staff. A bad back was a terrible thing to suffer, for him or his clients. Francis slowed himself down to a snail's pace gingerly placing foot after careful foot, and as he walked could feel the snow gathering and melting into his socks and shoes.

'Shoot,' he mumbled under his breath, 'son of a monkey,' the dentist having long ago erased blasphemous expletives completely from his vocabulary, except for the very occasion 'damn'. His father had been a swearer of the highest magnitude, almost priding himself on a wide repertoire of crude cuss words. He was also a classic drinker, perhaps both attributes pairing together well, but needless to say Francis promised himself that neither paternal traits would plague or ruin his own life. From a young age Francis focussed on different ambitions and drive to his father, and forged himself, not as an imitation of a father gone to seed, but rather on a much loftier path, hence the fiercely competitive need to finish top of his class in dentistry school. He was determined to make something of himself, in contrast to his drunken father who squandered every chance he had in life on a cheap bottle of rum and swore like bejesus. It was for this very reason that only on very rare occasions, did Francis utter a word as expressive or expletive as 'damn', and why he never touched anything harder than apple juice. Francis Grace was resolved to be nothing like Frank Grace.

The wet and anxious dentist reached the subway station after an arduous ten-minute crawl, brushed off his trousers, took a deep breath, and after counting to three, descended the stairs into the bowels of the underground. The next fifteen minutes went by in a complete blur. Somehow Francis managed to set himself onto autopilot, blocking out his surroundings as best he could, with just enough awareness to be able to negotiate switching trains and getting on and off at the correct stops. Finally, he found himself above ground again, taking sharp, shallow breaths, and reorienting himself to fresh air and his new surroundings. Once he got his bearings, he realised he was now just half a block from Mount Sinai Hospital. He could see it - just a short jaunt up the avenue. He carefully picked his way to the hospital entrance and walked straight to reception.

'Afternoon, I'm Dr. Grace and I'm going to be a father,' Francis blurted out to the bemused receptionist.

'Good day doctor, are you on shift today?' Francis suddenly snapped into focus.

'Heavens no! I'm a dentist not a medical doctor, and my wife is about to give birth. Perhaps you could point me in the direction of the maternity ward?' The young woman giggled, and Francis noticed how her remarkably unnatural blonde hair cascaded gently onto her curvy shoulders. She was wearing a tight-fitting yellow mohair cardigan which had a name tag that in clear red lettering read, 'Misty Monroe, ward clerk' pinned right there on her chest. Francis read the words out loud and couldn't help noticing her small, pert breasts.

'Why, Dr. Grace, the maternity ward is on the twelfth floor and the elevators are right over there,' smiled Miss Monroe. Francis returned the smile.

'That's a lovely name, Misty, and might I add your cardigan perfectly compliments your golden hair.' The woman blushed slightly.

'Right over there, Doctor,' said the ward clerk, pointing across the lobby, 'your wife, will no doubt, be expecting you.' Francis Grace strode confidently across the lobby to the elevators, no longer feeling anxious, instead, pleased that he had made it in time for the birth. He pressed the call button and waited. Soon the doors opened like a mechanical theatre curtain unveiling another off-Broadway extravaganza, as several colourful people stepped out and pushed past him. Francis stepped into the elevator, pressed number twelve and waited. The unwieldy doors slowly crawled shut, there was a click of gears, some sort of mechanical engagement, and then the lift began to lurch upwards. The elevator moved slowly, with purpose, up and up. Francis watched the floors arrive and pass by – three, four, five. . . It was only after the sixth floor that he noticed a tightness in his chest and a shortness of breath, a curiously similar feeling as he experienced being down in the bowels of the earth on a subway train. In his excitement he hadn't really considered that his claustrophobia would also occur in an elevator, yet given the confines of the space itself, it was reasonable enough to expect. But here he was, caught off guard. When was the last time he'd rode in an elevator, anyway? A slight wave of panic prickled the skin on the back of his neck, and he felt a bead of sweat forming on his brow.

'Corn nuts,' admonished Francis to himself, 'it's just an elevator, dagnabbit. And I'm almost there!' Francis stared yearningly up again at the lights that indicated the floors – seven, eight, nine. It wasn't until he was between the tenth and eleventh floors that he heard a loud sound, like the snap of a cable and the lift ground to a halt. Francis pushed the open button – nothing. He pressed the twelfth-floor button and then the open button in quick succession. Then again and again. Nothing happened. He tried pushing harder with all his strength, then holding his finger on the buttons. Nothing happened. The wave of panic now spread through his entire body, and he could feel the tremor of heart palpitations, the sweaty palms, and the light-headedness. He scoured the lift looking for any way out, any hope of deliverance. Nothing. Desperate now, he began banging on the door and yelling.

'HELP ME – GOSH DAMN IT!'

When Francis came to, he found himself gazing up into a halo of shimmering light and his first thought was that he'd passed on. He mentally surveyed his body to see if he could detect any feelings in his limbs. Feet – check. Arms – check. Fingers – he held his hand up in front of his face and wiggled his digits. All seemed to be present and accounted for and working fine. Perhaps the body transcends death, he thought to himself? Then something seemed to cloud out the bright light and he began to make out the blurry contours and lines of a face peering down at him. One he thought looked vaguely familiar.

'Francis? Francis, it's me, Nina.' The dentist focused his eyes. It *was* her. Had she died giving birth and gone to heaven, too? Then another face came into view – one he didn't recognise.

'Welcome back Dr. Grace. You took a nasty fall, hit your head. Nothing serious but just take it easy now, you're gonna be fine.' Francis groaned a little as the pain on the back of his head made itself apparent. Nina leaned in a little and pushed something towards him.

'Your son. Look Francis, your beautiful son has arrived.' Francis squinted his eyes trying to focus on the little pink blur that was dangled in front of him.

'Well, jumping jiminy crickets . . . so he has, Elijah is here,' was all Francis could stammer before a wave of euphoria passed over his entire body and, for the second time in one day, he blacked out.

And so it was, on January 24th, 1960, Francis Grace, non-swearing teetotaling dentist to the rich and famous, did make it to the hospital in time for the birth of his son. Unfortunately, he blacked out in the elevator, fell over and hit his head, which meant he missed the actual birth. He also needed treatment himself, so lucky for him he was in a hospital, but the fact still remained he did make good on his promise to Nina. Later the family would joke about how Elijah's mom and dad both spent their son's first hours in complimentary hospital beds. Like most children, Elijah learnt and memorised the stories he was told as a youngster and would later come to embellish them with his own made-up details. Sometimes interchanging the facts completely - how his father had been waylaid from his birth by having to save an old lady who passed-out in the elevator on her way to see her ailing husband. The heroics of which meant he missed his birth yet saved a life. But that was his pops. A heroic man. That was, until he went to prison for committing an unspeakable crime - but more on that to come. Like many a child, Elijah always liked his stories to have a courageous theme to them. But the fact still remained, once the facility engineers got Francis out of the elevator, he was taken to ER, received a few stitches in his head, and was left to recover on a gurney in the maternity ward, parked right next to his wife's bed.

Body & Soul

'Come on, darling, eat your supper. Be a good boy for momma, it's your favourite - macaroni and cheese.' Elijah sat rigid in his booster seat staring blankly at his mother and then pushed another piece of pasta onto the floor. Nina stubbed out her cigarette in the big glass ashtray that sat in the middle of the table and got up to refill her cup with coffee.

'Suit yourself,' she said, 'all the more for Desmond.' The Old English sheepdog, laying on the kitchen floor, upon hearing its name, peered up through its impermeable fringe with anticipation. Nina sighed heavily to herself, picked up the dog's bowl, walked over to her son, grabbed his little plate and scraped whatever was left into the bowl. She put it down on the floor and Desmond immediately appeared at her side looking up at her.

'Go ahead,' she said, 'someone might as well eat it.' Nina wiped Elijah's hands and face, got him down and walked through into the living room. On the way she lit another cigarette and then slumped down on the expansive sofa. Elijah followed her in, waddling the way toddlers do, and sat down at his little play table and began to sort through his toys and games. Nina picked up a fashion magazine and aimlessly flicked through the pages. Elijah looked over at his mother, and even at the tender age of three, somewhere in his still developing infant brain he knew he would have to entertain himself, his mother, although present, wouldn't be interested in playing games with him. And so, he picked up a toy car and making broom-broom sounds, started to drive it around his table.

'There's a good boy,' said Nina, looking over, 'just like your father, interested in bloody cars.' Nina laughed to herself. 'I wonder if you'll turn out to be a bastard playboy like him too, hmm?' Unlike her husband, Nina thought nothing of swearing and, in fact, believed that swear words had a particularity about them that was rather expressive. Take the expletive, fuck, for example. It could imbue all manner of different shades of meaning just from inflection alone. It could be nonchalant as in 'oh, fuck it', or aggressive as in 'don't you dare fuck with me', or even sensual, 'all I want is for you to fuck me in a field of wildflowers'. Nina took another drag on her cigarette and thought about her husband for a moment. When they had first met, he'd been like a knight in shining armour. So attentive, showering her with gifts and compliments, she was the centre of his world and above all else, Francis made sex fun. His spontaneity, alone, was impressive. They did in the back of his convertible, on his dentist chair when the office had closed, and many times while skinny dipping on a beach in Portugal, just barely out of sight of the other bathers. Since the birth of Elijah, however, it seemed like all the fun and sex had been sucked right out of their marriage, just like one of Francis' saliva vacuuming devices. All they seemed to do these days was pass the toddler back and forth to each other and exchange instructions, or child-rearing details.

'Elijah has already gone poo-poo,' or 'Mr. Ducky needs a wash, Elijah just fed him half his puréed pears.'

Some days they barely spoke to each at all. Nina worked nights and Francis worked days, and of course, Francis worked long hours. Sure, he was a bread-winner extraordinaire. He was, after all, the best and most sought-after dentist in all of Midtown. His net income was more than any other dentist south of 59th Avenue which provided Nina with all the creature comforts she could possibly desire. However, Nina also knew that Francis had a wandering eye. He liked the ladies, oh so much. She knew all about his insatiable sex drive, but sadly for them, the fact they had a kid around all the time just seemed like a contraceptive device. It was true that Francis had fucked Nina in a field of wildflowers. It happened in the south of France, and it truly had been a glorious thing. It happened on their honeymoon; a memory Nina would always cherish. The scent of lily of the valley wafting in the air as Francis' muscular body laid upon her and brought them both to climax. It was the stuff of dreams. But these days Nina had a strong hunch that Francis' late nights at the surgery meant that he was sure to be screwing his bevy of assistant girls. There did seem to be an on-going permanent advertisement for a 'dental assistant' at his clinic and Francis always insisted he be part of the interview himself. All of which was downright obvious. Girls came and girls went, an apparent revolving door – surely each one growing tired of being hit on by their boss. Nina took another drag of her cigarette blew the smoke out and watched it dissipate. Then quietly under her breath she said, 'well, fuck you, Francis Grace,' finding yet another expressive usage of her favourite expletive. She enjoyed the sound so much that she quickly added, 'two can play that fucking game.' She stared off into the distance and sang a few lines of a familiar song . . .

Good morning heartache,
You old gloomy sight,
Good morning heartache,
Thought we said goodbye last night . . .

At 5.30 p.m. Nina was still wearing her dressing gown and slippers having slept into her customary rising time of 1.00 p.m. The nanny had taken care of Elijah up until then while Mrs. Grace recovered from another late night of performing at the Smoky Slipper Jazz and Blues Club. Five nights a week Nina worked from 11.00 p.m. until the bar closed, singing American Songbook standards with a little combo of jazz musicians. Nina had a God-given voice, full of heartache and yearning, her natural alto gaining expressive rough edges from the endless cigarettes she smoked, and the drinks bought for her by the, mostly male, clientele. She cut a fine shape of a woman and was always turned out in one of her elegant figure-hugging sequinned dresses. Her hair would be teased up into a small bouffant, a style which took her plenty of time to prepare, and which was held in place with copious amounts of hair spray. Every evening the boys would start the set with a little instrumental, something by Coltrane or one of their own favourites - *Goodbye Porkpie Hat* by Mingus, warming up the audience before Nina would stride out confidently to centre stage and into the spotlight. She was the undisputed star of the show. Men were drawn to her, women, too. In her performances, she played it aloof, almost unapproachable. Then, closing her eyes in order to conjure up that raw emotion, she would bewitch all listeners with her interpretation of melancholy that drew gasps and cheers alike. There was no doubt that her performances were mesmerising and by the end of the night, the audience, well liquored up on whiskey and gin, would be eating out of her hand. And Nina always left them wanting more.

For her stage persona she had opted to use her maiden name – Black, along with shortening her given name from Clementina to Nina. She thought Black sounded more powerful and intriguing than Grace, and besides, Clementina Grace smacked of too much do-goody, like some sort of charity worker or Sunday school teacher. Nina preferred a name with more edge.

Nina Black. It was sharp and dark and suited her to a tee. But choosing to use a different surname upset Francis. In so many ways he was such a traditional man, not to mention jealous and possessive, and couldn't quite understand why she even needed a stage name.

'Grace is a perfectly fine name,' said Francis on the night she told him, 'it's my name, gosh-darn-it, and one in which you agreed to share when we married. And Clementina is positively lovely.' However, Nina was resolute. Francis' influence ended at the stage door and so, much to her husband's chagrin, she danced to her own drummer and insisted on performing under her chosen name.

'Don't be such a boring old bastard Francis. This is show business, not dentistry and I'm ditching the tiresome, tedious and tame, and sticking with Black – it's Nina-fucking-Black.'

'Really Nina-kins, do you need to swear like that all the time, hmm? And in front of Elijah too.'

'Eat me, Francis.' And that ended the discussion. Nina could, when she wanted to, have just as much a stubborn streak as Francis, and so in the end he simply had no say in the matter. He never quite understood why, after they married, she had been so insistent on maintaining her own career. After all, it wasn't as if they needed the money, and he would have much preferred her to be a stay-at-home mom. A Clementine Grace, mother – most certainly, but a Nina Black, singer – most certainly not. Nina had other thoughts though and wasn't interested in Francis' plan for a wearisome domestic life.

She craved the spotlight and attention it gave her. The only thing that could rival that was to be spread-eagled in a field of wildflowers, and that had been many years ago.

Most nights, her and the band played encores until after 3.00 a.m. and Nina would usually get home and then unwind with a few vodka tonics before finally crawling into bed around 5.00 a.m. - just an hour before her husband's alarm would go off. At. 6.30 a.m. each day Ingrid Norgaard, the nanny, would arrive in readiness to take care of Elijah. Ingrid hailed from Denmark and spoke perfect English. Just turned nineteen, she was enthralled by the vastness of America and the busyness and cosmopolitan feel of New York City. She particularly loved Central Park and often strolled with Elijah down East 65th St. to 5th Ave. where they could easily gain access to the park. It was just a fifteen-minute walk from the stylish four-story brown stone Francis and Nina owned. The home was prime New York real estate, with easy access to all the Big Apple had to offer, and easily commutable by taxi for both of them. Ingrid stayed in her own small studio apartment. At first Francis had suggested she live with them, after all, they had a spare attic that would make a perfect bedroom, but Nina, prudently suggested an alternative option, recognising all too well the temptation this young woman's presence would furnish, which would likely prove too much for her promiscuous husband.

The band were just finishing a credible version of *Take the 'A' Train* when Nina strode out onto the stage at the Smoky Slipper. It was Friday night, and the place was jam packed. There was the usual collective in-take of breath, a few whoops and wolf-whistles, as Nina walked out to centre stage and seductively adjusted the mic stand. She stood statue-still for a moment as her presence permeated over the room and the audience got a good look at her.

'Good evening,' she purred into the microphone, 'I'm Nina Black and these fellas are,' she paused for a moment, properly surveying the audience, and making sure to make eye contact, 'these fellas call themselves The Satin Sheets.' There were a few laughs from the men standing up at the bar and one guy whistled loudly. 'And trust me,' continued the songstress, 'ain't nothing Nina Black likes better than to slip between them satin sheets.' She looked around at her band. They'd heard the joke a thousand times, but still, they obliged her with wide grins. 'Why don't you count us in, Buddy.' With that, the piano player nodded his head in time to the unheard beat and then the band launched into a slow and sultry version of Billie Holiday's *Lover Man*. Nina pulled a cigarette out from inside her cleavage and held out her hand with it cradled between her slender fingers. One of the men in the front row stood up and reached out with his lighter. Nina stepped to the edge of the stage, bent down, grasped hold of his hand to steady it and leaned her head sideways to catch her cigarette alight. She took a long drag and blew the smoke in the man's face, then blew him a kiss. The club erupted in applause. Nina turned and sauntered back to her microphone confident in the fact that she already had total control of the room without even singing a single note. She waited for the music to circle around again, leaned into the microphone, and then treated everyone to her sultry alto.

I don't know why
but I'm feeling so sad
I long to try
something I never had . . .

From that point onwards Nina owned the joint and orchestrated the evening to her own desires and made sure the paying customers kept the band in drinks, herself included. The songs she sang covered a repertoire that was peppered with well-known ballads from Cole Porter to Duke Ellington and dipped deeply into the blues catalogues with renditions such as *Black Bottom Stomp* and *Oh, Didn't He Ramble* by Jelly Roll Morton. Billie Holiday, of course, featured often in the set lists, her songs of heartache and longing resonating deeply on Nina's weathered vocal cords.

'Why thank you so much,' said Nina, gracefully accepting the applause, 'we're gonna take ourselves a little break but we'll be back for one more set – so stick around. How about a big hand, and maybe another round for the hard-working boys in the band?'

On her break Nina sauntered to the bar to chat with her pal Diego, the Puerto Rican bartender. She sidled up to a space at the counter and nodded in the bartender's direction.

'Miss Nina, a mighty fine show tonight,' said Diego, as he shook his cocktail shaker and poured another long martini into a glass.

'How's tips tonight, Diego? These big spenders treating you right?' Diego Diaz free poured vodka into a tumbler and splashed in a couple of ice cubes, walked over, and handed it to Nina.

'There you go Miss Nina. Your usual, on the house. Tips have been good tonight. Your singing brings out the sweet charity in folk. You want a splash of soda in that?' Nina laughed, shook her head and put the glass to her lips and then fished for a cigarette in her purse. The man standing next to her turned around and pulled out a zippo lighter.

'Evening Miss Black, can I perhaps, assist you with a light?' Nina took in this stranger for a second or two. He was tall - six foot three, she figured, and had that weathered worldly look of someone who strode confidently through life. He was wearing a wide-brim cream coloured fedora and was sporting a black double-breasted suit, nothing too fancy, just one that looked like it had been measured to fit his large frame.

'Sure,' purred Nina, 'a light would be nice.' The man flipped open the top of his zippo, struck the wheel, and a little flame danced into life. Nina learned in, and with well-practiced style, touched her cigarette to the naked flame and set it alight.

'Your singing tonight is sublime, if you don't mind me saying so.'

'And who, may I ask, should I want to mind, is saying so?'

'Apologies. Name is Carter. Carter Ford. Pleased to make your acquaintance.'

'Acquaintance? My, how formal. Ford you say . . . as in the automobile?'

'Why yes, my father was from a long line of Fords, the very ones who started the automobile empire.'

'So, I take it you're a car man, Mr. Ford.'

'Why no, that would be the assumption most people make. I don't even own one.'

'Don't own a car? Why that is surprising, here I would have pegged you for a convertible man myself, but tell me Mr. Ford, what is a man of such vehicular pedigree interested in, if not cars?'

'Jazz music. A fine Tennessee bourbon, and I'd say, I have a penchant for honesty.'

'Honesty?' laughed Nina, 'why then, I'd say you're a man of many surprises, Mr. Ford – and how is the bourbon treating you tonight?'

'Carter. Please, call me Carter. I'd say this bourbon is hitting the spot.'

'And who is your preferred Jazz artiste?'

'Well, there are many people I admire, the American songbook inspires so many greats, lots of geniuses to be sure, but the way I figure jazz, it ain't so much about an individual talent, it's more about context, the

commingling of rhythms, notes and intentions, that, and hooking onto that transcendent musical experience.'
Nina took another sip of her vodka, looked at the glass, then shot the entire thing back in one go. She slid the glass across the bar.

'Diego – another, *por favour*.' Carter held up his wallet to the bartender.

'Here, I got this one.'

'A fascinating summation, Carter, and when did you last have a transcendent experience?' Carter Ford picked up his glass of bourbon and took a sip.

'Why, I'm having one tonight.' Carter smiled at Nina, and she couldn't help but notice how blue his eyes were. Paul Newman blue.

'Tonight? Well, I guess the bourbon must be alright?' said Nina. Carter Ford adjusted his hat slightly and leant his elbow on the bar.

'Oh, I don't mean the drink – it's alright. You know, I believe you can tell by the way somebody sings if it's authentic or not. When that joy or hurt comes from some real place. When someone is digging deep and turning that base metal into gold. That's what makes music transcendent.' Diego walked over and poured a new glass of vodka for her.

'There you go,' said the bartender, and then he tapped his watch, 'better watch the time Miss Nina, you still got one more set to play.' Nina took the glass from Diego and smiled at Carter Ford.

'I do believe you aim to flatter me, Mr. Honestyman, but I guess a girl gotta take men like you at face value. Otherwise, that bourbon really is shit and I ain't got no real stories to tell. Why don't you stick around for the next set and maybe you can see if we are mining real gold or fools. And then later perhaps you and I could find out what you really mean by honesty.' Carter Ford held up his glass and clinked it against hers.

'Break a leg,' said Carter, and Nina was sure she saw his blue eyes twinkling right at her.

Nina Black and the Satin Sheets ended the evening as they always did, with one final encore – a simmering rendition of *Body and Soul*. As people began to file out onto the late-night streets of Greenwich Village a single figure remained at the bar – Carter Ford. Nina hadn't forgotten her invitation and sauntered over.

'Can I buy you a drink?' said Carter.

'Why sure,' smiled Nina, 'another vodka soda would hit the spot.' Ford waved his hands to get Diego's attention and ordered a couple more drinks."

'Would you like to sit down a spell?'

'Alright.' They walked over to a small table and Carter pulled out a chair and offered her a seat.

'That was, by far, the best set of the night,' smiled Carter.

'So, did it hit all the marks - did you transcend?' Carter picked up his glass of bourbon and examined it.

'You married?' asked Carter.

'Married with child,' returned Nina.

'Happily?'

'Why now, I think you mentioned something earlier about honesty.'

'That I did. Your singing tonight, I do believe that comes from an honest place. I've heard a lot of singers to know the difference. There is a lot of heartache going on in your voice. If I was a betting man, I'd have to say – unhappily.' Carter looked straight into Nina's eyes and held her there with his stare. Nina couldn't help but smile at this brazen, intriguing, handsome man.

'Touché. Your perception comes a close second to your audacious curiosity.'

'You know Nina, I don't live too far from here and I have some jazz records I bet you've never heard. I also got myself a bottle of specially aged bourbon that was finished with mountain honey from bees that only pollinate wildflowers. I think the result, should you choose to join me, is sublime.' Nina couldn't help but feel drawn to this man and his temerarious overture.

'And if that wasn't enough, I do believe that Milt Jackson's vibraphone stylings will be a revelation.' Nina smiled and reached over to touch Carter's arm.

Francis Grace awoke to his alarm as he always did and quietly crawled out of bed as not to disturb his sleeping wife. He shuffled into the en-suite bathroom, closed the door, and stared at himself in the mirror. It had been another long week, business at the clinic had been brisk with lots of new clients coming to see him for their consultation. Word of mouth was everything in the dentistry world and even more so, amongst the actors and theatre impresarios who made their way to Francis' practice. More teeth whitening, thought Francis, more veneers, he could almost feel his bank account swelling at the mere thought of it and Francis already had his heart set on a new set of wheels - a sweet Jaguar E-Type, silver and blue. Perfect. What a riotous business dentistry had turned out to be. Cars, chicks and teeth. What a combo. He'd recently recruited a new assistant – Sandra, who had, arguably, the nicest derrière he'd hired in a long time. He smiled at the thought and brushed the sandy locks off his forehead. He flashed his teeth in the mirror. Today being Saturday, there was no need to hurry to shave, shower or ready himself, and in any case, Ingrid would soon arrive to take care of Elijah. Monday and Tuesday were her days off, but Francis loved Saturday's the most as he got to spend time with them both over breakfast. Sometimes the three of them would go to the park together, get a coffee and watch Elijah play on the swings. Ingrid was an enigma though. Impenetrable. Untouchable. She was drop-dead gorgeous and one of those young women who seemed almost unaware of her natural beauty. And unconcerned. Which was irritatingly appealing. She was one conquest Francis had not been able to realise. Francis checked the clock – 6.25, Ingrid would be here soon. He splashed some water on his face, ran a comb through his hair and made his way back into the bedroom to fetch his clothes. For the first time, since waking, he suddenly became aware that the bed was empty. His wife wasn't in it.

Francis, Ingrid and Elijah ventured to the park to feed the ducks and swans some bread crusts Francis had thought to bring along with them. The swans seemed to bully the much smaller ducks, jockeying for the best place to greedily snatch up the most bread. Ingrid took Elijah by the hand and walked him further down the pond so that the ducks could get a look in and at least some chance at some food. Elijah squealed with laughter every time he threw a handful of bread out and they frantically darted this way and that, desperate to get their fill. It was a cloudy, but warm spring day and after feeding the birds and some time on the swings, the three grabbed something to eat from a local food truck.

'Do you have hotdogs in Denmark?' asked Francis. Ingrid nodded.

'Yes, but in Denmark they are called rød pølse, due to their very red colour. But these are nice too.'

'American wieners are the best,' smiled Francis, thinking how his innuendo would likely go unnoticed by Ingrid. The three of them tucked into their hotdogs while they watched the ducks glide on the pond in the distance.

'What do you think, Elijah?' said his dad, patting him on the head.

'Grid, Grid,' said the young boy.

'What does that mean?' asked Francis. Ingrid chuckled.

'I think he's trying to say Ingrid.'

'Oh.' Francis turned to his son, 'can you say Daddy?' Elijah looked up at his father and then over at Ingrid.

'Grid, Grid,' he mumbled once again. Ingrid laughed.

'I'm sure he'll be saying that soon.' Ingrid wiped her mouth with her napkin and then turned to Francis.

'It's time for me to go now. Do you want me to clean him up first? He's covered in ketchup.'

'Nah, I got it. Come over here Elijah, come and say goodbye to Grid.' They both laughed.

'Bye bye Elijah, I'll see you next week, okay? Do you have a hug goodbye?' Elijah waddled over and hugged Ingrid around the thighs.

'See you later Mr. Grace, have a good weekend.'

'You too, Ingrid. Thanks for all your help.' Then Ingrid began her trek home. Francis wiped Elijah's hands and mouth and then taking hold of his son's little hand, father and son walked home together.

Nina eventually made it home a little after 10.00 a.m., had a quick shower to cleanse herself of any scent or trace of Carter Ford, then went straight to bed. When she finally roused herself, around three o'clock, she quickly pulled herself together, applied a little makeup and tied back her hair before making her entrance downstairs. Francis was lying on the floor playing cars with Elijah when Nina walked in with a cup of coffee.

'Late night,' said Francis without looking up. Nina had already rehearsed her excuse backwards and forwards and had devised something which would allow her additional 'late nights' so that her affair with Carter Ford could continue without the need to constantly explain her absence or cover her tracks.

'Vinnie wants us to work up a new set of material to make sure the regulars don't get bored,' said Nina, 'so we are rehearsing at the club after closing time. The band are already set up, so it makes sense to just stay a little longer.' Francis looked up at his wife.

'Be good if you let me know that. I was worried about you.'

'Ain't nothing to worry about darling, just breaking in some new songs.' Nina strode toward them both and kneeled down on the floor.

'We'll likely be at it for a few weeks,' said Nina, 'the boys are keen to work up a few trickier Monk tunes – *'Round Midnight* and the like.' Nina turned her attention to her son and his playing.

'Now how's my little angel?' Nina picked up one of Elijah's toy cars and ruffled her son's hair. 'What sound does this one make?'

Elijah, delighted to have both his parent's attention, pushed the car hard against the carpet, setting its wheels spinning and said, 'broom broom.'

'He said the word Grid today.'

'Oh? What does that mean?'

'It's Elijah-speak for Ingrid, I think.'

'Ingrid?'

'Well, it makes sense. She spends more time with him than we do.' Nina felt a twinge of something. Envy? Disappointment? Disapproval?

'I sing to him,' said Nina, despondently.

'And I'm teaching him everything he needs to know about cars,' laughed Francis, 'besides, he'll be saying mommy and daddy soon. You'll see.' Nina watched her son involved with his game and marvelled at just how big he was getting. Hard to think that he was two and a half already, and heading for three, and before you know it, he'd be starting school. He was such a pensive thoughtful child. Always contented to spend time playing alone. Sometimes when she was warming up her voice in the afternoons, he'd just sit and listen to her, absorbing things, taking in the music, entranced by his mother's voice. She never dumbed things down or simplified for his benefit, singing him nursery rhymes and such, instead she practiced sophisticated jazz compositions.

Nina looked over at Francis playing on the floor with their son. Elijah seemed contented. It was nice to see them together. He definitely had a strong resemblance to Francis with his sharp nose and arched eyebrows, even down to the shock of sandy wavy hair on his head. All from his father. From this vantage point it was obvious they were father and son, and it was hard to say who liked the toy cars more – Francis or Elijah. That made Nina smile. Her husband was a successful man, handsome, but for some reason that just didn't seem enough anymore. Or perhaps, in truth, it never had. Besides, his unfaithfulness was the final deal clincher. It made a mockery of their marriage. Then Nina's thoughts quickly turned to Carter. He was a different breed altogether. A man's man to be sure, he had a smoothness about him too, and a confidence that was appealing, not a swagger exactly, just a different kind of conviction that shone through. The way he had taken her to his bed without much persuasion. They had arrived back to his apartment, ignored his record collection and his premium bottle of bourbon completely, all in favour of a direct seduction and sex that was as liberating as it was voracious. It had been some time since Nina had felt the attraction of a man and it felt good to be wanted in that way again. To feel like a sensual woman and not just a mother or a wife. If it did turn out to be just the one night, then Nina was at least content to have felt the blood surge through her veins once again and be desired in that way.

The following Friday night, when Nina stepped out onto the stage, she glanced around the room to see if she could spot him and catch that sparkle in his eye as he nursed a good glass of bourbon in his large hand and tapped his shiny boots along to the music. But sadly, Carter was nowhere to be seen. Nina felt her heart sink a little, her expectations wither, but she steeled herself to the reality of the inevitable. So it was, Nina Black and the Satin Sheets did what they always did – launched into a heady set of jazz standards. It was her job, but even though, the songstress was a little more subdued in her performance, disappointed to have to admit that the brief fling had just been that. So, as the evening progressed, she loaded up on a few extra drinks in between sets just to dull her senses a little.

'You alright tonight, Miss Nina?' said Diego, as he free-poured another shot and pushed it towards her, 'you ain't seeming yourself.'

'The blues, Diego. Sometimes a woman sings 'em and sometimes she lives 'em too.' Diego touched Nina's hand.

'You need anything, you just holler.' Nina smiled at her friend. He was a good man and always watched out for her.

'You know what, the other thing about the blues is it don't tend to linger long. All character-building stuff. I'll be just fine Diego. Nina Black as the day I was born and Nina Black as the day I die too.' The two of them laughed and Diego filled a shot glass with whiskey.

'Well, cheers to them blues then,' said the bartender and he clinked glasses with her, and they both shot their drinks back in one go.

It was around the start of the third and final set when Nina opened her eyes after being deeply entranced by the lyrics she was singing when she saw a familiar cream-coloured fedora arrive and park himself at the bar. There he was. Her heart skipped beat, and she could feel her spirits lift as she sang the lines to the second verse.

It's autumn in New York
That brings the promise of new love
Autumn in New York
Is often mingled with pain . . .

When the song was finished Carter raised his glass in the air in salute to her and the band.

'Well, good evening,' said Nina into her microphone, 'I've been singing the blues all night, but now I think it's time we shake things up a little.' Nina turned to face her band mates, counted off the four beats and then the boys started in with their final number of the evening.

My life a wreck you're making
You know I'm yours for just the taking
I'd gladly surrender myself to you
body and soul . . .

When Nina went backstage to gather her few things there was a large bouquet of roses waiting for her. She smiled widely to herself and felt a strange mix fluttering in the pit of her stomach – the pangs of excitement combined with a strangely sad resignation all grounded with a sense of relief. She picked up the card, read it and put in her pocket, then gathered the flowers up in her arms, grabbed her purse, and headed out to the bar.

Over the course of the next few weeks Nina and Carter gave themselves over to each other like they'd never loved another before or would find another after. Late nights back at his apartment were the norm but they also ventured out during the daytime, to take in a museum, a late lunch, or immerse themselves and disappear into Chinatown, SOHO or the bohemian world of Greenwich Village. Places she and Francis had never been before. Places where they could be themselves, and their affair could bloom in public view. Whenever Nina could arrange for Ingrid to stay a few hours longer than usual, she took advantage. For his part, Carter played along too. He made whatever time Nina wanted available to her. They listened to some of his favourite jazz records, songs that would make their way into her nightly sets, he taught her how to like Italian espresso, and the two made love in ways that set Nina's soul on fire.

One morning Francis was up early as usual, quietly getting ready for work so that he didn't disturb his sleeping wife, and he began searching for his trousers. They were nowhere to be found. He looked in the laundry hamper in the bathroom to see if he'd accidentally put them in there, then he staggered around the bedroom for a moment in his shirt and underpants with only a shaft of light from the bathroom for illumination. Then he spotted them – a leg poking out from under a pile of Nina's clothes over on the chair. He gingerly picked up her things and something dropped out of her jacket and onto the floor. He picked it up. It was a small card, the kind you get with a gift, or accompanying some flowers. He couldn't make out the writing in the dimness of the light and so he shuffled to the bathroom, clutching his trousers in one hand and the card in the other. In the full light he began to read it.

To my jazz siren,
for our wonderful night together
may there be many more . . .Carter xo

Francis stood still for a moment letting the words and sentiment wash over him – Carter? Who the hell was that? Francis read the card again, studied the handwriting, each word isolated in his brain for meaning, each one linked together into one conclusive seductive statement. His mind began to blacken over as his thoughts swirled around and around in a torrent of mixed emotions. He pulled on his trousers, stuck the card in his pocket, and finished getting ready for work. He glanced into Elijah's bedroom and watched him for a few moments sleeping peacefully, then went downstairs to make coffee and wait for Ingrid to arrive.

The following Saturday Nina arrived at the club as per usual, in enough time to finesse her appearance for the paying customers and with time to spare to have a smoke and a drink to get herself into performance mode. Often, she would step outside into the back alley of the club where she could look up at the night sky and be unobserved and on her own. This was her meditative space and time before the show in which to focus herself. This evening the sky was particularly clear, and the stars were out in full force, despite the intrusion of city lights that usually hampered the showing. Nina sipped her vodka and pulled hard on her cigarette all the while staring into the depths of the night. She had a lot of things to think through. Her affair to Carter, her marriage to Francis, and what this would all mean to her life going forward. She had been in love with Francis once, but that had long since faded into non-existence. Meeting a new man, someone who appreciated her for who she was, had set something alight in her soul. There was no point staying in a relationship that was wrong, despite the turbulence leaving it would mean, and the ramifications for her and Elijah. Her resolve, however, was strong, as it is once you reach an impasse and she knew that whatever she did, whether right or wrong, her life was going to forever change. Carter had promised to come by that evening and said he had a special surprise for her. Nina wondered what it could be. One thing was clear, however, everything they did together just seemed to fill her with joy and anticipation. She looked up and thought she saw a shooting star crossing overhead, the image and thought filled her with happiness. Then she heard a voice speaking her name. A familiar voice. She turned around quickly, startled, and there he was.

'Francis! What are you doing here?'

'What, is that the best God-damn greeting you got for your husband?' Nina tried to collect herself. Francis never came to the club, ever. He looked different tonight, Nina couldn't quite make out how, just different.

'Well, this is a surprise. Who's looking after Elijah?'

'Our son. Now that's an interesting turn ain't it, your sudden concern for family matters.'

'What do you mean?' said Nina. Francis lurched forward, a little unsteady on his feet.

'Have you been . . .drinking?' said Nina. Francis laughed out loud.

'Well, Jesus-H-Christ,' sneered Francis, 'look at the pot calling the kettle black.' Francis pulled a little bottle of whiskey out of his jacket pocket, unscrewed the top and took a hit off it.

'Why are you here?' asked Nina. Francis pulled something out of his pocket.

'This,' said Francis, holding up the little card, 'to see how my little jazz siren was getting on. And to find out who the fuck Carter is!' Nina felt the blood stop cold in her veins, as a wave of panic washed over her. She stubbed out her cigarette with her heel and took a deep breath.

'There is something I've been meaning to talk to you about.'

'Really? Now pray tell, what could that possibly be?' sneered Francis.

'I want a divorce. I've met someone. Yes, his name is Carter, but that is almost immaterial. It could be anyone, because the main point is, this thing, our marriage, isn't working anymore. I'm sorry you had to find out this way. I'm really sorry about it all.'

'Sorry?' said Francis, 'you're sorry? You see the way I see things, sorry doesn't really cut it. You're a lying little bitch. Unfaithful and untrustworthy. You're a complete letdown to motherhood as well, what do you think our precious little boy is going to make of all this? His mother a cheating whore and his father, well, his father a vigilante doing the only thing he can do to put things right.'

'What? What the hell are you talking about, Francis? You've been drinking, you never drink. You're off your head. You need to calm down.' Francis pulled a gun from his pocket and waved it unsteadily in his hand.

'Oh, I've already thought things through. I can't abide by this, Clementina Grace, I really can't.'

'Francis – what the fuck! Stop this, you're really scaring me. Put the gun away, let's talk this thing through, okay?'

'Too late for all that. Goodbye, Clementina . . .' And with that Francis aimed the gun at Nina, pulled the trigger, hitting her in the chest. She fell over in a crumpled heap in front of him. Then Francis raised the gun under his own chin and looked up at the black night sky. His finger lingered a second or two on the trigger and just before he could squeeze a hand reached out and sharply knocked the gun away.

'I wouldn't do that if I were you,' said the stern clear voice of Buddy Washington, Nina's piano player. For a moment or two time seemed to stand still. Neither man said another word and from inside the club the echoes of a drummer and bass player rehearsing the opening bars of *Body and Soul* could just be heard as the strains of jazz music floated on the nighttime breeze.

Shotgun Superstar

'Hello,' said Elijah, picking up his phone.

'This is Nick. Nick Bravado. Are you the guy who's got the ad looking for a singer who aims to be the next big thing? If so, then I'm that guy.' Elijah took note of the voice on the other end of the phone, a voice that was cocky and full of swagger.

'Hi Nick. Yeah, that's my ad. I'm a guitarist and songwriter, working on some interesting original material. You sing, you say?

'I sing. I shout if I need to. I plead, beg, cajole, seduce, do anything I need to do to bring a lyric to life. Make the listener believe in me.'

'So, what kind of music are you into?' asked Elijah. There was a sudden silence on the other end of the phone, then a little shuffling noise, then the distinct sound of someone lighting up a cigarette.

'I'd say I'm mostly drawn to The Velvet Underground, Iggy Pop and Buck Owens.'

'Buck Owens?' said Elijah, laughing, 'the country singer guy?

'Buck Owens is righteous. Country music is outlaw music. Two chords and the truth. What are you into?'

'I'm really digging what's going on in England right now – the Sex Pistols, the Clash – you heard any of that?'

'There is a fucking righteousness bomb going off right now, music is changing, the scene is opening up. And thank God, cause it's about time, and I aim to be part of it,' said Nick. 'So, what kind of songs you got?' Elijah thought about his response for a moment then said with renewed confidence.

'I'd call it outlaw punk if I had to label it, but I hate labels. Do you live downtown, Nick, cause maybe we should meet up for a beer, talk a little more about what I have in mind?' Elijah heard the sound of him pulling hard on a cigarette.

'I'm just off Queen Street.'

'One question for you,' said Elijah.

'Shoot.'

'Is that your real name - Nick Bravado?'

'You know I once read an article about Johnny Cash, he got fed the same question - is Johnny Cash your real name? You know what he said? It's as fucking real as I aim it to be, next question.' Elijah smiled.

'The Cash part is true but his real first name was JR,' said Elijah, 'his dad wanted to call him Ray, but his mother liked John. So, they settled on JR. But when he went into the army, they wouldn't let him use that. So, that's when he became Johnny.'

'You're a fucking encyclopaedia,' laughed Nick, 'you know where the Horseshoe Tavern is?'

'Yeah, I think so,' said Elijah.

'See you there in an hour,' said Nick.

'Okay. Hey, how will I know who you are?''

'I'll be the only one who looks like a fuckin' star,' said Nick, 'you got a tape of your songs?'

'Of course,' said Elijah.

'Bring it with you.' Then Elijah heard the click of the phone being hung up.

'Nick?' said Elijah to the coolest-looking punk-rocking guy he could see sitting in a darkened corner of the Horseshoe Tavern.

'You must be the songwriter dude I spoke to earlier,' said Nick, taking a drag off his cigarette and reaching out his hand.

'Yes, Elijah Grace – it's good to meet you.'

'Well, that's not going to work for a start – Elijah Grace? Don't you get called something cooler like, Ely maybe?'

Elijah shrugged. 'Sometimes, I suppose.'

'Grab a seat, here, have a beer,' said Nick, filling up a glass from the pitcher that was already sitting on the table and pushing it towards him.

'See, the way I see things, you have to consider everything as part of your packaging. Your name included. It's all about what you aim to represent, your vibe, and your name is definitely a starting point. Johnny Rotten, Sid Vicious, sells it doesn't it? Even before you hear a note. But then . . ..' Nick leaned back in his seat, a smile spreading across his face, 'then once you hear it – *Anarchy for the UK*, you know you got a fucking revolution going on. But you already knew what some guy called Rotten was gonna bring to the party.' Elijah picked up his glass of beer and took a swig.

'Black,' he said.

'Black?' repeated Nick, 'what's black?'

'My mother's maiden name was Black. She was a jazz singer; she used that name to perform.'

'Well then, I'd say it's gotta be Ely Black. That's your name from now on,' said Nick. He grabbed his glass and clinked it with Elijah's. For the next few hours, the two drank pitchers of beer; talked music, bands they loved as well as artists they loathed, finding common ground and hatching a plan of sorts. One of how they would put a band together, a band that would blow the doors off the music industry and make stars out of both of them. Nick was unwavering in his belief in himself, and his inherent destiny and Elijah got swept away, having found a kindred spirit who shared the same goals and could express them with such clarity and belief. The two ended up back at Nick's small apartment and Nick quickly produced a bottle of rye whiskey while they listened to Elijah's demo tape of his songwriting efforts. The first song up was a hard-hitting piece of garage rock he'd called, *Queer*.

I'm a little queer
I'm a little queasy
Don't come too near
You might feel uneasy,
I'm a little queer . . .

'What do you mean by queer?' asked Nick, 'are you saying faggot or is it about something else?'

'Queer - as in different,' said Elijah, 'sometimes you meet someone who makes you feel a little uncomfortable. No real reason why. I've often felt like an outsider, like I didn't fit the mould. That's what queer means, but I suppose it could also mean gay.' Nick smiled to himself.

'I get it. And I like the ambiguity.' The second song contained a swirling guitar riff and seemed to invoke religious imagery within the lyrics, albeit, peppered with a healthy dose of cynicism.

If I walk upon the water
What kind of man will I become?
If I squander my religion
Is the best still yet to come?
Jerusalem.

'You ever been to Jerusalem?' said Nick.

'No, I haven't, but I've read lots of things about it. Jesus as mystic or messiah, I'm not sure about any of that, but it sure conjures up some interesting imagery.'

'My old lady is Jewish. I guess that makes me one, too,' said Nick. 'But I don't bother with all that religion crap – nice guitar riff, though.' The final song on the demo tape really caught Nick's attention – *Spunk Junkies*. Not least for its X-rated lyrics, and for its raw honesty and hooky guitar riff.

Spunk junkie, read your magazine
Spunk junkie, always leaves it clean
Sweet lover, taste my sweet perfume
Sweet lover, leaves me black and blue
I just wanna get some down
And spill the rest upon the ground

'Now that song has fuckin' hit potential,' said Nick, 'that's like the Velvets and Iggy smashed together – very cool.' Elijah smiled and nodded.

'Don't know where that one came from. Sometimes things just jump out and land, ya know?'

'You got a lyric sheet?' Elijah searched in his guitar case.

'Here,' said Elijah, handing Nick a dog-eared piece of paper. Nick read the words to himself.

'Can you play it for me?' said Nick, handing him a battered acoustic guitar. Elijah launched into the opening riff of *Spunk Junkies* and within a few seconds Nick was singing along. The result was fantastic. There was a load of personality and swagger in Nick's voice. Elijah was floored. His little song was coming to life before his very eyes. For once it wasn't his own tentative voice that he heard, but something with authority and conviction. Nick Bravado. They finished the song, high-fived each other and both knew they'd hit upon something special.

'We gotta get a band together,' said Nick. 'This is what I've been waiting for, this is what I was born to do, and you, my friend, got the songs.'

'That'd be amazing,' said Elijah, 'I always dreamed of playing in a band.'

'I know a couple of guys I hang with sometimes, lots of people on the Queen Street scene will be digging this – we'll need a drummer, a bass player,' said Nick. Elijah couldn't believe his ears. All that time he'd spent in his bedroom woodshedding things on his acoustic guitar. Little ideas for songs, musical snippets, lyrics, all being finessed one at a time. And now his creative ideas were finding purchase with someone who could actually sing. Someone with a big personality.

'You and me, Ely Black,' said Nick, pouring them both another shot of whiskey, 'we are gonna take this thing to the top.'

Two months later and the band were playing their first gig. The tiny Queen Street venue was packed with the band's friends and supporters and Nick was on fire, pacing the stage like a panther. Screaming lyrics when it felt right and whispering lines too, each performance tactic drawing listeners into his web of mystery and intrigue and bringing Elijah's songs to life. Elijah was floored with the experience, the sound of his guitar ringing loud and snarky behind him as he worked his own corner of the stage and every now and then he felt the band lock into a groove that felt so tight, so sure footed, it was nothing short of primal. The audience were collectively moving to the music, and it seemed like all eyes were mesmerised by Nick. At the end of their short and fiery set there was a standing ovation of enthusiastic audience members clapping and cheering for more. In the dressing room after the show, the band were feeling ecstatic and toasting themselves with beers when Nick dropped some news.

'Okay, listen up. At our gig next Saturday, I got some record company guys coming out to see us. I want us to knock their fuckin' socks off. We gotta be on fire.'

'Record companies?' said Elijah, 'like, who?'

'Seamus O'Donal, the A&R rep from Sony is coming, and I got Harper Greenberg coming out too.'

'Who's he?'

'Only the head of licensing for Atlantic Records in New York.'

'No shit!' said Elijah, 'Atlantic?'

'And that's why we gotta be hot. So, I want you to call all your friends, relatives, round everyone up you can, I want this gig packed to the rafters with enthusiastic fans and supporters – show these guys what we're all about. This is our shot!'

When he returned to his little apartment, Elijah could barely contain his excitement. Within a few short months he'd met Nick, adopted the name Ely Black, was part of a band, and now record companies – real record companies - were coming to check them out! And, at the heart of it all, were his own songs. Songs he wasn't too sure about at first, but now, with Nick and the band on board, sounded strong, convincing, the real deal. Elijah wanted to call someone to share his incredibly good news with. Carla . . .

Eight months ago, the two of them had been an item. She worked evenings at the local repertory cinema, where Elijah would sometimes go on his own to watch foreign films for cheap, but during the day she was studying graphic design at Ryerson College. She was cute, interesting, creative, had similar taste in music, dressed a little new wave, and the sex was easy-going and plentiful. It didn't take long before the two got serious, and before he knew it, Elijah was moving his scant belongings into her place and the two set up sharing an apartment just off Carlton Street. Elijah played her his songs as each one was emerging. She was encouraging, gave him feedback, told him what she liked and what sounded forced or pretentious. He took it all in stride, glad to have found a sounding board that was honest and forthright. She also turned him onto books, authors, indie theatre, and art films he should watch. His world opened up and he took it all in with ravenous eyes and these new influences soon found their way into his music. Then a few months later when she didn't get her period, she bought a little home test, and there it was – a distinct blue line.

It didn't take long for the relationship to unravel. Carla decided on her own that an abortion was the most realistic option. After all, she was still in school, and he wasn't about to find a permanent full-time job. She still had another year of college to go, and he was a fledgling musician with his dreams set on making it in an industry that appeared to be as fickle as it was unreliable. It all seemed way too much. How could they possibly manage, yet alone, afford to raise a child under those circumstances. But despite a sensible decision being made, after it was all over, it still struck deep into Carla's core and left a hurt she struggled to come to terms with.

Elijah picked up his phone and stared at it for a moment or two. Part of him wanted to show Carla that his dreams were coming true after all, and that success was just around the corner. There was also part of him which hoped that, with this turn of good fortune, they could pick things up where they had broken off. Start over again. They had loved each other, after all, hadn't they? He dialled the number he still knew by heart and held his breath. It rang five times before it went straight to the answering machine, and he heard the tinny sound of her voice.

The band rehearsed once more before the Saturday night arrived, paring the set down to only the best songs, the ones which had seemed to elicit the most audience reaction. As they hit the final chords on what would ideally be their encore song, it was clear that everything rocked with a wild abandon and just enough ragged edges to make it all feel authentic. The band took a break and Nick and Elijah stepped outside to have a smoke. Nick pulled a small vial out of his pocket, dipped in a little spoon and snorted some white powder.

'You got blow, Nick?'

'It's what makes Nikolas Dziedzic from Scarborough Ontario into Nick Bravado, rock star of the world. You want some?' Nick dipped his spoon into the vial and offered it to Elijah.

'This, my friend, will show you the future.' Elijah hesitated for a moment and then lowered his nose over the spoon and snorted back a hit of cocaine. Almost immediately he felt a burning sensation inside his nostril before a numbness replaced it extending down into his throat, but then the euphoria kicked in. A feeling he'd not experienced before. A feeling that he could be and could do anything.

'You really think things are gonna work out next Saturday, Nick?' The singer looked at him.

'I was born into a shit-hole existence in a shit-hole family in a nothingness suburb of Toronto. My old man used to regularly beat the shit outta me and my brother. He was nothing more than an asshole immigrant factory worker going nowhere, taking his frustrations with the world out on his wife and kids. Am I gonna show him I'm worthy? Fuck, yeah.'

'Shit, said Elijah, 'I had no idea about any of that stuff.'

'The sound of my voice, all that edge, that snarl – it all comes from that,' said Nick, taking a long drag on a cigarette, 'it's where I get my energy from. Piss and vinegar – that's just teenager angst bullshit – now anger and retribution, that's where I find my mojo.' Nick stepped closer to his bandmate and grabbed him by the back of his neck and pushed his forehead right onto Elijah's.

'And you my friend, are gonna be by my side the entire way. You just keep writing me those brilliant songs of yours and it's a dream come true time.' Elijah felt slightly breathless. He wasn't sure if it was Nick's overwhelming personality, his forehead pushing into his own, his piercing eyes just inches away, or the effects of the cocaine – or likely, a combination of all of it, but either way, there was something new coursing through his veins. Belief. Nick Bravado pulled back from Elijah and slapped him on the shoulder.

'C'mon, let's run the set one more time,' said Nick, 'I got a few moves I wanna try out.'

The following Saturday at ten-to-eight Nick strolled into the dressing room. With heavy eyeliner and gelled spiky hair, he looked like some kind of wired-up raccoon. Behind him was another youngish man, perhaps in his early thirties, sporting a fedora and wearing a sharkskin suit jacket over a Ramones t-shirt.

'Hey everyone, listen up,' said Nick, 'bringing the band to attention. This here is Mike Bishop, my manager.' Elijah looked up, a little surprised.

'Your manager?'

'Yeah, he's got a great track record dealing with labels. In a few minutes time we are gonna blow the roof off this joint and Mike is gonna be out there schmoozing like a sonofabitch making sure all them record folk are fighting for the right to sign us. Ain't that right, Mike?' Nick's manager took a step forward into the dressing room, glanced around at everyone like he was addressing a high school football team at halftime.

'Great to meet you guys, but listen up, here is the same thing I tell all my clients – just forget about those guys out there, blank it out, do whatever you need to. The only important thing is to do what you guys do best and play the greatest gig you ever have. Break a leg!' Mike shook Nick's hand whispered something in his ear then left the dressing room. Elijah's mind took a spin for a moment – where had this guy come from, and how come Nick had never mentioned him until now? The information jarred a little, but still, there was less than ten minutes before they would be face to face with a room full of fans anticipating an evening of great music. Elijah reeled in his thoughts and parked them, instead focussing on the job ahead, and the destiny that included.

Then, before he knew it, Ely Black, rock star in-the-making, was on stage plugging his trusty Telecaster into his amp and dialling in his usual snarly sound. He quickly scanned the room for any sign of Carla, he had left her a short message about the gig, but he couldn't see her anywhere in the crowd. Nick was already leaning on the microphone leering at the audience, making eye contact with as many as he could. Then the drummer counted off the opening song with four clicks of his drumsticks and Elijah hit the opening chords to *Vampire Girls*, another of his own tunes. The audience were immediately entranced by the wall of noise and the energy coming off the stage. Nick paced from one side to the other, getting well into character and channelling his own demons. His voice was a strangled powerhouse of emotions.

You made a meal of me
Down to my flesh and bones
You made desire bleed
Then left me all alone
Oh no, oh no
I'm Valentino with a knife behind my back.

A few days later and Elijah got a call from Nick inviting him down the Carlo's pool hall to shoot a game or two. Elijah was feeling buoyant when he walked in, keen to hear how their performance had gone down with the industry reps. He spotted Nick over in a corner deep in conversation with Mike Bishop.

'Hey Ely,' said Nick, once Elijah made his presence known, 'good to see you, man.' Mike immediately grabbed his jacket and looked set to leave.

'Great show on Saturday, Ely. Really impressive. I gotta hit the road here, but nice to see you again.' And with that, Mike Bishop scurried out.

'Hey Nick, so what's up? You become a pool shark now, or what?' said Elijah trying to make small talk. Nick lit a cigarette and racked up the balls.

'Why don't you break,' said Nick. Elijah found himself a cue and tentatively put a little chalk on the tip. He wasn't much of a player but had shot enough throughout his teenage years to play a decent game. Elijah steadied his hand, resting the cue between his arched thumb and finger and with a swift stroke, broke up the triangle of balls. One of the balls managed to make its way into one of the corner pockets.

'Lucky break. I guess I'm stripes,' said Elijah.

'Guess you are. You know, Ely, I always think that pool is a metaphor for life.' Elijah gave Nick a quizzical look.

'How so?'

'Well now, there is a whole lot of chance involved - the way the balls break, the lay of the table, that's pure luck. But then comes the skill, how you line things up, take advantage of a good shot, pot the black when the time is right. But the way I figure things, guys like you and me, we make our own luck.'

'Okay, not sure I follow, you saying that was a good break, I got lucky, or what?' Nick took a long drag on his cigarette.

'I've been waiting a long time, Ely, for things to change, to get my kick of the can.' Elijah could see from Nick's expression that he was leaning into something serious.

'Yeah, like you said you had it rough, but that's in the past now.'

'That was a great gig last weekend, indeed it really was,' continued Nick, 'it achieved everything it was meant to. Both Sony and Atlantic were mightily impressed, and even Epic are now showing interest. In fact, I now have been offered a four-album deal with Atlantic that I'm about to sign.'

'Well, that's fantastic news, Nick.'

'Yes, it is, and I have to say I couldn't have gotten there without you. The kicker is . . .' Nick leaned his cue onto the table and swiftly sunk a solid ball in a corner pocket, 'the deal is just for Nick Bravado - not the band.'

'What?' said Elijah, 'I don't understand.'

'I really hate this, Ely, I really do and if there was some way I could change things I would. But Harper was really clear, and it turns out he has lined up some session guys, really great players, all set to go in New York just waiting for a frontman like me. I'm really sorry, man.' Elijah stopped hearing Nick's words, excuses, protestations, after that. Instead, everything swirled into a black void of emptiness, disbelief, and betrayal.

'And you are gonna be by my side the entire way . . .' Nick's vacant words were left ringing in Elijah's mind for the rest of that night. A promise, now hollow, untrue. Nick was getting his shot, claiming his prize, but Elijah was being left high and dry.

When Elijah finally got home, pissed, disillusioned, and broken, he trashed his prized Telecaster against the wall in a fit of anger and frustration. Slumped on the floor amongst shards and pieces of guitar, Elijah picked up his phone and dialled Carla's number. It was two in the morning, but she was the only person he could think of to reach out to. The phone rang several times before a sleepy voice answered it.

'Yeah,' said the voice. It wasn't Carla, it was some guy. Elijah could hear Carla in the background, sounding disoriented.

'Who is it, Jack? Who's calling?' Elijah looked blankly at the receiver for a moment, then hung it up. He picked up a shard of smashed guitar that was laying on the floor next to him, held it up in the faded light. The edge looked ragged and sharp, resembling a serrated knife as he turned it around in his hands. Then Elijah pulled out his little notebook and wrote down a few lines that had suddenly flown into his mind.

We live in the danger zone
With a fire licking at our feet
Bad luck breaks you down again
Real life - it's a bad disease

He wasn't sure if what he was writing was the beginning of something, an ending, or his own epitaph. Nick's voice jumped in his mind, 'guys like us make our own luck . . .' Elijah could almost feel Nick's head pressed against his own, his eyes piercing into him like crazy demonic daggers. Elijah finished scribbling down two more lines . . .

Cold steel with a big guitar
I'm your shotgun superstar

George and the Dragon

It was threatening to snow, the temperature having dropped over night to the minuses, but then it was mid-January, after all. George, who had just turned ten, and Finn who was one year older, were scrambling across Petteril Common looking for games to play or anything else that might pique their mischievous interest. The two lived next door to each other in almost matching council houses on Maitland Street and so, come weekends, it was natural they would play together.

'Hey George,' shouted Finn, 'wanna see something cool?' George poked at the ground with the toe of his trainer, always curious, yet wary of Finn's suggestions as they usually went one step beyond his idea of fun.

'Sure,' replied George, tentatively.

'Check this out,' said Finn, pulling a shiny object out of his jacket pocket.

'What's that?'

'It's a vape, stupid.'

'Where'd you get it?'

'I nicked it off the old man,' sneered Finn, 'he has so many lying all over the house, he'll never miss this one.'

'What do you do with it?'

'You really are such a kid, aren't you, George? You inhale it, pinhead. Don't worry, this one's a real pussy flavour – rhubarb and custard, even you'll like it.' Finn set about firing up the device and was soon inhaling a good lungful of the flavoured smoke. He blew out a big puff which quickly covered George in a cloud of enticing aroma.

'You wanna try?' said Finn, holding out the vape. George cautiously took it from his outstretched hand.

'Just press the button and inhale, it won't kill ya,' laughed Finn. George pushed the firing button and sucked hard on the mouthpiece. A little too hard for a first timer. He was suddenly taken aback by the overwhelming sensation of a warm rush of fumes filling his lungs and the uncomfortable scratchy feeling that caught the back of his throat, and he immediately began to cough uncontrollably. Finn laughed again and slapped his knee.

'You're such a lightweight, George, here give it to me.' Finn grabbed the device from George's hand and began to expertly inhale vape fumes. Then without hesitating he began to blow smoke rings out of his mouth towards his friend's face. George just stood there mesmerised by the perfect round shapes that wafted gently through the air.

'I learned it watching my old man – pretty cool, huh?' George looked sheepish but nodded his approval.

'Yeah, vape rings are dope,' said George, trying to regain some composure.

'C'mon,' said Finn, 'let's go build a hideout – over there.' He stashed the vape back in his jacket.

'I'll race you,' and with that Finn took off running across the grassy common towards the scrubs and trees that lined the south perimeter. George had no choice but to follow suit, but he knew his chubby legs would never allow him to catchup Finn.

'Wait up,' called George, as he began puffing his way into a slow jog.

When they reached the wooded area, they noticed that it had become an unofficial dumping ground of sorts. The scrubby land was strewn with all manner of rubbish and discarded things: parts of electronic devices, bin bags spilling out with unwanted belongings and old toys, a shopping trolley laid on its side, rusting and seemingly being engulfed by the surrounding undergrowth. Along with this were piles of decaying wood, fencing posts, plastic containers and all other manner of detritus likely offloaded from the nearby allotments. Finn found a brick and an old computer monitor. He set the screen up against a tree stump and launched the brick with all his might, smashing the screen into several pieces.

'Cool,' said Finn. Meanwhile George had rummaged a sword-shaped stick from a pile of wood and raised it up in the air admiring it – Saint George about to do battle with the almighty dragon. This was one of his favourite stories that his dad would often read at bedtime to him and his younger brother, Peter, and one which fired up his imagination to no end. A victorious George saving the princess and villagers from their imminent demise by slaying the fire-breathing dragon.

'What's that?' yelled Finn.

'A sword. Here, there's another one for you,' said George, plucking another piece of wood from the pile.

'We can be knights of the round table; you can be Lancelot if you like. I'll be Galahad.' Finn took the wooden sword off George and gave it the once over.

'Who is Lancelot?' asked Finn.

'Only the most dope knight of them all,' smiled George, 'c'mon, let's build a fort.' The two then got busy collecting wood and bits and pieces of other debris and were soon piling everything into a barricade they could hide behind. George was plucking another piece of wood from a discarded pile when he noticed the rounded spiny body of a small creature that was just visible - a hedgehog.

'Hey Finn, come see this, quick.' Finn sauntered over and went to poke his stick at it.

'No, don't wake it,' said George, 'it's a hedgehog and it's hibernating, sleeping through the winter. It's bigger than I thought, I've never seen a real one before.'

'Why are they called hedgehogs?' asked Finn.

'Because they like to live in the hedgerows, they usually only come out at night, and they roll into a ball when they feel threatened. This one will likely sleep through to March.'

'Hedgehogs, you say?' said Finn.

'Yeah, and their babies are called hoglets. Cute, huh?'

'How come you know so much about 'em?'

'I did a school science project on them last year, but I've never seen real one before. We should cover this one back up.' With that George carefully started to place some leaves and small twigs over the sleeping animal.

'There you go Mr. Hedgehog – enjoy the rest of your sleep. I can't wait to tell Mom and Dad about this.' Finn gave George a baleful look, then pulled out the vape from his pocket, hit the button, and inhaled a lungful. George watched him closely.

'Wanna try vaping again?' sneered Finn.

'No thanks – actually, I think I should get going home,' said George, 'it must be getting close to teatime.'

George excitedly told his mom and dad, along with Peter, over his tea of fish fingers, chips and peas all about the creature he had found on the common.

'That's wonderful,' said his mother, 'so nice that you finally got to see a real one.'

'They've been diminishing in numbers in England for a while now,' said George.

'Why is that?' asked his mom.

'Well, what I learned was it's due to loss of habitat, people living in the areas where they live, and I suppose, pollution too.'

'That's sad,' said his mother, letting it sink in.

'We all have a responsibility,' said Doug, his father, 'to make sure we protect our wildlife. I'm proud of you for spotting it and taking care to protect it.' George blushed slightly and felt a twinge of guilt about not telling his folks about how he had also tried vaping.

'Why don't you run upstairs,' said Dad 'run a bath and then I'll read you and Peter a bedtime story, it's early to bed tonight - school tomorrow.' George did as he was told and once the two brothers were bathed and dried and into their pyjamas Doug sat between them on the couch and the two boys cuddled up close.

'So, what story would you like me to read tonight?' George blurted out straight away, 'George and the Dragon.'

'Well, wait a minute, what does Peter want to hear?' asked Dad

'C'mon Pete,' implored George, 'it's got a real dragon in it. Swords and slaying, a princess and everything – please.' His brother leaned into his father's shoulder and nodded.

'Okay, I guess tonight it's your favourite again, then,' smiled Dad picking out the book from a pile. It was only halfway through the story when they became aware of a noisy ruckus coming from next door – Finn's house. Shouting and banging followed by the unmistakable screams of a woman in distress and then more thumping against the walls and shouting. Dad tried to continue with the story, but the domestic dispute raging next door was hard to ignore.

'What in Christ are they up to over there?' said Doug, 'bloody Catholics, always drinking and fighting, that's all they ever do.' George's father didn't get angry often but when he did the result quite shocked and scared George. Although he didn't quite understand their full meaning, as he listened to his father's angry divisive words, he was aware that Finn went to the other school, the one further up the road than his. But he didn't really understand the differences between the two schools, just that some kids went to the Catholic school, and he didn't.

'What are Catholics?' asked George, innocently.

'A bloody nuisance,' said Dad before his wife, Sandra, appeared.

'Catholic is just another type of religion,' said Mom, 'they are Christians like us, but different. They have a pope.' George looked confused but knew by the furrowed look on his mother's brow it was better not to ask any further questions.

'They're at it again,' said Sandra, to her husband, 'do you think we ought to ring the police?'

'Damn lot of good that will do,' snapped Doug, 'it'll be right as rain in the morning, same as always happens. Shelia O'Donnell always takes that damn Seamus back. Maybe he'll break her arm or something this time, and then finally we might see a different outcome.'

'Doug, please,' admonished Sandra, rolling her eyes, 'the children.' Doug shrugged his shoulders.

'C'mon boys, I think it's time for bed. Kiss your mom goodnight and I'll come up and tuck you in.' George kissed his mother's cheek and lingered a little really wanting his mom to hug and kiss him back, but she just distractedly accepted his kiss and turned away, consumed with her own thoughts. The two boys climbed the stairs and clambered into their respective bunk beds, George, afraid of heights, opting to sleep on the lower bunk. Doug leaned in to kiss his sons goodnight and as he kissed him, George threw his arms around his father's neck hugging on tightly.

'Goodnight, kiddo,' said Dad.

'Dad?'

'Yes.'

'What are they fighting about next door? Is it because they're Catholics?' Doug looked at his son.

'I think that Mr. O'Donnell gets a little frustrated by things sometimes, that's all. It's nothing to worry about. It'll be all quiet come morning, just try to ignore anything else you hear tonight – Mom and I are just in the other room. Okay?' George turned over onto his side and clutched tightly onto his stuffed seal.

'Goodnight,' whispered Doug, then he turned off the light, closed the door and left the room.

'Dad?'

'What is it now, George?' said Doug, opening the door a crack.

'Can you leave the door open a bit?'

George was sitting at a table at school, but it wasn't his school, it was a different school, familiar, yet not so. He turned to a stranger standing beside his desk.

'Excuse me,' said George, 'what school is this?'

'St. Mary's,' said the stranger, smiling, 'the Catholic school.' George looked around. There were lots of people milling about talking to one another, grownups as well as kids. So many people in fact, the room was full up. A man who he didn't know, but who looked like he could be a teacher, was walking from desk to desk handing out paper and pencils. He stopped at George and put a sheet in front of him and said, 'you can draw your favourite animal.' George was thinking about what to sketch for a moment or two when the girl sitting next to him held up her paper for George to see.

'Look at mine,' she said, and George saw it had a drawing of a hedgehog on it.

'That's what I was going to draw,' said George, but the girl had already turned back to her desk and completely ignored him. George picked up his pencil and began to trace the outline of a creature when suddenly there was a loud sound, like the sound of a gun going off, or fireworks, and everyone stopped talking, froze, and turned to look at the doorway. Standing there was a man with a black balaclava over his head and face, his body was covered in combat fatigues, and he was holding a machine gun, pointing it in the direction of the people. He yelled something, but George couldn't understand what he said, and then he started firing. Randomly at all the kids and the people in the room. There were screams, terror, adults and children trying to flee. People were being shot and some were dying right there, in the classroom. George didn't know what to do. He turned to look at the girl next to him, but she had already been shot and was slumped over her desk - dead, on top of her drawing, in a pool of her own blood.

George tried to get up, move, but his legs wouldn't work. He started to panic. He tried to shout for help, but no sound would come out of his mouth. Then the man with the gun started walking towards him, slowly, raising his rifle, taking aim, and all George could do was watch . . .

His cries had awoken his mom and there she now was, sitting on the side of his bed talking to him, stroking his sweating brow.

'It's okay George, you were just having a bad dream. Mommy's here now.' George felt such an overwhelming sense of relief to have the dream stop and go away, and to have the comfort of his mom nearby, that he just hugged onto her waist and cried.

'It was so awful, Mom, they were shooting and killing people,' sobbed George.

'I know, I know, but it was just a dream. Shh now, Mommy's here. Try to think of something else now – something nice, maybe daffodils, or how about one of your stuffed friends.'

'Like Sealy?' said George, his nose streaming with snot. Mom pulled a paper hanky out of her dressing gown pocket and wiped at his nose.

'Yes, like Sealy – where is he?'

'He's here,' said George, reaching over to grab his stuffed toy that was down the side of the bed, a small smile beginning to return to his face.

Two days later, George and Peter were walking home from school together when George suddenly got an idea.

'Hey Pete, want me to show you the hedgehog?'

'Yeah!' said his brother, 'I really wanna see it.'

'C'mon, I know a shortcut to the common,' said George, tugging on Pete's arm, 'this way.' The frost and dusting of snow of the previous weekend had completely disappeared being replaced by the usual overcast and mild January weather. The trail to the south side of the common was now wet and muddy and everywhere they tried to step were the large footprints of dog walkers and other ramblers squished and outlined in the mud and trampled bracken.

'Try not to get your shoes dirty or Mom will kill us,' said George, aware that there would need to be some explanations when they got home, not only for being late, but why their good school shoes were mucky. When they finally reached the far side of the field George could see the things that he and Finn had collected and piled up to make their fort were still intact.

'Where's the hedgehog?' complained Peter, tired from the long muddy walk across the common.

'C'mon, it's just over here,' pointed George, leading the way. When they got to the pile of wood and leaves, however, things didn't look the same. Everything had been disturbed. The place where the hedgehog had been sleeping had been torn away and there was no sign of it.

'He was right here,' said George, a note of disappointment in his voice.

'Great - so all this way and there's no hedgehog to see,' sighed Peter. George swung around to face his brother when something caught his eye. Lying in the grass, a few feet away was something that vaguely resembled a spiny creature. George stepped a little closer to get a better look and when he did, he realised it was a hedgehog. Only thing was, this one was dead. In fact, it looked like it had been bludgeoned to death with the big stick that was lying on the ground nearby. The thing was so bloody and misshapen it was clear someone had purposely massacred it. George could barely believe his own eyes. Gone was the nice round ball of spines that George had seen before, tucked up into itself for protection from intruders, in its place was a bloody, pulpy mess. He was aghast, stricken. The poor thing. George's mind flew off in all directions. Why would someone do something like that to an innocent creature? One that was only sleeping, one that is endangered, and one that doesn't do any harm to anyone. Then George saw something else nearby, something shiny poking out of the mud. He reached to pick it up; it was a vape, a familiar looking vape. Finn's vape.

George did finally get to see inside St. Mary's Catholic school. Later that same year, in February, there was another cold snap. More arctic air moved down across Scotland and the north and the school's old pipes simply gave up and froze. Instead of suspending school indefinitely while the plumbing was fixed, all the kids from Thornhill Elementary, including George and his brother, were sent to sit in with the kids at St. Mary's. Space was certainly tight, but the teachers and maintenance staff found extra desks and chairs, and everyone did their best to share what they could, chip in and help out. Since the pandemic of 2020 and the shambles that home schooling turned out to be, children's education, along with their mental wellbeing, was seen to be of the upmost importance. 'Keep our kids in school', was a motto and priority that all head teachers, these days, needed to subscribe to. George's parents were a little apprehensive to say the least, as St. Mary's was generally acknowledged to be the rougher of the two schools, but the three weeks went by quickly and everything soon returned to normal. George did cross paths with Finn at St. Mary's a few times, silently passing each other in the hallways, with only the briefest nod of acknowledgment, but in the playground, they generally opted to stay segregated into their own circle of school chums - the visiting Protestant kids and the Catholics. George still liked to hear his dad read 'George and the Dragon' before bed, but something had shifted in him that year. He never did return to the common to built forts and avoided playing with Finn completely. And, as for swords, well, after the hedgehog incident, he never looked at long sticks the same way again.

Silloth Sunset

The front door slammed shut with a force that could have busted its hinges. She knew it had to be Frank.

'I'm back here,' she yelled, 'in the kitchen.' Rose quickly topped off her glass with a little more gin and doused it with some slimline tonic and lit another cigarette. She blew the smoke out the side of her mouth and fixed her face so it wouldn't show nothing. Disappointment or anger. Frank's sharp profile appeared in the doorway. He just stood there leaning against the door jam, watching her, not saying an effing word. She always hated him when he applied the silent treatment, but she figured everyone have different ways they fight.

'So,' she opened, 'is it done? Why don't you pull up a chair and join me in a drink.'

'Christ, it's barely noon,' cracked Frank, a little sneer spreading across his tight lips, 'you starting in pretty early today?' Rose shrugged.

'How much you get?' said Rose. Frank said nothing, just took off his jacket and cap, threw them on the counter, pulled out a kitchen stool and plonked himself down.

'I'll have a beer,' he said, his dark eyes piercing into her. Rose stubbed out her cigarette and shuffled over to the fridge.

'You want a Special Brew or a Stella?'

'Gimme a can of both and bring the whiskey and a glass.' Rose did what Frank said and slid the beers and bottle in front of him.

'I was thinking,' said Rose, 'now that we're flush, maybe we could take a little holiday. A weekend getaway somewhere – like we used to.'

'Jesus Christ woman,' erupted Frank, 'the cheque hasn't bloody cleared and you're already spending it.' Rose lit up another ciggie and let the silence ease into the space between them.

'Remember that time we spent the weekend in Silloth? Remember how the clouds and rain cleared, and the sun came out all bright and hazy and that rainbow stretched right across the horizon? It was so beautiful; I can still see it now like it was yesterday. You bought me ice cream, mint chocolate chip – my favourite, and we sat on the grass like teenagers watching the waves crash against the shore. That was the best time ever. Do you remember it, Frank?'

'Why you always gotta live in the past? We got real shit to deal with right here, right now, ain't no good burying your head in the sand, Rose.'

'You'll get another job,' she said, touching his arm, 'you'll see, things will come round.' Frank jerked his arm away and Rose noticed another tattoo there.

'You got some new ink?'

'What's it to you?'

'Show me. I wanna see what you got.' Frank hesitated a moment then pulled back his sleeve and turned his arm over.

'An orchid? Why'd you get that flower? Why not a rose, huh?' Frank rolled his eyes and cracked open the beer.

'Is it for that stupid Asian cow you were two-timing me with?' Frank looked down the end of his nose at Rose and shook his head slowly from side to side.

'Don't fuck with me Rose, not today, not ever, understood?' Frank reached inside his pocket and pulled out a pile of crumpled bank notes, chucked them across the table at her.

'That's your share - a hundred and fifty.' Rose stared at the money then at Franks tattoo.

'You said you was through. You swore to me, Frank.' He pulled down his sleeve and downed his shot of whiskey and poured another.

'Are you screwing her?'

'Ain't none of your damn business.'

'None of my business!' Then years and months and days and hours, and infidelities, and lies and violence all seemed to simmer up in that moment and then that was it - Rose leaped up, grabbed her glass, and launched it straight at Frank's face. It hit him hard, right between the eyes. He screamed, clutched at his gashed forehead, kicked the table over, then threw himself at her. Rose's head hit the wall with the sheer force splitting it open, while Frank's fingers clasped firmly around her throat, squeezing tighter and tighter.

The sun was a glorious yellow orb floating in a speckless blue sky. Silloth was literally a-buzz with people taking advantage of the unseasonably good weather. Couples, arm-in arm, and families with little ones in tow all strolled the promenade watching the dinghies bob and roll on the gentle waves. The sea lapped against the shore, turning the pebbles over and over, then over and over again, creating an unhurried rhythm like life itself. The shrill voices of excited children rang out across the town square as they played football, tig, and hide-and-seek. The ice cream van that had parked near the sea front had an endless queue waiting patiently for their sweet treats, and from her vantage point on a park bench on the green, Rose drank it all in - the tranquillity, beauty, and familiarity.

Her half of the money had bought her a bus ticket from Carlisle to Silloth and a sweet little room in a B&B. Next to her on the bench was her empty ice cream tub. This time she'd gone for two flavours – mint chocolate chip and peach melba. Both were as satisfying and good as she'd remembered. She knew they wouldn't discover Frank's body for a while and by then it wouldn't matter anyway. As the day began to wane and the sun began to set, the sky was awash with brilliant colours that slowly changed from bright yellows, dusty oranges and finally into rosy hues. And as if the sunset was calling her by name, Rose slipped off her shoes, walked into the sea fully clothed, and slowly began swimming towards the point where the sun would finally sink beyond the horizon.

Ice

'I have to say, I think it's really positive and healthy that you're playing music again,' said Meredith, the words an easy flow of counselor-speak.

'How do you feel about it?' Andrew looked at Meredith with a blankness that was beyond resignation, more of a bone-weary tiredness. A lethargy born of listening to too many mental health counselors feedback his own feelings to him with the thinly veiled superficiality of psychoanalytical therapy. Andrew saw it all too clearly. The absurdity of spilling your guts to a complete stranger, only to have your words, your thoughts, your innermost feelings annotated and then fed back to you as some pseudo-caring mumbo-jumbo. At one time these thoughts would have incensed Andrew, would have found vent in the sort of sarcasm he often applied to things he found overly trite or sentimental, but right now he just felt worn down by it all. *Yeah, it does feel good to play again*, he thought to himself, but managed only to mutter - *good*. Meredith nodded thoughtfully and scribbled some words onto a notepad. Behind her, on her expansive desk, stood the gold-framed evidence of a well-adjusted successful life: two smiling children, a loyal and loving husband, a university graduation portrait. A single bloodless yellow rose stood mockingly aloof in a crystal vase, and a child's spirited and unselfconscious artwork hung framed alongside numerous degrees and accreditations - a vision of near-perfect balance between family-life and career. Andrew looked at his watch. Almost closure time, he sighed to himself with tired relief. The inevitable wrapping-up of the therapy session that always occurred at exactly ten minutes to the hour. He calculated the time in his mind; he still had time to pick up a present for his daughter's birthday and make it to the party.

Andrew stared blankly at the icicles dripping outside the window, marking time, drip, drip, drip. . . Meredith put aside her notepad and carefully removed her reading glasses. They were the modern kind, with frames that manage to look both trendy and dowdy at the same time.

'Well, we seem to be making some real progress,' she finally announced. 'You've reconnected with your family and you're playing music again. I'd like you to do something though, something for our next session.'

Andrew studied her for a moment. On the outside she was the very picture of control and authority; the sharply crossed legs, the bluntly cut hair, the immaculate clothes and makeup, a body that exercised more than it consumed calories, it all read: flawless, in control. The office, too, was a natural extension of her personal and professional self. There was something so balanced, so perfectly right, so feng shui about it that it made Andrew feel nervous and suspicious. He wondered what darkness lurked below the picture-perfect surface of her life, concealed and contained. What was the crack? Everyone had something in their life that wasn't quite right, didn't they?

'I want you to write a letter Andrew, a letter to yourself. In it I want you to explain to yourself why you think this happened.' She uncrossed her legs and leaned forward in a well-practiced gesture that said, 'I care'.

'Then I want you to give yourself permission to heal that hurt, to bandage the wound. Forgiveness, Andrew. I want you to write a letter of consent to forgive yourself.' Jesus Christ, thought Andrew, that's it. . . fucking forgive myself?

Music had always been Andrew's passion. Who he was was inseparable from what he did. At school he was always a natural, the best by far amongst his peers. It came easy for him. Piano lessons were a breeze, and he nurtured a dream of becoming a writer. As he immersed himself deeper in music it soon became his total focus, his identity. He played in all the school bands, accompanied the choir, and even formed a rock band with some friends. Music was fun, inspirational, a solace. After high school Andrew went to university. It seemed like what you should do and besides, his parents had convinced him that that was the right path to take, if he wanted to become a professional musician. He stuck it out for a few years, before realising that music schools were mostly interested in conformity, a 'this is how you must play it' sort of mentality. It seemed to Andrew that music school was all about practicing scales and theory; possibly because technique and theory were the only tangible parts of music that could actually be taught, and probably because most music teachers were spawned from a great tradition of historical musical reference points. From Mozart to Miles, it was all sacred ground. Music that must be revered and then imitated. Creativity was encouraged, but only under the oppressive weight of tradition. Music education was self-perpetuating industry - an institution fed fat on mediocrity. Besides, he'd convinced himself at the time, if none of his favourite musicians had gone to music school, then why should he?

Making a living from music, though, proved to be a difficult and tenuous road. To make ends meet Andrew worked at a seemingly endless array of low paying and demoralising jobs. You name it, and he probably did it, albeit briefly. He worked by day, wrote by night. All the time, honing his skills, working on his next great piece, writing the kind of music that he liked and was proud of. He was soon to discover, however, that the music business was a callus industry that had no patience for another young musician who showed little concern for playing by the rules. Talent was only one part of the game. Knowing the right people, making the right connections, and tenacity and perseverance were as much a part of the formula for success as God-given talent. One thing was for sure though, without the support of the industry, reaching an interested and supportive audience was next to impossible. Eventually he learned that compromise was the name of the game; one could, after all, only hold on to one's lofty ideals for so long, if one wanted to eat, that is. Andrew dumped the day jobs and found work and temporary gratification playing in piano bars and on cruise ships. Performing music was better than being a line cook any day, but still, people only really wanted to hear the hit songs, music that was familiar to them. But the money was steady, and the readily accessible free alcohol was a fringe benefit that helped to take the edge off things. He became quite adept at covering other people's songs with a precision that was as remarkable as it was hollow. And then the years quickly piled on top of each other as they so often seem to do once you pass adolescence, until one day Andrew realised that he had been eking out an acceptable existence performing music for over a decade. It was at his thirtieth birthday party that he met Pauline, the woman who would become his wife.

Pauline was born and raised in New Hamburg, a small rural town in southwestern Ontario, the only daughter of a factory foreman. Her mother had died unexpectedly from a brain aneurysm when Pauline was young, leaving her and her father to forge an existence together. Her father was never the same after she died, and home life for the young girl became a dreary and cheerless existence. As time went by and Pauline reached her teens, she took on the role of mother for them both. She was a real homebody; satisfied with the simple way of life, cooking dinners, tending to the house for her and her dad. Excitement consisted of going to the local movie theatre on Friday nights with her girlfriends. Since high school, she had worked in a florist's shop in the town's only shopping mall. In some ways it was the perfect job for her: relatively stress free, some interaction with the public, and consistent hours. Mostly, though, she enjoyed immersing herself in the solace of making the beautiful floral arrangements that were the store's specialty. The store did most of the town's weddings, graduations and funerals. From birth to death, the cycles of everyday life seemed to be depicted by flowers: roses for graduations; spring bouquets of freesias, tiger lilies and wild daisies for Mother's Day; and carnations for funerals. An old school friend of hers had moved out to Calgary a few years previously and had been begging her to come out west and join her. Calgary was exciting and full of friendly people she'd said, with lots of available guys. Pauline joked about going but always felt great trepidation at leaving her hometown, especially leaving her father all alone. Then one Christmas her father surprised her and bought her a Greyhound bus ticket. He gave her his blessing and after convincing her that he would be alright on his own, she decided to give Calgary a try.

It was strange to be leaving her hometown, not to mention the florist's shop, which had been so much of her daily life for nine years. As she travelled on that Greyhound bus, she was a mix of excitement and nervousness. She watched in awe at the sheer vastness of the Canadian landscape as it rushed past her window. She arrived in the Calgary bus depot at 6:00 a.m. on a rainy March morning, feeling weary and dirty, and glad to see a familiar friendly face. Calgary was a change all right - a bustling, fast-growing city, not at all like her sleepy little New Hamburg.

Emma was busy helping her mother prepare for her sixth birthday party.

'Is Daddy coming?' she innocently asked.

'Daddy said that he was going to try to come,' answered Pauline, but refrained from adding, 'but don't get your hopes up.'

'Mommy, can I do the candles now?' asked Emma, satisfied with the answer.

'Okay sweetie, they're over there, in the second drawer, only six now, remember?'

'Mom,' came the exasperated reply; 'I know that!'

Pauline and Andrew's marriage had only lasted two years, two long years of struggles and heartaches. Like most relationships, things had started off well enough. Pauline had met Andrew at his birthday party; her roommate had been dating Andrew's friend at the time. Pauline was trying hard to fit into her new life and meet new friends. She'd found work in a local Safeway supermarket in the produce section, which included the responsibility of tending to the stores' somewhat limited flower selection. At the party, Pauline accidentally spilled a glass of wine on Andrew's piano and spent the rest of the evening apologising, while he spent the rest of the evening teasing her about it. The two hit it off and started dating each other. Andrew introduced her to the Calgary hot spots, and Pauline made him home-cooked meals. They were only together for three months before Pauline found out she was pregnant. For a Catholic boy there was only one thing to do. They married, and Pauline gave birth to Emma three months after the wedding ceremony. The ceremony itself wasn't a particularly happy affair. Money was tight; Andrew sold his treasured upright piano to pay for it and Pauline did the flowers herself. The reception was a small gathering of mostly Andrew's friends and relatives at Andrew's parents' house. The atmosphere of the devoutly Catholic household had a definite cheerless undercurrent since it hadn't been a proper church wedding not to mention the much frowned upon pre-marriage pregnancy. Pauline wept lonely tears on her wedding night. Here she was living in a strange city, married to a man she hardly knew, with a baby on the way. She missed her father. She missed her friends. She missed her life in New Hamburg. She knew, even then, that the marriage was a mistake.

With a new baby and limited family income, the marriage didn't get off to a very good start. At first it seemed that Andrew embraced the whole fatherhood thing, changing diapers, bathing the baby, going for walks to the park. But the novelty soon wore off as the drudgery of it all set in. The sleepless nights, the responsibility, the lack of freedom. Living in cramped quarters with a demanding infant wasn't easy and trying to write music was next to impossible. The baby only increased Andrew's growing frustrations about his career, or lack thereof. He began to spend more and more time away from home, seeking solace in the adult-only environment of the piano lounges he played at night. These became a haven for him; the free drinks and camaraderie somehow felt comforting to the discouraged musician. Andrew hadn't exactly meant it to happen, but like so many affairs, perhaps it was more a matter of timing than a real attraction. Whatever the case, one night at the Avalon Lounge, Andrew met a divorcee named Caroline. She was brash, fun and definitely out for a good time. She had one of those ashtray-alto voices, like Kathleen Turner, sexy and lived in. She smoked endless cigarettes and laughed loudly at all of Andrew's jokes. It didn't take long before the two were sharing the innuendo of flirtatious conversation oiled by plenty of cocktails. At closing time, the drinking continued at her apartment. Caroline had a sexual appetite and quickly took what she wanted from Andrew. He felt a selfish sort of liberation, pure lust and fun, no strings attached. Here was a woman that just wanted to have sex, without placing any other expectations on him; no crying baby to interrupt their egocentric lovemaking, no discussions about rent or groceries, and no bleak future to disdain. The affair, however, turned out to be more pathetic than passionate, lasting a mere two months. Caroline soon tired of Andrew's negativity, and with the thrill of the chase over, quickly became bored with the predictability of their lovemaking. For Andrew, the let-down was hard. He was crushed when Caroline unceremoniously dumped him, and worst of all, Pauline found out about the whole thing. The marriage managed to limp on for another six months. Pauline tried her best to get over the affair and Andrew did what he could to make amends, but with the combined stresses of raising a young child and the unrelenting financial strain, their already frayed relationship began to unravel.

The doorbell rang.

'Mommy, Mommy can I get it, can I?'

'Sure honey,' Pauline replied. The excited little girl ran to the door and pulled it open.

'Mommy, it's Daddy!' exclaimed Emma, delightedly.

'How's my birthday girl?' said Andrew, holding out a gift to her.

'Daddy, Daddy!' she squealed, and ran to hug her father's legs.

'So, you made it?' said Pauline, giving Andrew the once over.

'Well, I guess you'd better come in.' Andrew shook the snow off his hat, stamped his boots on the doorstep.

'This is for you,' he said, handing over a brown bag containing a bottle of wine, 'hope you still like chardonnay?' The divorce had been amicable enough, after all there hadn't been much to fight over, and he didn't contest the custody of Emma. Andrew eyed the wine glasses with bemusement.

'Only glasses I've got,' motioned Pauline, aware of the irony of using their wedding gift. Emma opened her present gleefully and started playing with her new Barbie doll.

'It's Malibu Barbie,' said Andrew, 'I thought you'd like the one that swims. Do you still go to swimming lessons Emma?' Emma didn't answer, she was lost in her own world of make believe.

'We can't afford it right now,' answered Pauline.

'Oh, that reminds me,' said Andrew, and he dug into his pocket and pulled out the crumpled-up family maintenance cheque.

'I'm a little short this month . . . sorry . . . I'll try to make it up.' Pauline took the cheque and put it in a kitchen drawer. It wasn't the first time he'd been short with the money, and she knew it probably wouldn't be the last.

'So how are things with you?' asked Pauline, tentatively.

'Oh, alright I guess, you know, the same old same old,' Andrew took a big gulp of wine. He topped up his glass and offered the bottle to Pauline.

'No thanks. Are you still . . .'

'Seeing a shrink,' finished Andrew, 'yeah, I'm still seeing the damn shrink, but apparently, I'm making progress,' he said, sarcastically, 'they have high hopes that I'll be all better soon.'

'I was going to ask you if you're still playing at the Avalon,' said Pauline. The doorbell rang.

'That'll be Emma's friends.' She stood up and moved to the door to greet the guests.

'Christ, what an asshole,' Andrew chastised himself under his breath. He glanced at the excited happy little faces arriving for his daughter's birthday party. All that potential, he thought to himself, all those little dreams of being actresses, singers, dancers. The archetypal little girl's fantasy. In that instant his whole life seemed to bear down on him with an unbearable weight: his own dreams of making it, the music that he had fastidiously crafted that expressed his innermost soul yet went seemingly unnoticed. A marriage gone down the tubes. And now, a daughter who was growing up, and inevitably was growing further away from her own father. No wonder - he was a loser.

'Father,' he sneered to himself, 'can't even do that right'. He gulped back the rest of his wine and stood up to leave.

'You're not leaving, now, are you?' asked a surprised Pauline at the door, 'the party's just starting. . . there's birthday cake.' Andrew stared at his ex-wife. It was too bad things hadn't worked out, she was a good person and deserved more. Maybe she'll meet a good guy, he thought to himself.

'Gotta go, gotta gig, ya know, same old same old?' He glanced back at Emma in the living room, surrounded by all her friends, eagerly ripping the paper off birthday presents. A picture of innocence and happiness.

'Thanks,' said Andrew.

'For what?' replied Pauline. He had the urge to say something like, *for being a good mom for our daughter*, but at that moment he couldn't find it in himself to say those words, 'for the drink,' he said, flatly. Then he buttoned up his coat and set off on the long, cold walk home alone.

Andrew braced himself against the cold January wind, the wine had warmed him. The air was heavy, and you could almost smell the impending snow. He looked up at the sky - must be getting warmer, he mused. As he walked beside the frozen river, he watched two groups of teenage boys playing ice hockey on a makeshift rink. Straight ahead, just across the river, was home. He put his head down and trod along the icy path.

After his marriage ended, things seemed to get a little better for a while. Being a bachelor again he could pretty much do as he pleased; eat when he wanted, sleep when he wanted, and drink as much as he wanted. He was able to write music again too, whenever he had the urge, without disturbing anyone, or being disturbed. But somehow it didn't feel right anymore. The spark was gone. Maybe it was the constant struggle for recognition, or maybe he just didn't give a shit anymore. As the months, and eventually, years tolled on, he became more and more despondent, finding little interest in friends, relationships, or anything else. He was caught on the treadmill, spinning his wheels, getting nowhere. He wasn't a has-been; he was a never-was. Then one morning he woke up to the realisation that he was a thirty-seven-year-old divorced dad, without a steady job, with little prospects. His youth was gone. His family was gone. Even his precious music had deserted him.

He looked up and felt the gentle, cold kisses of snowflakes on his face. *Forgiveness*, he mumbled under his breath, *bloody forgiveness*. Six months ago, he had reached a point of no return. He decided on that day that he just couldn't take it anymore. What was the point of it all? He'd read all the self-help, positive thinking, affirmation-bullshit books. He'd bought into the maxims do what you love to do, and the money will follow, and create your own destiny, but he decided that it was all a load of new-age nonsense. He'd even reluctantly gone to see a couple of counselors, but none of it took away his feelings of failure. That day Andrew took a walk with the intention of never coming back. He left no note, no explanation, no goodbye. He simply found an old, abandoned house, broke into a side door, went down into the basement, and slashed both his wrists. There was no ceremony, no hesitation, no pain. He had become numb to pain, numb to life itself. He watched detachedly as the blood dripped steadily onto the dirty concrete floor. His unfulfilled, unhappy life, draining away, into a pool of liquid at his feet.

Andrew was unconscious when the paramedics arrived. A neighbor had noticed him enter the house, and when he hadn't come out again, called the police. The one thing left he thought he could control, succeed at, he couldn't. Even death had ignored his careful orchestration. He stayed in hospital for a while. Pauline brought Emma to visit a couple of times. Everything felt awkward. Everyone seemed to overcompensate. He felt like the narrator in Sylvia Plath's poem, 'The Tulips' - *I didn't want any flowers, I only wanted to lie with my hands turned up and be utterly empty*. Empty and numb. After he got out, the counseling sessions came on good and heavy, after all, suicide is really just a plea for help. They all wanted to psychoanalyse, interpret and probe his mind. They all wanted to help him feel good about himself. Get himself back on track. The probing went deep: back to childhood, anger, resentment, parents, relationships. . .you name it. And how does *that* make you feel, and how does *this* make you feel? Didn't they get it? He wanted to scream it in their faces, LIFE SUCKS, AND THEN YOU DIE!

The air was quiet and still. The snow seemed to absorb all the usual sounds of life and bring a peacefulness to the world. Andrew liked the snow. It blanketed everything with a sameness that was comforting. Snow made Andrew think of happy times: snowmen, sledding, children. Emma. When he was a kid, snow was the one thing that could interrupt his piano practice to go sledding down undulating snow-covered hills and build snow forts. Andrew looked across the river at the little row of houses. Almost home. The snowy streets criss-crossed this way and that like veins draining from the heart of the city, emptying out into the river. Andrew was feeling cold; it would be good to be inside again. He decided to take the shortcut, skip the bridge, and cut across the river. He was nearly halfway across when he thought he heard a crack below his feet. He stopped to listen: no sound. He took another step forward and the ice below him suddenly gave way. Before he knew it, he was crashing through the frozen surface and was submerged in frigid water. He opened his eyes and desperately searched above him for the hole in the ice. He could see it just to his right, but he was already starting to drift under the ice down the river. In seemingly slow motion, he began thrashing, kicking, and flailing his entire body in the frigid water. His lungs ached, and his eyes burned, and his heart pounded in his chest like a drum. The weight of the water felt like a slab of concrete lying on top of him, pushing him down and his clothes, like anchors pulling him down to the bottom of the river. In a final burst of desperation, he kicked and swam with all his might upwards toward the receding light - toward life. Suddenly his lungs burst open sucking a gulp of lifesaving air. His fingers clawed numbly at the ice until he caught hold and clung precariously onto the frozen surface of the river, gasping for breath. His mind was racing. It would only take minutes before hypothermia set in. The fading winter daylight was quickly giving way to the encroaching shroud of darkness. His eyes scanned the riverbank, desperately searching for someone to help.

The snow didn't let up for the whole day. By nightfall, Andrew's footprints had disappeared. Snow had an uncanny way of wiping out one's presence, leaving behind no trace. The hole in the river quickly froze over, while underneath the ice, the frigid water flowed quietly. For a moment in time, everything was covered up with a white snowy blanket of sameness and perfection.

The Questionnaire

'Can you believe that?' said Ralph, as he shuffled into the kitchen to get a refill of morning coffee.

'What's that, honey?' said Gloria, looking up from her *Woman's Day* magazine.

'That's the third email I've had from the car dealership. This one was from one of the head honchos himself. I mean, all we did was have our annual service checkup - how many surveys does a guy need to fill out?'

'Maybe they're trying to have us upgrade and go electric?'

'Thing is, they said they are aiming for a ten-out-of-ten service, anything less and they wanna hear why.'

'Well, what did you give them?'

'I gave them a seven.'

'Why, honey?'

'Why? I'll tell you God-damn why. They used to run a drop off service, pick you up and drop you back at home, save you wasting three hours waiting around in the nearest McDonalds while your car gets serviced.

Now it's gone. Just like that,' said Ralph, snapping his fingers to emphasise his point. 'You want a lift, now it's gonna cost you eighty bucks – that's robbery, and you get to waste your life away while they change your oil. Some bright spark at corporate head-office's idea of how to put more profits into the shareholder's portfolios. Whatever happened to putting the customer first? And,' said Ralph, on a roll, 'now they have an automated check in too. A little touch screen thingy you gotta navigate, share your details, first born and all that. Can't speak to a human. No way - gotta use the check-in. In fact, come to think of it, there might have been a survey on there – how we doing so far? It took me twice as long to hand over my keys than if I coulda just spoken with one of the knobheads loitering over at the counter. Seven-out-of-ten? Should have given them a five.'

There was a tentative knock on the front door.

'Want me to get that?' asked Gloria.

'Nah, I got it.' Ralph walked to the front hall and tugged open the door and there was his neighbour, Ken.

'Morning Ralph. See you already got the joe going on.'

'The what?'

Ken pointed to the coffee cup in Ralph's hand. 'Coffee,' smiled Ken, 'joe. I'm just about to hit Tim Hortons myself, hey, you want me to pick you up anything. Pack of Tim Bits?'

'No, that's okay, Ken – we're good. What was it you wanted?' Ken looked sheepishly down at his feet.

'I just returned your lawn mower, it's in your

garage.'

'Great,' said Ralph, 'you're welcome, anything else?'

'Thing is, I didn't see the rock until it was too late. The blade took the worst of it. Sorry to tell ya Ralph, but it's busted. The blade broke right in two. The Chinese - they sure don't make stuff like they used to.'

'Busted? Well, perhaps while you're out filling up on donuts you could stop by Canadian Tire – they're sure to have replacement blades.'

'I'd love to do that, and I will, I swear - thing is, I'm a little behind on the maintenance cheques for Charlene. She's really bitchin' on at me this month, threatening me with child services and everything – can you believe that? So, needless to say things are a little tight, so if I could fix you up next month, that would be real neighbourly of you.' Ralph just stared at Ken for a second or two.

'Well, I guess that's that. I don't seem to have much of a choice, do I?'

'Knew you'd understand,' said Ken, 'are you sure about them Tim Bits?'

'I'm sure.' Ralph closed the door.

'Who was that, honey?'

'Our no-good neighbour, Ken. Returning my mower. Broken.'

'Oh, that's too bad.'

'Too bad? He's such a good-for-nothing bozo. I just know that I'm going to end up having to fix it myself. And look at our lawn – it needs a damn mow. Why don't we go into town today? We could hit the hardware store, get a new blade then maybe grab a little lunch out? A piece of pie might cheer me up.'

'Sure,' said Gloria, 'don't forget, my new desk is being delivered today. You said you'd put it together for me. I already got a text from Amazon – it's not coming until this afternoon, so lunch should be okay.'

'Be okay?' said Ralph, 'damn straight it should be.'

By the time they had taken Samson the dachshund for his business walk, driven and got parked downtown, Ralph and Gloria had to line up and wait thirty minutes just to get a table in their favourite lunch joint, Jitterbugs Cafe. When they were finally ready to place their order the specials board had already sold out of several items including the daily special sandwich, and Ralph could only see one piece of lemon meringue pie left sitting under the covered glass container over on the counter.

'Damn it,' said Ralph, 'I just know that piece of pie is gonna get snapped up, where the hell is the waitress?'

'Sure is a busy one today,' said Gloria, 'what are you having?'

'Well, if we ever get to order, I'll have one of whatever they got left.'

'I'm going with the soup; I haven't had split pea for ages,' said Gloria, closing her menu.

'Yeah, soup sounds safe. Me too. Wanna split a sandwich? I got a real hankering for a Reuben.' Ralph rubbed his stomach.

'No, but you go ahead, hon.' Finally, a waitress showed up and Ralph ordered for the both of them. He was right – all the pies had already sold out. After another fifteen-minute wait their soups finally appeared and Ralph's sandwich too – a corned beef on white bread – all the pastrami and rye had already gone in the first round of lunch rush.

'How's your soup?' said Ralph, 'warm enough? Cause mine is sorta tepid.'

'Warm enough to eat, I guess,' said Gloria, 'you always complain that it's too hot, now it's too cold, sheesh, just eat why don't you.'

'You're missing the point. You should be able to wait for a soup to cool down to the right temperature. That's the sign of a good soup service.'

'Well, eat your sandwich then.'

'I had my heart set on a Reuben.'

'Ain't that what you've got?'

'Nope. This bread is crap, a Reuben is supposed to be on rye bread. And I don't think that is even Swiss cheese in there either.'

'Geez hon, someone sure woke up on the wrong side this morning.'

'I beg your pardon. Someone did not. This food and service is a joke. They'll be bringing along a bill for this garbage in a minute or two, expecting me to pay it in full. And I tell you something else, I ain't leaving a God-damn tip. I ain't hardly seen the waitress.' Gloria rolled her eyes.

'Why don't we go through Tim Horton's drive through on the way home, maybe a donut will cheer you up, huh?'

'What is it today with donuts? C'mon, let's get going,' said Ralph, pushing his plate away. He was just putting on his jacket when he felt a tap on his shoulder. Standing behind him was the waitress waving his bill.

'Excuse me sir, but aren't you forgetting something?'

Ralph felt in his pockets – there was his wallet, reading glasses, car keys. 'I don't think so, sweetheart.'

'You didn't leave me a tip.'

'Well, that's not me forgetting, I didn't mean to leave one. Sorry to tell you this, but everything was crap today. I only tip for the good stuff.'

'I got a kid to feed, mister.' said the waitress, folding her arms, 'what am I supposed to feed him: your annoyance, or your unreasonable expectations?'

'I'm sorry, my what? Last time I checked I was the customer here. Tips get earned, they ain't a done deal.' Heads in the restaurant started to turn round upon hearing Ralph's raised voice, but he was just getting warmed up.

'It's people like you that make coming into work a real chore, you know that mister?' said the waitress, 'we get less than the minimum wage for putting up with jugheads like you and we depend on tips to make ends meet.'

'Well honey, perhaps you should have stayed in school, then?' said Ralph, 'graduated onto something a little loftier than waitressing perhaps, and maybe, while we're on with it, you should have thought twice before you got saddled with a mouth you can't afford to feed.' The waitress glared at him, then suddenly Gloria stepped forward.

'Here,' she said, pushing a twenty-dollar bill into the waitress' hands, 'he's sorry, please, take this.' Gloria pushed past them both and without looking back was straight out the door. The waitress stood there smirking at Ralph and all he could do was eat crow and follow his wife.

When they got home, they went their separate ways for a while. Ralph choosing to cool off and tinker in the garage, while Gloria settled in picking up where she left off with her magazine, Samson snuggled next to her on the couch. Finally at around 3.30 p.m. there was a loud banging on the front door. It was the Amazon delivery guy – Gloria's new desk had arrived. Flat packed, naturally. Gloria took Ralph a cup of coffee to warm him up to the task at hand.

'I'm so excited,' said Gloria, 'finally, I'll be able to have a dedicated space for all my arts and crafts projects. Do you need a hand, hon?' Ralph eyed up the big cardboard package laid out in the hallway. Then looked over at his wife.

'No, I think I got this.' Then Ralph set about putting the thing together. Ralph had done many-a-flat-pack before and so knew the strategy down pat. After opening the packaging, he checked that all the pieces were there and accounted for. Check. He opened the little plastic bag containing the screws and handy little tool they always gave you and lined everything out into small piles. Check. Then finally he smoothed open the instruction manual and turned to diagram number one. These instructions appeared to have been printed in a foreign language. Not a single word of English in sight.

'Crap,' said Ralph, 'what is that Spanish, or something? Damn Chinese manufacturers,' he muttered to himself, 'well, I guess these pictures are gonna have to do.' Then Ralph painstakingly began to decipher the drawings. The whole thing took longer than he thought it would. He was second guessing himself and double checking as he went along, the drawings not being exactly idiot-proof. Finally, two hours later and he was just down to the last step of putting in the four caster wheels that made the desk moveable.

'How's it going in there?' came the voice of Gloria, 'ready for dinner?'

'I'm pretty much done,' said Ralph, snapping in the wheels one by one. The door swung open as Ralph pushed in the final wheel. There was a louder than anticipated snap. The little plastic moulding broke off in his hand as he pushed.

'Shit,' said Ralph, 'that wasn't supposed to happen.'

'What's that?' asked Gloria. He held up his palm with the little broken plastic wheel sitting there.

'Definitely not my day today,' said Ralph, 'we got any beers in the house?'

Two days later and Ralph had Gloria's desk set up where she wanted it in the spare bedroom right up flush against the window. He'd managed to jimmy together a block of wood, the same height as the other wheels so as long as she didn't try to move it, the desk was stable enough. The next morning as the couple ate breakfast together, checked the weather and emails Gloria turned to her husband.

'Well, there you go. That's sure quick service for you.'

'What's that?' said Ralph, looking up from his bowl of cornflakes.

'Just got an email from Amazon about the desk. Looks like there's a link included.'

'A link to what?'

'Looks like a questionnaire. It just says - tell us how we did. Maybe I should forward it to you, Ralph?'

The River

The summer sun slants through the branches and cuts golden slices of shimmering light across the surface of the river. The water sparkles and dances, creating ever changing diamonds of reflected light. A graceful ageless beauty. Its journey began high in the mountains; streams and creeks traversing the sharp rocky ridges, falling in cascading waterfalls. Tumbling and bubbling, rushing down to the flat lands where the meadow fields stretch out for as far as the eye can see. Here it curiously meanders where it will: round bends, spreading out through fields, curving and arching this way and that, never in a straight line. Along the banks, majestic willows dip fingertip branches into cool pools and playfully stroke and caress the passing water. Small fish, wary of its transient nature dart back and forth gulping at small decaying particles of life; resting now and then in small eddying pools, safely hidden behind rocks and stones, or fallen branches caught along the mossy bank. On the river's glistening surface leaves drift and meander, dreamily pirouetting as they journey downstream like matchbox ships. In the deep narrows, the river runs clear, cool and resolute. But down towards the silty muddy bottom, the water moves in stronger currents. A watery snake body twisting and turning this way and that, making whirlpools that suck and pull downward. Suffocating, constricting, squeezing the life from anything that gets caught in its grip.

Upstream along a sandy strip of beach, people gather at the water's edge to beat the summer's incessant heat. A natural harbour eroded by many moons of currents and carved away by storms and rain. Children paddle in the shallows and play at filling buckets with pebbles, sticks, grasses and water, mixing potions and making spells, stirring and dumping then refilling and mixing over and over again. Pink plastic spades dig and claw in the sand and castles are piled up then knocked down again. The day becomes lost in a world of imagination and timeless games. Mothers watch within arm's reach from the bank, chatting to each other about this and that - husbands, groceries, vacations, home improvements. Life slows to the river's cold-blooded pulse as hours drift past in languid slow motion. There is no breeze, and the sun beats down unforgiving in its determination and heat. The water is cool and inviting, a welcome respite from the relentless hotness, but no-one moves out past their depth. They stay safe in the shallows. The river serpent coils and twists, slowly winding its way past the scene, surveying it all patiently from the dark murky depths.

Later in the afternoon teenagers arrive in carloads in an unspoken agreement - the handing over of the space. Time snaps back into sharp focus - the afternoon quickly changing into early evening. A timeless routine. The mothers hastily pack up bags, toys, and blankets. Sandy feet are dried with sun-warmed towels, and soggy bottoms changed and put into shorts. Little hands clutch granola bars and fruit juice boxes with little straws. Coolers, inflatable toys, chairs, and belongings are hurriedly packed into the trunks of family vans and SUVs. Windows are rolled down in readiness for the long, hazy ride home. The mothers ease their way from crude gravel parking lots to sticky tarmac roads, turn on car radios, and let satnavs steer them towards home. The teenagers control the beach now. The scene comes alive with the sounds and happenings of youth. There is loud music which echoes in the trees and bounces across the water. Their beatboxes pulse with seductive hypnotic rhythms as instruments bump and grind, blip, and scrape, making a modern tribal beat. Beers are passed around from Styrofoam coolers and the talk becomes animated and loud. Girls strip down to impossibly tiny bikinis, their thin, pale bodies laid out on beach blankets like long-legged antelopes. The young men cajole and out-macho each other, strutting and posing for the females. Wrestling and splashing about in the water - an absurd ritual mating dance, shared by species all over the world. They are animals gathered at the watering hole in the waning afternoon sun. The river snake stirs to life again and watches and waits.

Night falls and the riverbank becomes quiet. A restless uncertainty pervades the storm that is brewing in the West. Darkness descends. Birds fall eerily quiet and settle in their nests. Creatures take refuge. The river shows little interest in the impending change but continues its unhurried journey. The young folk have gone leaving behind their debris. The first drops of rain fall almost unnoticed in the shallows, a premonition and a promise. The air changes shape. Soon the wind begins in earnest, gathering momentum, battering through the tops of trees. Nervous branches creek and groan, some snap and fall. They lie discarded and broken around on the ground like twisted arms. Some fall in the river and get tossed and smashed on rocks. Those that survive get taken by the surging water to become deposited somewhere far away, somewhere downstream. The rain falls heavy now in pendulant drops and soon drives and slashes across the river in heavy sheets as the wind whips everything into a frenzy changing the landscape from the stillness of the afternoon into a scene of violence and foreboding. The storm blows for two hours or more and the incessant rain swells the river to overspill her banks. The beach where the children played has disappeared as the river erases all evidence of life. The fast-flowing water churns up the silty bottom into a cloudy slab-grey colour. The river serpent is at its most dangerous now. Gathering power from the storm. Growing to a magnificent size. Fully awake and hungry.

In the morning, calm has returned. The day breaks in the east, a redness that slowly extends its welcoming arms across the landscape and lighting up the world with its beckoning warmth. The storm that ripped its way through so violent and indiscriminate, has been and gone. In its wake, a trail of battle scars. The ravaged world of the night before looks strangely peaceful now. Nothing remains the same, yet nothing has changed. A tree uprooted from the ground, lies with its arms and head submerged in the river. It stares blankly up at the sky, its branches reaching out in a useless cry for help, its trunk making a slippery bridge across the water which almost reaches to the far bank. The river is calm again but swollen and deep, flowing heavily with a renewed force and drive. The current pushes hard at the tree trunk determined to find a way around this new lumbering obstacle. The river will not be detained. The river will not be denied. A young boy sits astride a bicycle and watches from the bank. He surveys the scene with excitement. All around are items which fire a child's imagination. Branches and sticks in which to fashion make-believe swords, fishing poles, boomerangs, pistols. Places to hide-and-seek. Stones to skip and rocks to plummet into the river's depths. The boy spies the fallen tree, and already in his mind he is building a fort, a bridge of adventure, a vantage point to fish from. His bike lies discarded in the long grass, exactly the same place it will be found, in two days' time.

A few small fish gather in a small mossy pool. The water is still here and gently reflects the images of life around it: swaying branches, a mother bird feeding its young, long grassy arms that wave hello and goodbye. Food is plentiful in this part of the river, there is no need to hurry and search. The fish can simply live, and grow, and reproduce. There is an order at work. A symmetry to life. Miles away the searchers work night and day. They drag the riverbeds and scour the countryside. The ashen faces of neighbours, friends and volunteers bear the lines of tired desperation and prepare themselves for the inevitable. The river serpent lies quiet now. It only needs to feed its hunger once in a while. It can return to the depths again, to doze, and digest its prey.

Obituary

Elliot Noble sat at his desk, laptop open, coffee cup now bereft of caffeine, staring into the void of his blank computer screen desperate for any glimmer of inspiration. All he'd typed thus far was his name and a few scant sentences about where he was born before he'd struck a creative dead end. He knew, though, from the two screenplays he'd written and the best-selling memoir he'd mostly penned himself, that inspiration doesn't jump out from a computer screen. Inspiration needs to be coaxed and invited into being. With that thought, he headed to the kitchen, surveyed the display of cut-crystal drinking glasses and opted for a rather large tumbler to save himself from unnecessary trips for refills. He topped up the glass a quarter full of ice and then with an unopened eighteen-year-old bottle of Glenfiddich under his arm, he returned to his writing desk. He poured himself a healthy shot, took a good belt, and then picked up the story thread where he'd left off.

'Born in Hartlepool, Elliot Noble grew up . . .' Elliot abruptly stopped typing, 'Hartlepool? God, that just won't do, will it? Perhaps a little creative fiction is in order. Let's see now – where should I be from, Durham or Harrogate perhaps? Hmm, Durham me thinks - it's historic, has a grand cathedral, tons of prestige, yet still carries a healthy cache of that Northern credibility. Perfect.' Elliot began backspacing and replacing the sentence he'd written. He read the new words out loud.

'Hailing from the northern city of Durham, nestled on the meandering River Wear, Elliot Noble first caught the acting bug whilst attending Grammar School.' He picked up his glass in quiet celebration.

'Yes, that's better, that's much, much better.' Elliot took another sip of his peaty inspiration and then noticed his phone vibrating – it was Chris Goodfellow, his agent.

'Elliot, I hope you're sitting down?' said the voice on the end of the phone.

'Oh, thank God it's only you, Chris. Why should I need to be sitting, darling?'

'Because Neville Fisher has just accepted our terms, that's why. You got the role *and* the fee we asked for. No negotiating involved.'

'What! You mean I'm getting two million dollars for playing a doddering old fool who keeps going on walkabout? What is the film world coming to?' exclaimed Elliot.

'That's right, and don't we just know how the Academy loves nostalgia; this role has Oscar written all over it.'

'Did you read the script, Chris? It's about as ambitious as a crate of over ripe melons; the writing is positively juvenile; and the character of Zachery is one-dimensional. Believe me, a couple of million isn't enough for the sheer embarrassment.'

'Oh, don't be so dismal and dramatic, Elliot, Neville just cast Taylor Jordan as your daughter. She's the hottest thing in Hollywood right now.'

'Taylor Jordan? I'm going to have to play opposite that lightweight. She doesn't know how to act; she only knows how to look good in a selfie.'

'She sells tickets, though. Bums on seats. That's what producers like.'

Elliot poured himself a large refill of whiskey.

'Why do you always have to be so crass, Chris? Money, money, money, whatever happened to the good old days when acting actually meant something?'

'Boy, someone is sure Mr. Crabby today, why don't you let me take you out for dinner - my treat. We'll celebrate, and you can make all the jokes you want about lightweight actresses. How's that?'

'I'm busy right now.'

'Oh, what are you up to?'

'Writing my obituary, darling.'

'You're what?'

'I'm having a small procedure next week and I can't bear the thought of someone eulogising me inappropriately.'

'What procedure? Are you okay?'

'A tummy tuck, darling.'

'Elliot – that's just God-damn plastic surgery. No one dies from a tummy tuck in Tinsel Town. Your obituary? You're just being grandiose and morbid - not a good combo.'

'Still, you never know, do you, and when my time does come, I want the tribute to be worthy of my career. Did you read that dreary piece in the Hollywood Reporter last week about Calvin Russell's sad demise? So, pedantic. It didn't really celebrate the man at all. All it did was make a big deal about the fact he was a gay actor.'

'Elliot, you are gay, and the entire industry knows it.'

'That's exactly what I'm talking about. These things have to be handled sensitively - not some homophobic strap line running rampant across the internet. We're talking about people's lives here, their legacies. *My* legacy.'

'Elliot – you aren't going to die, for Christ sakes!' yelled Chris, down the line.

'But what if, Chris, what if?' The phone went silent for a moment while Chris Goodfellow collected his thoughts and figured out how to pacify his most lucrative of clients who had potentially just bagged him a sweet commission.

'Tell you what, when you have a draft of your obituary why don't you send it across and I'll have Tina go over it for you – if you want to, that is?'

'Thanks Chris, but please don't patronise me, it's so unbecoming.'

'I wouldn't dream of it. Tina proofreads all my stuff – she's got a brilliant eye for these things, trust me.'

'Oh, alright. One thing though,' said Elliot, stirring the ice cubes round the glass with his finger, 'in my *best of* section would you highlight my role as Sergei Petrov in the *Russian Doctor* or Detective Frank Holloway in the *Cruel Hoax* miniseries? I can't decide which is my most revered work.'

'It's your obituary, Elliot, why not include them both?'

'Always the voice of reason, Chris. I guess that's why I pay you the obscene amounts I do.'

'I only aim to please,' said Chris.

Elliot swore he could see his agent's shallow little smile spread across his face, even through the phone line.

'Listen, I hope your surgery goes well, and I'll make sure we take out the additional insurance, just in case.'

'Always a prick, Chris. You know you never disappoint, it's what I love about you. And who, if not yours truly, doesn't appreciate a good prick?' Elliot laughed and took another mouthful of whiskey.

'Well, on that positive note, have yourself a good evening, Elliot.'

'I aim to, darling,' said the actor, eyeing up his bottle, 'oh, I aim to.'

A week later and Elliot Noble was laid out in a hospital bed, groggy and disoriented.

'Afternoon Mr. Noble,' said an unfamiliar voice, 'you've just come round from your surgery.'

'How did things go?' asked Elliot.

'The procedure went well and you're just in recovery now, in an hour or so we'll be moving you to your room.' A while later and Elliot was propped up in bed, sipping on water and getting used to the idea that he was still alive.

'You have a visitor, Mr. Noble,' said the nurse, gently pulling back the curtain, 'are you up for that?' Elliot nodded and took another sip of water. Within a few moments Chris Goodfellow sauntered into the room, proffering a bouquet of flowers and a small basket of fruit.

'Elliot – they tell me you are a model patient, and look at you, you look like a million bucks.'

'Well, I'm alive and kicking, if that's what you mean.'

'Touché,' said Chris, finding an empty water jug to put the flowers in.

'How long until you're out?'

'After a daunting surgery like this one,' said Elliot, 'another day or so, at least.'

'Neville is keen to get started on pre-production. Will you be up to flying in a week or so?'

'Flying? Why, where am I going?'

'He wants to shoot the entire film on location, in London, he said it will add to the authenticity. Which means that you get to go to your homeland, all expenses paid – which part did you say you were from again?'

'Durham, darling. It's all there, in my obituary.'

'Right, your obituary, by the way I enjoyed reading the thing, quite the career you've had,' smiled Chris, 'sadly, no Oscar. But I'm telling you, this role could be the one.' Chris pulled a few sheets of manuscript out of his jacket pocket, 'and here is the finished article. If I do say so, I think Tina has improved things immeasurably.' Chris handed the pages to Elliot who feverishly began to read them. When he'd finished, he dabbed at his eye with a tissue.

'I'm so moved,' he managed, 'Tina really has tightened everything up, hasn't she?' Chris smiled widely at his client.

'But here is my favourite part,' said Elliot, clearing his throat and reading a few lines from the new draft.

'Elliot Noble not only talked his talk but walked his walk. Citing his role in *The Custodian* as his finest piece of celluloid artistry and his finest philanthropist moment, this indie film inspired him to start the South Bronx School for the Creative Arts – an opportunity for under privileged children to gain an education and pursue their dream of a career in the arts. It is for this singular thing that Elliot Noble was the proudest and which will undoubtedly remain his true legacy in a long list of illustrious career highlights.' Elliot let the pages fall onto his lap and beamed his proudest smile.

'Simply sublime.'

'Bravo maestro,' said Chris, 'and if perchance I do outlive you and all your horrendous plastic surgeries, I will be sure that your own sentiments are heard clear and strong.' Elliot dabbed away another tear and reached out and took hold of Chris' hand.

'But for the time-being,' said Elliot, 'let's talk about that pre-production schedule and getting me to London.'

The filming of *The End of Days* staring Elliot Noble and Taylor Jordan began innocuously enough. Elliot started each day with two hours in makeup, making sure that he looked the part of a distinguished gentleman in the autumn years of life. Neville Fisher was a sensitive and supportive director allowing Elliot to improvise when he felt the urge, as he surely grew into a deeper understanding of the role of Zachery, and just how the ravages of senility can tear relationships apart. Elliot was working at the peak of this abilities, hitting his stride but it didn't take long before the notoriously cantankerous thespian began to find working with an inexperienced actress like Taylor Jordan, more than a little trying. The ingenue constantly forgot her lines and when she did attempt to act was about as engaging as a wet rag. Beyond this, she was constantly late to the set, and generally, acted like a diva who didn't really know how a proper diva was supposed to act. All of which incensed Elliot. It all erupted one day when, rehearsing an emotionally charged scene for the umpteenth time, she once again, appeared to bring up the script on her phone.

'For fuck's sake,' said Elliot, making sure the entire cast and crew heard him, 'is it just me or are you checking your insta-twitter thing again? Would it be too much to fucking ask, that we actually get this scene shot today, hmm?' Taylor threw Elliot a insolent glare and then stormed off the set followed by her entourage. The next day Chris Goodfellow received a pointed letter from Taylor's lawyer. The general gist being that if Elliot didn't reign himself in, then Taylor would walk, and the entire production would grind to a halt. Taylor Jordan, despite being only in her mid-twenties and one of the newer kids on the acting block, had far more celebrity selling power than Elliot Noble ever did, or would. That same night Neville Fisher visited Elliot's trailer to see if he could smooth things over - anything to keep the production on track. The two shared a good portion of a bottle of Scotch, while commiserating with each other about the current generation of acting wannabes and their general lack of resilience or work ethics. Neville left with Elliot promising to at least try to be on his best behaviour for the remainder of the shoot. There was only another three weeks to go, surely even Elliot could manage that. For the remaining schedule of *The End of Days* the atmosphere on set was frosty, to say the least, if not sometimes completely non-communicative, but Neville deftly played referee and the two camps kept a judicial distance from one another. However, after the shooting wrapped Elliot outright refused to do the usual promotions routine – there was no way he was interested in singing the praises of the film on the late-night TV show circuit, seated next to his vacuous co-star. No one questioned his decision. He gladly forfeited a percentage of his earnings, and he took an almost sadistic pride in wilfully sucking up the loss.

The film hit cinemas just in time for the holiday season and Elliot was thrilled for the resurgence the film gave to his sagging celebrity. So, with a gorgeous new toy-boy in tow, he took off to France to celebrate his unexpected success with a skiing vacation. It was during the Christmas break that Chris got the phone call. A freak accident, a one in a million chance, or sheer bad luck, but the result was still the same. Elliot's new lover, Marcelo, had challenged him to go skiing in the uninhabited back country. Virgin powder, ski trails all to yourself, and that undeniable spirit of *carpe diem* was tempting but perhaps more than any of that, Elliot just wanted to prove to Marcelo that he still had what it takes. And, so it was, he launched himself head-first down the steep, ungroomed slope with gusto. Halfway down his knee gave out, he lost his balance, hit a rock, and ended up face first inside a tree well. Suffocation was the official cause listed on the death certificate. Elliot Noble, died within minutes - a life ended, an acting career over.

Chris Goodfellow flew out to London for the BAFTA awards. It was both solemn and poignant to be there on behalf of his client who had been nominated posthumously for best actor at both the British and American film awards. It had been just over a month since his death, so there was a high level of interest and speculation as to whether Elliot Noble would finally get the recognition everyone thought he deserved. Chris arrived early and as is the protocol at these types of events, groups of people were seated together, as much for the sake of the watching television audience as for the convenience of making it to the stage together when accepting an award. Chris was one row from the front and directly to his right was none other than Taylor Jordan. Chris had the finished obituary in his pocket, which he'd read and re-read, on the flight over, just in case.

'Evening Taylor, you look stunning tonight. That's quite the outfit - Prada?'

'Actually, it's Louis Vuitton, turns out he's a big fan,' she shrugged, 'I just posted a pic of this little number on my Instagram and already I've had a million hits.'

'Amazing,' was all Chris could think to say.

'Listen, I'm so sorry to hear about Elliot's accident, he was such a talent.' Chris looked her over and thought back to the disagreements she and Elliot had had during the shooting of the film. He'd had to listen to Elliot's complaints about her on a daily basis, just to keep him on an even keel and able to keep working.

'Ignore the little bitch, think about the bigger picture Elliot, a couple million dollars buys a lot of freedom' is what he'd said, 'once this thing wraps you can treat yourself to a gorgeous holiday, as far from the madding crowd as you like.'

'God, I hope she detests skiing,' said Elliot, 'there is a sweet makeup artist I've just met who has never seen the alps before. And I intend to educate him. It will bring new meaning to the term ski bum, darling. But mostly I simply can't wait to be away from that little insincere starlet.' Chris smiled quietly to himself recalling their brief exchange, and at the irony that here he was now, sitting right next to that very same insincere little starlet.

'You think he'll win the BAFTA?' he asked.

'Oh, I'm sure he will,' said Taylor, checking her makeup with the camera on her phone.

'Well, Elliot was a complex man, but one thing is for sure he knew how he wanted to be remembered. His legacy is everything to him.' Chris patted his jacket pocket.

The show started and, as per usual, it took some time before the big hitter awards were announced. In the Best Supporting Actress category, Taylor Jordan narrowly lost out to the seasoned veteran, Melanie Pickford, for her commanding performance as a matron in the period drama, *The Conscience of War*. Finally, the Best Actor nominees were announced, and a hush fell over the entire auditorium. Chris Goodfellow could feel his pulse racing and his palms sweating. Then, as time seemed to stand still for a moment or two, before the words registered in Chris' brain, he heard '. . .and the winner is . . . Elliot Noble!' The entire audience were immediately applauding loudly, but Chris sat numb for a second or two before snapping back to reality. He pulled the folded obituary out of his pocket, his thoughts still reeling, when Taylor snatched the pages out of his hands.

'Great, a speech,' she said, rising to her feet, 'I think the co-star should accept this one, don't you?' Before Chris could say anything, Taylor Jordan strode confidentially towards the stage, with Elliot's obituary in her hand. Then all the eyes in the theatre, indeed, on television sets all around the country, watched with bated breath as Taylor Jordan carefully manoeuvred her way up the steps and onto the stage, demurely setting herself in readiness to accept the award on Elliot's behalf.

'Good evening,' said Taylor, straightening her gown, 'what an evening so far, and now this,' she said, raising the statue into the air. The audience cheered and clapped back its approval. The television cameras zoomed into closeup mode on the striking actress as she worked the room.

'During the making of *The End of Days,* Elliot and I bonded and got to know each other really well. I don't think it would be wrong to say that he became like a second father to me. Such an amazing actor, such an amazing human being. He told me, in our final days of shooting, that this film was his most gratifying experience ever and the finest moment of his career. I'm so proud, and he would be so happy that you all are recognising him for this achievement tonight.' She looked up toward the heavens, then placed the award on the podium.

'I have, right here in my hands, some words, written by the man himself, of what this meant to Elliot Noble.'

Taylor straightened the pages on the podium, stared squarely down the camera lens, and began.

'Hailing from the northern city of Hartlepool . . .'

A Wish

It was hard to ignore the smell. It caught you the minute you opened the door despite your face covering and your PPE - sickly sweet, earthy, something that seemed to imbed itself into the very insides of your nostrils. The odours of illness, death and dying. There were other smells too, antiseptic, the harshness of Dettol and bleach, the tang of constant cleaning, scrubbing, a pandemic being scoured away after every innocent touch. Every cough and sneeze, disinfected. Every benign interaction wiped away. Each surface of the hospital shone; every crevice constantly deep cleaned.

'Hi, can I help you?'

'I'm here to see my mom, Meghan Spencer, I think she's on E floor, room 314. She gets called Megs.' The ward clerk gazed deeply into her computer screen trying to connect the dots, while I stood watching, numb and slightly frazzled. Several nurses walked past, quiet and serious. Their full regalia of PPE couldn't hide their weariness. The nurses and healthcare assistants, the doctors and even the porters just doing their jobs but showing signs of deep fatigue. Fear too, in some of their eyes. So obvious, that look scared people get when they are back at the coal face about to fall over and break. But here we were, the pandemic on the rise again, the dreaded second wave already upon us with more people infected, more vulnerable dying, and the daily stats and death tolls mounting exponentially. Who knew we would end up adding all these new words into our ordinary vocabulary – PPE, deep cleaning, social distancing. Worse still, how could something like this be happening to me?

'She's been moved,' said the clerk solemnly, 'this morning - to ICU.' The woman in front of me attempted a weak smile. 'But,' she paused apologetically, 'we aren't allowing visitors right now, the new restrictions just came into effect today. There's been an outbreak on one of the wards.'

I felt the baby stir and turn right over in my uterus. Maybe it wasn't a turn, it's just how it felt to me, the times you get those big fluttery feelings, sharp kicks and elbows perhaps, as Charlie (as we had already decided he would be called) made himself comfortable, settled in, or indeed, turned over. This far into my pregnancy and his movements always felt big, magical, a lovely connection between us. Danny had wanted to name him Colin after his uncle, but I wanted something more regal sounding, a name that resounded, had a history to it but something that could also be shortened to sound more familiar. Charles on the birth certificate, but we would call him Charlie. That ticked my boxes. To be fair, Dan came round to it pretty quickly as we both revelled in saying his name in those intimate moments where we relished the everyday miracle that was occurring.

'Hey there, little Charlie,' Dan would say as he gently spread lotion on my extended stomach, or when he felt the baby kicking into his back as we languished in bed, blissfully sleeping late on a Sunday morning. That wouldn't last for too much longer, as we'd been warned, babies change your life forever, right? I felt Dan's hand reach around for my breast. His usual morning greeting.

'Hey, you awake?'

'Yeah, for over an hour now. Charlie was pretty active around five a.m. Think that's a sign?' Dan laughed, 'guess we'll find out soon enough, eh?' I reached for Dan's arm, pulled it tightly to my chest. I needed to feel him, make a connection. I was worried sick about Mom and scared about giving birth. We had both tested negative for the virus, but it still seemed like there was so much that could go wrong. I wished it would all just go away. In another month we would be parents, baby Charlie would enter our lives, draw his first breath and take his place in our family and hearts. But what a world to enter into all because of this stupid pandemic. For now, at least, he was safe inside me. No viral invaders in there, no germs being spread by a simple loving kiss, the touch of a hand, or by sharing the same air. No, for now, Charlie was safe, and we were all excited to meet him, but no-one more so than his grandma.

I had imagined walking slowly, purposefully, absolutely filled with dread and fear towards Mom's hospital room. The lights shining down, casting an impersonal glow, whitewashing everything with a fluorescent ordinariness, a cold medicinal reality. But the real reality was there was no walk to her bedside. No holding of her hands. No personal space to say what you wanted and needed to express, or to let the tears come when they wanted. Instead, there had been an arranged Skype call over some nurse's phone held at Mom's bedside. It probably sounded like I was calling from the moon. I'd already had the daily stats about the blood clots, the now failing kidneys, the ventilator barely keeping pace with Mom's incessantly weakening breathing. A virus ravaging a life, a family coming to awful terms. Surely, this can't be happening.

'Can I speak to her now?' The words sounded brittle and tinny, coming out of the little device that was being pushed towards the woman I barely recognised. So shocking to see her right there on my phone, my own mother in such a state, so frail, so hopeless.

'Hold on, I'll just get you in a little closer so she can hear your voice,' said the nurse as she moved the phone up towards Mom's face. She looked gone already. Her skin the colour of grey slate, her body, a feathery dead-weight - light, but already deeply embedded into the bedclothes, the standard issue sheets and blankets that seemed, already, to enshroud her. Had she already made an exit? Was she looking down from above, watching to see how things played out, observing her own body expire, these futile attempts to keep life alive? Those were the only thoughts that flew into my mind. Was she already free of this?

I could still taste the lingering flavours of almond, cherries, and custard. What is it in human nature, the need, the urge, the eat more than we should just because it's a celebration? Mom's sixtieth. A big deal. Maybe not to her but it was for those who cared about her. We threw her a party, invited some of our friends, her neighbours. We made a big fuss, baked a big cake, cooked a roast dinner with all the fixings and bought her a gift. She seemed happy. Not so much for herself, more for Dan and me. It may have been her birthday, but we were having a little boy. Her first grandchild, maybe her only one, who knows? She was so excited about the future - our little family growing. We'd lost Dad years ago to cancer. But Mom was stolid and just got on with life. I'm sure she had her moments, but she didn't let it show, she simply put on her game face and made sure the rest of us were fine. Mom was always like that though. Unselfish. Ready to help people, a neighbour, friends. Everyone knew you could count on Megs Spencer when you needed something. A cup of tea or a someone to listen, she was always there for others. I got the call three days later. Mom's neighbour, Janet, had tested positive.

'I'm really sorry,' she said, her voice sounding apologetic, like it was her fault.

'How are you feeling?' I asked.

'Like shit, actually. We had a rough night. Doug's got it too, but he seems to be feeling a little better this morning. I thought we should phone, let you know. How are you guys?' asked Janet.

'Us?' The question caught me by surprise. Us? Well, obviously we'd been in contact now too, was there a chance we might get it?

'Dan and I are fine,' I said, but my mind was already blurring over with other thoughts and the rest of the conversation got lost in the deficit. I hung up the phone. My mind was reeling. Dan was making lunch. Neither of us had shown any signs, no coughing, no fever, but it still felt a little surreal to find out you could be part of the stats. A pandemic that knows no bounds, shows no mercy, being innocently passed around between friends and family.

'Who was that?' called Dan from the kitchen.

'Janet.' I paused for a moment letting her news sink in. 'She's got covid.' Dan poked his face around the door.

'Covid? What the . . .'

I cut him off, 'where's my phone, I have to call Mom.'

The pain was incredible. I know they tell you, warn you, but what can ever really prepare you for childbirth? I was in good hands, though, the nurses, the midwife, and all the others who seemed to just float in and out like medical ghosts. Just folk doing their jobs. The NHS was under great strain. We'd all heard about that; it was a constant on the news. The battle against the pandemic, to save lives, save the NHS, on constant and endless repeat. It wasn't the most ideal time to be having a baby. Dan wasn't allowed in, to be part of it, the rules were explicit: no visitors even your partner or family. So much for the plans we'd made way back when things were normal. He would have to wait to see the bundle of joy that was now sleeping, all cosily bundled up, against my chest. Charlie. Our son, here at last. Seemed like these days everything was just one long list of unfulfilled wishes. Like how I wish Dan could be here with me right now, or how I wished the world wasn't battling this stupid disease right now. But mostly, I wished we'd never thrown that party for Mom.

I kid myself she died peacefully, but how could she, afraid, alone and struggling for each breath? They said that in the end it was her heart that gave up. To think, her kind heart. I know that when I spoke to her, that horrible day, through that God-awful impersonal device, urging her to fight and get well, I couldn't say what I really wanted to. Goodbye just seemed so wrong. Yet, I think I knew it then that's what it was. She was there, but not. Some say that the recently deceased can stick around for a while following the moment of death. Who knows about these things for sure? I do know that Mom was so looking forward to meeting Charlie, holding him, and doing all those grandmotherly things she loved so much. It just doesn't seem fair, her dying barely two weeks before he was born. After the call that day, I made a wish. A secret desire I held in my heart; that mom would get to watch her grandson, even if it was from afar. I know it probably seems daft, but I remind myself of that wish every time I look at Charlie sleeping peacefully in his crib. His life just getting started. Surrounded by his teddies, the handmade quilt, and the framed picture that smiles, lovingly, at her grandson.

Electric Chair

1959 - Bismarck, North Dakota. Prison guard, Bo Jefferson, hand-cuffed inmate, Joe-The-Werewolf-Walters, then began leading him from his cell on death row, down several corridors, two flights of stairs, then finally past Warden O'Leary's office, for an initial run-through and viewing of the execution chamber and to make sure they'd set Old Sparky's electrodes in the right place ensuring that when Walters was fried for real, that no further adjustments would be necessary. There were the usual jeers and cussing from the other inmates as the ersatz death parade strode past.

'Alright,' said Jefferson, banging his baton authoritatively against the bars, 'this ain't no cake walk, keep it down in there and keep that jealousy to yourselves.' With that, Bo smiled quietly to himself, as he always enjoyed having the upper hand. For his part, Walters didn't show anything. No fear, anxiety, and not a single hint of remorse. But then again, Joe Walters had always maintained his innocence since day one when Judge Augustus Carmichael handed down the guilty verdict for the brutal murders of six young girls whose bodies were found decomposing along the banks of the Missouri River. The way the bodies had been ripped apart, desecrated, and only partially buried was what led to the media dubbing these, the Werewolf Killings of North Dakota and how Walters got the nickname. No, as he practiced his death-row walk, Walters kept his self-professed innocent eyes facing forward, his head down and simply placed one foot in front of the other, showing no fear about what he was about to see or what would happen. Jefferson opened the double locked execution chamber door, heavy and a little stiff from underuse to the plain, well-lit room. The walls were whitewashed, and in places slightly flaking. In the mirrored viewing window that allowed the small group of invited witnesses to watch the carrying out, the reflection of the electric chair shimmered slightly like some distant oasis mirage instead of an instrument of death.

In the middle of the room was the chair itself. Of simple design and construction, made from seasoned oak, it didn't evoke anything more or less than something you'd see around your grandparents dining table at Thanksgiving, except there would be no turkey and fixings. This chair had leather straps fastened to the arms and a little brace for the legs, all to make sure the prisoner was secured and still while the 2000 volts was sent through the waiting electrodes and into the convict's body.

'If you don't mind now Walters, I need you to go ahead and sit down and try out the chair,' said Jefferson, keeping his words slow and steady. Joe Walters, sedately did what he was told to, shuffled over, turned himself around and then sat down. The chair was a decent fit all right, neither too big nor too small. Sturdy as the day it was made. Next, Jefferson undid the prisoner's cuffs so that he could rest his arms on the wooden armrests and Jefferson quickly winched over the straps and tied them off. Then he pulled on the wires and attached one electrode to Walter's temple and another to his right shin. Everything seemed to reach okay, and fit. So far, so good, thought Jefferson to himself. Throughout the process Walters never said a single word, instead he just stared straight ahead. No one could ever figure out what Walters was thinking or what he fixed his mind to throughout the entire trial. He never, once, showed even a glimmer of emotion. It was partly this cold-blooded, relentless, and seemingly composed demeanour that had tipped the scales of justice against him, and convinced the judge and jury that he was guilty. The evidence, at best, was only ever circumstantial. He was never placed at the scene; no weapons were found, but he had spoken to three of the victims. All young girls who didn't deserve to die. But when those bodies were found, murdered in such a brutal manner, the public outcry was as incessant as it was aggressive. Someone had to pay, and Walter's inscrutable demeanour did him no favours on that score.

Once Walters was good and properly fitted and secured in the electric chair the chamber door opened again and in stepped Reverend Harley. Of medium to slight build, pale complexion and with a sharp nose that hooked beak-like right under his simple spectacles, the reverend was fairly new to the world of preaching having only recently graduated from theological college in Ellendale, North Dakota. Upon finishing he'd gladly accepted the posting of counselling and rehabilitating prisoners as he felt this to be a calling from the Lord himself, and at worst, he figured a role such as this would allow him to find his feet and put into practice everything he'd learnt.

'Morning, Reverend.'

'Morning, Officer Jefferson. And who do we have here?'

'This,' said Jefferson, 'is the notorious murderer, Joe-The-Werewolf-Walters, and what we are engaged with today is a dress rehearsal, if you will, just to make sure everything goes to plan on the day of his actual execution. That day being a week on Thursday.'

'I see,' said the reverend, surveying the convict and scene, 'the notorious Werewolf Killings of North Dakota - my my, those murders sure shocked people in these parts. The work of a brutal monster, truth be told, and here is the man responsible.' The reverend stopped for a moment to get a good look at Walters. 'And I'm to give final counsel to the prisoner, is that correct?'

'That's right, Reverend. The warden thought that given the immediacy of the event, it would be wise for

Walters to have the opportunity to settle his score with God. Make amends, so to speak.'

'Make amends?' said Harley, 'if this man is guilty of the atrocities he has been charged, then I think that making amends rather underplays the gravity of things. Perhaps he'll be needing to seek atonement instead.'

Jefferson shrugged. 'Whatever is needed. You'll have half an hour with him. Be careful, Reverend, this man is not to be trusted. A guard will be posted should you need anything. Any questions?'

'No, I think everything seems clear enough.' Harley moved a chair so he could directly face Walters and sat down.

'My name is Reverend Harley, but you can call me Stephen, if that's more comfortable for you.' Walters said nothing, just stared down at his feet.

'I suppose the purpose of me being here, as you heard, is to give you the opportunity to relieve yourself of the burden of sin and to ask for forgiveness before you meet the Lord himself.' There was a long silence before anything further was said.

'Do you have anything to say for yourself?' Finally, Walters slowly looked up.

'I never done it.' Harley had to take a breath in, firstly because he'd never expected the notoriously uncommunicative prisoner to say anything, and because if he did, then he never expected that utterance to be one of a complete denial of guilt.

'But you have been convicted by a judge and jury in a case that was undeniably clear cut. You have been proven a guilty man, Mr. Waters.'

'I ain't,' said Walters, 'I've been charged and convicted but no proof has ever been shown that I did it. I never laid a hand on a single one of them youngsters.'

'Well now, that's sure some claim you're making. You do realise that we are in the presence of God, Mr. Walters, the all-knowing, all-forgiving God. If he hears your confession, he will undoubtedly take things into account. You are still able to receive God's forgiveness. Even now.' Harley leaned forward in his chair. 'For God's sake man, I'm here to help you, this is your time.'

Walters stared straight at the reverend. 'I already said I ain't done nothing I need to ask forgiveness for.' The reverend leaned back in his chair.

'But you also killed another man, didn't you? Here in prison. I mean, surely that can't be under any debate?'

'It was self-defence.'

'Self-defence! You are a killer, Mr. Walters, whether self-defence or not, you are still capable, rather culpable, of murder.' Walters stared at the reverend, almost like he was looking straight through him.

'There is an order in prison. On the day in question, it was me or him. Simple as that.'

'Would you like to talk about it?' Walters glanced at his arms tied tightly to the chair.

'I was working my usual shift in the laundry. It was just another day, but once Johnston and a few of his sidekicks came in and locked the door I knew what was going down. You see, until you mark out your own territory then you ain't got your place in the pecking order.'

'Pecking order?'

'Call it what you like, it's just the way it is,'

'And so, what happened?'

'Child killers, Reverend, are thought to be the lowest of the low.'

'You're saying that these men were coming to get you because of your conviction?'

'Like feral dogs marking out their territory, only one of us was gonna be left standing.'

'And so, you killed him?'

'Like I said, self-defence, Reverend.'

'My God.'

'After that, they left me alone. But I ain't no serial killer. I never touched those kids.' The Reverend looked Walters straight in the eye.

'Well, someone did.'

The rain began to fall, gentle at first then heavier as the storm quickly, predictably, moved in. It hadn't been hard to convince the girl, Mary-Ellen, to come with him. After all he was known to her, a family friend. Trusted. The rain had been on his side, too.

'I can give you a ride home. Your mom said if I saw you, I was to pick you up, okay? No sense in getting drenched.' He laughed; the girl smiled. Mary-Ellen had felt the first drops land on her arm and then her hair, which was long and golden, just like her mother's, as she left school that day. She didn't recognise the car, it looked new, shiny, and nice. It was a rental, something to make sure he wouldn't be recognised driving out to the place he already had staked out. The place where he'd raped, dismembered, and then buried three other girls. But still, the rain was really starting to come down, and if her mother had said it was fine . . .

For some, killing was like a fever dream, something that got into your blood and never let you alone. The power and control of it all, the desire and surge of adrenalin you got. That ultimate special moment when you slid the knife into soft flesh and ended someone's existence. Once you'd gotten away with the first one, and a second, it was hard to deny the urges.

'Where are we going?' said the girl, as they veered past the outskirts of town.

'I have an errand to run, I promised I'd feed a friend's dog. Do you like dogs?' Mary-Ellen nodded.

'What kind is it?

'A Lab. He's called Spenser.'

'Good name for a Lab,' laughed the girl. They drove further out into the country. Further away from anyone who might witness what was about to happen. Once he finally pulled over the vehicle, she had no idea where they were. The rain seemed to have let up some.

'Why don't you come with me. Spenser is in a cabin just over there, I'm sure he'd like to meet you,' he said, pointing into the distance. Mary-Ellen looked out at the sky that was clearing, then over at the man, and for the first time that day she had a small tight feeling inside her that something wasn't quite right. It was too late; within ten minutes Mary-Ellen would be no more.

It was one day before the scheduled execution when Joe Walters banged on his cell bars, trying to get the attention of Bo Jefferson.

'What is it, Walters?' said the officer, once he'd made the long trek down the corridor, 'this better be important, I was having coffee.'

'I want to write something.'

'What does a man like you have to write about?' said Jefferson, laughing aloud, 'your confession? It's a little late, by all accounts, the Reverend has been and gone.' Walters stared back at the officer.

'I believe it's my right as an inmate on death row.'

'Been doing your homework, have you? I suppose you'll be putting in your order for your last meal too?' Walters shrugged.

'I just want some paper and a pencil. An envelope too.' Bo Jefferson understood how things worked, he'd been parading convicts up and down death row for years, and requests such as these were customarily granted.

'I'll see what I can find. Anything else? Steak and ice cream?' Jefferson turned on his heel and was chuckling to himself all the way back down the corridor. Twenty minutes or so later and he returned.

'Here you go, Walters. Everything you requested. You got an hour with that pencil then I want it returned.

No funny business, understood? There'll be a guard watching you' Walters took the things and nodded.

The day of execution had finally arrived. At half past ten Bo Jefferson handcuffed Joe Walters and, just as they had rehearsed, they made the slow and steady walk to where the termination was to be completed. This time, however, the other inmates were quiet as the solemn parade passed by. Already gathered in the witness room was Warden O'Leary, Owen Graves, the county sheriff, along with Reverend Harley in readiness for the eleven o'clock execution. No friends or family of the convict had accepted the invitation to come.

'What time you got?' asked the Sheriff.

'Just gone ten fifty' said O'Leary, checking his watch, 'they'll be arriving soon, we should be on time.' And almost as if on cue, the chamber door swung open and in shuffled Walters, Jefferson and a couple of other officers. Jefferson nodded his head towards the glass window, acknowledging the crew he couldn't see, but knew would be there, then set to work getting Walters settled in the chair and the electrodes hooked up. No one said a word, everyone just went about their tasks diligently in silence. There was a knock on the witness room door, and an officer entered the room.

'All set to go, Sir.' O'Leary checked his watch, one minute and counting.

'Oh, and this is for you,' said the officer, handing Reverend Harley an envelope.

'What is it?' The officer shrugged.

'Something from the prisoner, it's addressed to you.' Harley stared at the handwriting for a moment. In bold upper-case letters, in heavy pencil, it plainly read - REVERED HARLEY.

O'Leary checked his watch once more.

'It's time,' he nodded, 'let's get this over and done with.' The officer returned to the chamber to pass the final instructions on to Jefferson. Meanwhile, Harley had begun to carefully tear open the envelope and pulled out a letter.

'Dear Reverend,' it began, 'on this, the morning of my own death, I thought it only right to put down the truth of the matter once and for all . . .' Harley stopped reading for a moment, interrupted by a loud urgent grunt and the sound of wooden chair legs banging against the concrete floor as 2000 volts shot through Joe Walter's body, making it shudder and shake - the normal and expected death throes of electric chair executions. The witnesses sat up and took note as was expected of them, and then within a few moments it was all over. Walters had paid, with his life, for the murders of those six young girls. Harley continued with reading the letter, the words jumping out at him like little sparks. Then he put a hand over his mouth, to make sure no gasp or other sound escaped it, as he continued to read the truth, at least as one man told it to be, of one of the worst crimes in North Dakota's history.

Old Vinyl

'Shall we do this box next?' Margaret began to pull away the cardboard tabs that had been neatly tucked inside each other and peered inside.

'Natalie, come and look at this.' She handed her daughter a couple of vinyl records – T-Rex, David Bowie, Roxy Music.

'Wow, these are so cool,' said Natalie, turning them over in her hands, admiring them.

'Records,' said Margaret, 'your grandfather was a collector, a real music nut.'

'These are really old,' said Natalie, looking over the back covers, 'early seventies.'

'Grandad would have been eleven or twelve at the time, likely the first music he ever bought.'

'Did you have records in your day, Mom?' Margaret shook her head.

'It was CDs by then,' she said, 'vinyl wasn't very common when I was a teenager. CDs were supposed to be an improvement in sound quality, indestructible they claimed, and that's how we played our music. The

Black-Eyed Peas, Jay-Z, Kanye West. Great memories that really take me back.'

'Can we play one of these?' said Natalie. Margaret moved over to where her father's stereo sat on the dusty sideboard and flicked the on switch.

'God, lemme see if I can remember how to do this,' she said, taking the record out of its sleeve and carefully placing it onto the turntable. She lifted the arm and moved it across the black plastic disc, the record began to spin, and she gently placed the needle down just as she'd watched her father do so a thousand times before. Nothing happened. There was no sound.

'It doesn't seem to be playing,' said Margaret, 'not sure why not, I don't really know how these things work, if I'm being honest.'

'Don't worry,' said Natalie, 'maybe I can find the song on my phone.' She tapped and swiped a few times, and soon had Bowie's *The Man Who Sold the World* playing out of the tinny phone speaker. The two of them listened for a minute or so.

'Nirvana did this song,' said Margaret, 'on their unplugged album. I still have the CD.'

'Who are they?' asked her daughter.

'Nirvana – they were grunge music, the sound of the nineties really. Kurt Cobain was a tortured genius, but I thought he was kinda cute.'

'Are they still around?'

'No,' said Margaret, lifting the vinyl off the turntable and carefully placing it back into its sleeve.

'Kurt Cobain killed himself. He left behind a wife and little girl. It was such a shock - a real tragedy.' Natalie switched off her phone and returned it to her pocket.

'Mom,' she said, 'how did Grandpa die?' Margaret stared at the old piece of vinyl in her hands, it really was a thing from an era gone by, although, vinyl records were making a comeback, or so she'd read somewhere.

'I think Grandpa died of a broken heart,' said Margaret, putting the record back into the box, 'after Grandma passed away, he didn't have the will to carry on anymore. You could say that he simply lost hope.'

'But didn't he . . .?' Natalie let the sentence hang in the air, unfinished, and then mother and daughter, without speaking, began to re-tape the box closed, in readiness for drop off at the charity shop.

Lazarus Sky

February 14th 2062, and what used to be known as Valentines came, on this day, with no particular fanfare. Not too many remembered much about the early ways and besides, no one really cared about meaningless celebrations anymore. It had just turned 8 a.m. and was already thirty-four degrees Celsius. If the BBC had still existed, they would have reported that today's temperature was due to reach a high of forty-six. Not too extreme for mid-winter, and nowhere near the record-breaking peak of fifty-four, from two years ago. Summer was a different kettle of fish, however, where temperatures could easily soar above sixty. This was the time when any of the remainers would have already migrated as far north as they could. Some to the tip of the Orkneys or some even farther into Iceland or Greenland, anywhere they could find a reprieve of ten or so degrees. All of which could mean the difference to survival.

There had been some rain the previous week that had pooled in the deep tracks of what had once been the

Eden River. Whoever or whatever was left would have taken their fill straight away, for today it was back to being a barren trench, a pock-marked mud-less scar that ran through, what remained, of the city once known as Carlisle. A rabid dog stood at the crusted edge chewing on something hard and decaying. Likely the carcass of another dog. Or the remains of some hapless human desperate for water.

Water. The stuff of life. And now the world's most precious commodity.

Caleb raised his gun and looked down its sight at the shadowy figure that was bobbing and weaving in the distance.

'Damn it,' he spit, 'those bastards come within fifty metres, I swear they're dead meat.' Yael carefully got up out of her chair, all the while holding onto her engorged belly and walked over to where Caleb was standing guard.

'Maybe, we ought to pack up and leave soon? Otherwise, it's going to be a long trek with a baby in tow.' Caleb didn't take his eyes off the shadowy shapes in the distance.

'Aye, maybe,' he said, 'what do ye got, another month to go?' Yael rubbed her bump.

'Three weeks, although, I feel as if he could come at any time.'

'He?' said Caleb, 'how do ye know it's a boy?'

'I don't, it's just a feeling I have. Call it a mother's instinct. I was right about Atarah, though, wasn't I?' She put her hand on Caleb's shoulder.

'I want to call him Lazarus.'

'Lazarus?'

'It means resurrection. That life will go on. It'll be a good omen; we could use one of those.'

'Aye, well let's hope you're right then, and it is a boy,' smiled Caleb, 'Lazarus, ye say.' He turned to look at his partner. Yael had the darkest eyes; looking into them was almost like diving into black pools of deep, cool water. He knew they held many intuitions just like they held a fathomless beauty. He wanted to kiss her right then and there. No, what he wanted to do was lay her down and enter her, feel his own lifeforce moving inside her, experience the electric sparks of love and desire as they climaxed together. There had been no sex for a while now. There were too many distractions. The need to be constantly on guard, that and because Yael was feeling so big and ungainly at this point of her pregnancy, she didn't feel sexy at all. Caleb let go of the thought then scanned the horizon again for any more movements. The scavengers in these parts were getting wilier and more dangerous. Taking more risks, throwing caution to the wind. Desperation was pure motivation when it came to stealing water or other supplies.

'Know what today is?' said Yael. Caleb wiped at his brow and shrugged.

'Valentines. The day of lovers. And it's love that gave us this,' said Yael, placing Caleb's hand carefully on her belly.

'Feel that?' Caleb nodded.

'That's a boy's kick. I think Lazarus is getting set to meet us.'

'Then I say we ought to stay put. Wait things out. It's a long slog of a journey and we'll be less vulnerable traveling if we wait for the baby to arrive.'

'That'll take us into March,' said Yael, 'the weather will already be on the turn.'

'Aye, but once we start the trek, we can't be stopping for anything, especially to have a wean. We'd be like sitting ducks.'

'Whatever you think is right. I trust you, Caleb.' Yael leaned in and kissed him on the cheek.

'Maybe I should make a tonic of raspberry leaf tea, see if we can't quicken things along.'

Caleb picked up his binoculars. It looked quieter now. Not always a good sign.

'I'm going to check on Atarah,' said Yael, 'fix her some breakfast and maybe her and I will go and see if we got anything interesting in the stores so I can make us something special for dinner tonight. For all my valentines.' She smiled while rubbing her stomach once again then turned to leave.

'I can go for you later,' said Caleb, 'I think ye should stay put for now, I dinnae like the look of things today.'

'We'll be alright; we've gone to the bunker many times, and besides I want tonight to be a surprise for you.'

'Well, if ye are hell-bent on it then you be careful out there. And here, take this,' said Caleb, passing her a hunting knife. She held it up to the light, checked it for sharpness, then tucked it into her boot.

'Don't you worry, I will.'

Atarah wiped the sleep out of her eyes and yawned as Yael pulled a simple handmade cotton dress over her head.

'Do you wanna help Mommy find some raspberry leaves? We can make some tea together?' The three-year-old threw her arms up in the air - her signal for wanting a hug. Yael picked her up and wrapped her arms around her.

'C'mon, you can have something to eat on the way.' Yael unlocked the back door, looked around the barren yard, then the two of them stepped out into the relentless sunlight. The stores bunker was an old shipping container that Caleb had half buried in the ground at the back of their compound. The steel made it extremely sturdy not to mention bullet and flameproof, and there was only one way in and one way out, and that was bolted and locked tight. No one was going to get into it without the key. Caleb had covered it over with dirt and patches of grass were growing so from a distance, at least, it wasn't really that visible. Yael put the key into the padlock and was soon pulling away the heavy chain that looped through the handle. She lit her lantern and tugged open the door. Inside they had set up rows of shelving they'd made out of discarded pallets, and these were filled with all sorts of dried and canned goods. Some were items they'd rescued from the supermarkets and warehouses before they'd been abandoned and burned. Many other things were the result of careful planning, hydroponics and harvesting. Down towards the back was the most important resource of all - a well. Caleb had discovered a spring and had painstakingly drilled and dug down fifty metres or so, creating a source which gave them a constant supply of fresh water. A precious commodity hidden inside the steel shell.

'You wait here for Mommy,' said Yael, sitting Atarah down at a small bench near the door and handed her a piece of fruit.

'Eat your apple. Mommy won't be long, okay?' The girl nodded and bit into the flesh of the fruit. It was sweet and delicious, and a little sticky juice ran down her chin. Yael was soon rummaging the shelves for some inspiration - there were cans of corned beef, beans, tuna, peas and corn, along with jars of different types of fruit in syrup. They had a supply of flour and rice too. Maybe a corned beef curry would be nice, she thought to herself. She could make some fresh naan bread and she'd spotted a can of coconut milk which would make things silky and sweet. As Yael was gathering together these few items, she suddenly heard the sound of bootsteps behind her and quickly turned around. Standing in the doorway, facing her, was a tall, shady, skinny figure. In one hand was a knife and in the other . . . the other was clutched around the small, dimpled hand of her daughter.

Caleb put down the spade and looked out across the inlet. The sun, as always, was relentless in its desire to scorch all it touched. Despite that, the view in this part of the Orkneys could have been considered idyllic. The sea gently lapping against the shore. The grasses that swayed in the ocean breeze. The sea birds that circled the rocky cliffs. And for as far as the eye could see, there was just water, sand and sky, unadorned and unaffected by the chaos that had dramatically changed life on the planet. It had taken him several hours to dig the dirt and pile the stones on top of the burial mound that would forever mark the place where his partner, his daughter and unborn child were laid to rest. But he knew it was better to have been able to bury them here, himself, rather than let the scavengers find and dig them up.

Caleb took a moment to drink in the view. The colours were just beginning to change and deepen into pinks and crimsons – *red sky at night, sailors delight*. If that were true then tomorrow promised to be a good day and, in that moment, he was sure he heard Yael whispering in his ear – see, Caleb, it's a Lazarus sky

A Future Unwritten

The kettle turned itself off automatically. Hannah heard the click and returned to the kitchen to the waiting teapot that was rinsed and at the ready. There were already three teabags out on the counter. The place looked orderly, the work tops all wiped down, the dishwasher unloaded, just the breakfast dishes to be dealt with. They could wait. The small Murano glass vase, a memento of their anniversary trip to Venice, now filled with simple garden flowers sat neatly in the windowsill and the calendar on the fridge door had all their doctors and hospital appointments circled and highlighted. All of which made life for Hannah, somehow, more manageable. She stopped for a moment to ponder the ordinariness of everyday things. The tea for a start. It was always the first thing that happened each day. Kettle on, warm the pot, one teabag for each person and one for the pot, then after a few minutes to brew, there was nothing quite like a cup of tea to start the day.

Things didn't seem right without it. Besides, tea seemed to have two opposing properties, it could be a right pick-me-up after a busy day of shopping or such, and conversely it could also have such calming properties too. A drink to settle the nerves, quiet the disposition, something to be taken in the evenings, even. Nowadays more and more people were sworn coffee drinkers. Costa, Starbucks and all the rest of the High Street shops doing stellar business. Perhaps this was a symptom of modern life? How everyone needed a real jolt of caffeine just to be able to face the day ahead. And another thing - coffee was bought in individually ordered servings: Short, Tall or Grande, and everyone had their own individual drink, their own preference – latte, skinny cappuccino, flat white, whereas tea was made in a pot, one type, something meant to be shared.

'What a busy day, shall we have a pot of tea, dear?'

Simon had awoken from his afternoon nap agitated again, he hadn't slept well the previous night, which was becoming the normal pattern these days, but it was hard to say if it was the slowly creeping onset of mental deterioration or his physical decline that set him off with these, almost, daily episodes but either way, a cup of tea was what was called for.

'I won't be a minute, Simon, I'm just letting it steep a little.' Hannah soon returned to the sitting room with a small tray containing two sets of proper cups and saucers, a little jug of milk, the teapot covered by a well-worn knitted cosy, and a few chocolate digestives laid out on a plate. After pouring the tea she placed a cup on her husband's side table along with two biscuits.

'There you go, a proper brew, just as you like it. Shall I turn on the TV, there might be some snooker on?'

'What's for supper?'

'I bought us some cod fillets from the supermarket, the battered kind, I thought we could have them with some rice and peas.'

'I'd rather have beans. Beans on toast,' growled Simon.

'But darling, we had beans yesterday, wouldn't you like a nice piece of fish?'

'Beans.' Hannah sighed heavily. These days, more often than not, Simon seemed to dwell mostly in childhood memories. Beans on toast must have been a staple back then. A cheap and yet satisfactory teatime meal to serve your kids in 1950s Britain. Simon always seemed to be plucking things - favourite food, songs, places and times, out of that juvenile memory bank. Besides this, he had more or less become immobile these days. With each passing month it seemed he was more incapacitated than the month before. It was like watching a cliff crumble away in front of your very eyes. Not a landslide or an avalanche per se, but more a small constant erosion. Her husband slipping away, piece by tiny piece, falling away into an endless nothingness, never to return. Not fair. On top of that, her life was now almost consumed with being a full-time carer for a man who had always been so full of life: the main breadwinner in the household; a father of two; a husband; an engineer; a fit tennis player; an assured dancer; a man of sharp mind and wit, always quick with a dad joke or two. Now this.

'I need a wee,' said Simon. Hannah put down her cup.

'Do you want to try the walker, or should I fetch the wheelchair?' Simon turned his head to face her. There was still enough cognition left for a wave of embarrassed anguish to appear in his defeated eyes. She saw it too. A man who now needed help getting to the downstairs loo. Some days he needed help with his trousers, his zipper, wiping himself. Dignity, it would seem, was a thing of the past.

The doctors couldn't really pinpoint a time scale for how these things would play out. What would do him in first, the dementia or some physical ailment? How long would this continue? Hard to predict. While there was a common trajectory for these things based on historical patient data, every case was different, individual. One thing was for sure, whatever time he did have left was diminishing into smaller pieces of unsatisfactory living. Beans on toast, seven days a week. The dining room made over into a bedroom. The simple joys of life and everyday communication chucked headlong off that ever-eroding cliff top. All that seemed to be left was the constant bleakness and inevitability of the situation.

The local vicar had called a few times, to see how they were getting on, the new church outreach programme providing parishioners like them with a lifeline to the church community. Vicar Brown was cheerful man, a glass is always half full, sort of chap, he naturally had advised her not to give up hope.

'Allow hope to rise up like a phoenix, Hannah, and resonate with your being,' is what he actually said. After some tea and biscuits and an encouraging chat with Simon, Hannah stood on their front step to wave goodbye as she watched him leave, likely onwards to the next family in need. She stood there for a good few minutes, just watching the world pass by. Cars driving down the road, people at bus stops huddled together sheltering from the rain, mothers bringing kids home from school, delivery drivers, neighbours going places, and unknown others walking their dogs. But inside the house, things were different, life had taken a distinct turn. Hope, he had said. She wondered what it was exactly she should be hoping for.

The phone rang, it was Angela.

'Hi Hannah, I thought I'd ring and see how you are getting on. How are you, dear?' Hannah looked at the yellow rubber gloves on her hands, the dishrag and bucket of water by her feet. Another accident on the toilet floor mopped up.

'I'm doing alright, I guess. How about you?'

'Now listen here, I can even tell by your voice that you're in need of a little pick-me-up. Now don't say no, but I'm coming over this afternoon, I have a bottle of Prosecco that has our names on it. And a lasagna you just need to heat up, so you don't need to cook tonight. It will be just what the doctor ordered. What time does Simon usually nap?'

'That's really kind of you Ang but . . .'

'No buts allowed! You need some you time as well you know. Richard is out of town, and I have the afternoon all to myself. And you, my dear friend, are on my mind.' Hannah smiled to herself.

'Simon usually has a lie down after lunch, around two-ish.'

'Great,' said Angela, 'I'm bringing lunch for us, no need to bother with anything, it's a nice day, we can sit out in your garden, it will do you a world of good. See you around two.'

Hannah turned off her phone. When was the last time she'd had a glass of wine, and during the daytime, too? She didn't mention anything to Simon, what would be the point? She just got him his lunch and then afterwards settled him for his usual afternoon lie-down. Angela arrived as promised; the shrimp sandwiches, couscous salad and Victoria sponge cake she brought were delicious. They were onto the second bottle of Prosecco, when Hannah realised it had been ages since she'd felt a freedom like this.

'I don't know how you manage, Hannah, I really don't,' said Angela, 'how do you keep going with it all?'

'I just do what I have to.'

'Yes, I can see that, but it must take its toll, surely?' Hannah shrugged.

'What else can I do?' Angela topped up both their glasses.

'I hope you don't mind me asking, but do you every think about the future?'

'The future?'

'Yes, you know once . . .well, when you won't have to live such a rigid life anymore.'

'You mean once Simon is gone?'

'I suppose so, yes. Oh, I don't mean to be morbid or a busy body, it's just that at some point the inevitable will happen, and you will still be here. You are still young enough, Hannah, to have a life you know.'

'I have a life now,' said Hannah. Angela raised her eyebrows and took another drink of her Prosecco.

'Of course you do, dear, but anyone can see how it's wearing you down - how it would wear anyone down. You know, it's okay to have other feelings about all this. It's perfectly natural.' Hannah looked up at her friend. Perhaps the wine was starting to take effect, but she did feel, for once, like speaking openly about things.

'Some days,' said Hannah, 'I really hate it.' She stared off into the distance.

'I hate him, for being this way, for doing this, for putting us both through hell.' Angela reached out her hand and put it onto top of Hannah's.

'Oh, Hannah.'

'Not all the time, though,' said Hannah.

'Of course not,' said Angela.

'Then I realise how selfish that is, how selfish I am. We made a promise, didn't we? A vow. To look after each other, come what may. How this must be for Simon, I can't really imagine. It's all so bloody sad and horrible.' A tear made its way down Hannah's cheek.

'The thing is,' said Angela, 'as awful as this is, for everyone, you will survive this. And life will go on, as hard as that may seem in these darkest of days.' Hannah looked up at Angela and nodded.

'Yes, I do realise that. It's just . . . almost too difficult to think about right now.'

'But in the meantime, you need to take care of yourself.' Angela raised her glass and they both clinched glasses.

'I wasn't going to mention this, but now I'm here and have seen for myself. Well here goes, in a fortnight's time a few friends and I are going to Malaga Spain for a long weekend. Why don't you come with us? It would do you a world of good.'

'But how?'

'You have a grown daughter and a son, surely one of them could look after Simon for a few days? Give their mother a break.'

'I don't know,' said Hannah.

'C'mon, just imagine sitting looking out over the Mediterranean, sunshine warming your face, a drink of spritz in your hand. And the best part - no one to look after for a few days. Tell me you wouldn't love that.' Hannah took a sip of her wine, and a smile began to spread across her face.

Once Angela had gone home and Simon was awake Hannah busied herself getting his supper ready. Angela was right, the lasagna was a welcome gift and made a nice change from cooking. Hannah was still feeling quite tipsy from all the wine, as she hadn't drunken that much in ages, and her mind was still turning over the exciting possibility of a weekend away somewhere warm. She put a plate down in front of Simon and a plate for herself and sat down. Simon stared blankly at the food.

'It's lasagna - you like Italian food, Simon.'

'I don't want to eat that,' said Simon, after a moment, staring down at his plate.

'It's a nice change for us, I'm sure it will be delicious. Just try some.'

'I want beans, beans on toast,' said Simon, and with that he swiped at his plate of food and knocked it onto the floor.

'You miserable bastard,' said Hannah, the wine freeing her inhibitions, 'Angela made that just for us. It's perfectly decent food. You can't have beans-on-bloody-toast every night; I can't take this Simon!' He stared blankly at her.

'Beans . . .'

Two hours later after the mess had been cleaned up and Hannah had felt the guilt wash over her like a wave, she sat on the couch nursing a cup of tea. She picked up her phone and dialled Angela.

'Hello,' came the voice of her friend.

'It's me – Hannah.'

'Is everything alright?'

'Well actually, no. I don't think I can come on the trip.'

'Oh no, why not?'

'It's just that, I have to see this thing through, Ang. I really have to.'

'Oh dear, has something happened?'

'No, not really. I heard what you said, and I agree, there will be another time when I can embrace a new life, it's just . . . not right now. This is something I have to do.'

'Are you sure?'

'I'm sure.'

'Well, if you change your mind, there will still be space for you.'

'And about today. I had a really nice time – thanks.'

'You're welcome. Look, call me anytime, okay? Even if it's just to offload.'

'Thanks, Ang. Bye.'

The next day, Hannah busied herself with the daily routine. Tidying the house, running the errands, and of course, attending to all of Simon's needs. She knew what had to be done and so she put her head down and just got on with things. But despite all of that sometimes it would hit her at the most unexpected moment. You couldn't label it grief as Simon wasn't gone yet. Pre-grief? Anticipatory grief? Whatever it was, it was a wave of complicated and mixed-up emotions that crashed down on her when she least expected it. Hannah pulled the quilt up over her shoulders and stared at the ceiling. Simon had settled early and gone to sleep and tonight she had decided to return to their upstairs bedroom. The bed they had shared for forty years. She yearned for a sense of normalcy. To be off the carer hook for just one night. The light was still on as she had intended on reading her book, but she couldn't focus. The bed felt cold and too big without him beside her, yet somehow it was a relief to be there alone.

Alone.

What was it going to be like when she truly was alone. No more needing to shuttle Simon off to doctor's appointments, hefting the wheelchair in and out of the car boot; no more beans on bloody toast; trips to the loo and back again; 'here lift your foot and we'll get your other sock on'. The endless taking care of someone else. Day in, day out. That would all come to an end.

But then her husband, partner, friend, and lover, would be gone.

Forever.

They had met at a party. Sharon, her best friend, had invited her and a few others round for nibbles and drinks on Christmas Eve. A gathering of single friends, a time for a few laughs, adult conversation, wine and all those goodies that M&S made oh-so tempting to buy at

Christmastime. The eve of the big day itself - when you were unencumbered by all those pending family commitments. Nieces and nephews overrun by sugar and excitement, listening to your least favourite aunt complain about the price of everything, while you helped your mother in the kitchen pull together hours of cooking and preparing the same predictable meal she pulled together every year. Surely never worth all that effort? Simon was handsome in his own way. Not a real looker, but there was a twinkle in his eyes, he looked fit and comfortable in his own skin wearing those Levi's and that tight-fitting jumper over a simple black t-shirt. And there was a definite flirt in the way he topped up her glass and smiled at her. A smile that was warm, friendly, and lit up his entire face. He told jokes and made observations that made her laugh. He could skewer things, not in a mean way, but in a way that assured he saw the absurdities of life, knew how to spot the real treasures, and had a zest for adventure and fun. He'd already travelled to Morocco, Italy, and New York. He knew lots about all sorts of things, had favourite music and books he could quote, and even dreams and aspirations for the future. She was smitten straight away. Like only happens once in a lifetime.

Hannah was awakened in the middle of the night by a loud noise. She was disoriented. Where was she? Where was Simon? Then she realised she was upstairs in the old bedroom. She heard a groan coming from downstairs. Good God, not Simon? Already she felt pangs of guilt as she grabbed her dressing gown and flung herself down the stairs. She switched on the dining room light and there he was. On the floor, a tangled heap of arms and legs. A pool of urine leeching out from under him across the floor.

'Simon! Are you okay? What happened?'

'Wee. I had to go wee.'

This time it took all the strength she could muster to get him up off the floor and finally moved and comfortable into his armchair. When she came back with the tea he was slumped over asleep. Luckily, he hadn't broken anything as far as she could tell, just a silly trip, an unfortunate attempt to do something for himself. But later in the morning, she would call the doctor's office and see if they could get an appointment to have him checked over. Just in case. He looked peaceful sleeping there. The agitation, fear and frustration gone from his countenance. For a while at least. If she squinted hard enough, she could almost recognise that youthful face, the same one she had looked into all those years ago. She took a sip of tea and let her head rest back a little.

There had been a moment, a crossroads, when life could have gone in a different direction. Paul was a colleague from work. Five years younger than her. They were tasked with developing and completing a project together, which meant spending lots of time together.

Hannah was project manager and part of the plan was to mentor Paul with project work. He was different to Simon. Less self-assured, but funny and curious. Mostly the attraction began as a physical one. He had the bluest of eyes that seemed to see right into her very soul when he stared at her. She let down her guard. There was a touch of an arm here, a few hugs goodbye there. You could always tell when a hug was more than just friendly. But it felt nice to be wanted in that way once again – desirable and alive. Office time soon spilled over into drinks at the pub after work to discuss and celebrate the projects on-going strategies and success. She knew what was happening but let it anyway. Simon and she had been on a plateau for several years now, the kids, already off to college, needing them less and less, and life had become somewhat predictable and repetitious. Then came the invitation. A weekend away to Cornwall, together, to see where this thing could go. She thought it over, should she, or shouldn't she? Nervous, unsure, but excited, she accepted, none-the-less. Her overnight bag was packed and ready, excuses to Simon made, delivered and believed. No turning back now. Perhaps this would be a true fork in the road or perhaps just a brief detour. Either way, there was only one way to find out. Then just before the taxi arrived, she heard it. Simon had fallen or done something equally stupid out in the garden. Twisted his ankle, a sprain or perhaps a fracture. He was so sorry to spoil her plans, no need he said, he was sure he could manage the weekend by himself. However, that was it. She would have to stay, call things off, take care of him, she really couldn't find it in herself to leave him to fend for himself.

Hannah cleared up the cups and took them to the kitchen. It had just gone 5.30 a.m. and dawn was just starting to break. From the window over the sink, she could see right into the garden. Over the years they had transformed it into such a tranquil space. On a fine day it was a pleasure to sit out there in one of the several seating nooks they had created, enjoying the ambience, the sound of birds, the gentle rustle of leaves being brushed by the breeze. Hannah had already decided to create a new space once Simon was gone, dedicated to his memory. Perhaps there would be a new sapling planted, perhaps this would be a place for ashes. These thoughts didn't feel morbid or trouble her, instead they gave her some sort of sense of sway over the future. When everything else was so out of her control, this plan brought a small feeling of peace. Hannah thought about what she could make for breakfast. Simon's mother would sometimes make cheese scones on the weekends as a treat. Hannah mentally checked the ingredients. They were simple enough to make; she was sure she had everything to hand she needed. It only took half an hour to prepare and bake a batch. Now the sun was really starting to turn into, and warm, the garden and fingers of light were reaching out to touch the kitchen window. It promised to be a fine day. Once the scones were out of the oven the house was quickly encompassed by the earthy aromas of baking. Of home. In a while, once Simon woke up, she would surprise him with a couple, still warm, buttered, just like his mother used to make, along with a pot of tea that they could share. Perhaps it was, after all, all about seizing the day, living in the moment. The road ahead may have been inescapable, but perhaps it was here, that hope could be found in a future that, while inevitable, was still unwritten.

A Decent Rack of Balls

Ian Keswick awakened, sweating and clearly agitated from the dream he'd just had. It had been so violent it had literally broken though his deep sleep. He'd been having these types of nightmares since being a child - monsters lurking under the bed, knife-wielding killers hiding behind lamp posts, and airplanes set on fire plummeting to the ground. This time the dream was that psycho guy who lived across the street, whose windows stared directly across at his. In it the guy was skinning something, hard to say if it was a person or an animal, but it was still alive whatever it was.

Ian shuddered, jumped out of bed and went to the bathroom to get a drink of water. He peered out of the corner of the curtains over at the guy's place. It looked quiet, but he was sure he did strange things in there. Weird visitors who came and went at odd times, and the tortured sounds of wild creatures, chickens and rats screeching in terror. And odd smells too, like lab animals being steeped in formaldehyde, snake skins being hung up and dried, and the sickly-sweet aromas of offal meats cooking and the smells of burning hair. Besides this, his neighbour always seemed to be watching, staring, observing. Taunting and resenting him, but for what? Having a bigger house than the council flat that he lived in? Being gainfully employed by the city council? Where was this guy from anyway? Not from around here, obviously. Likely an immigrant or some refugee. Legal or illegal? Hard to say, but it was obvious he didn't work a straight job. I mean, how many snake skins do you need to sell in a month? He had one of those dogs, too. Big and vicious. What were they called - American X Bully? Yeah, that was it. Like a pit bull, but on steroids and more aggressive. Deadly, even. Recently there had been reports in the news of mauling and actual deaths from these types of animals. Middle-aged mothers minding their own business getting caught in some angry dog crossfire. How do you even die from a dog attack? Ian shuddered again and tried to erase that image from his mind. Anyway, aren't dogs supposed to be reflections of their owners? Sometimes they even resemble each other. You see it all the time - Poodles out strolling with some puffy hairdresser type, Pugs with their equally pugnacious keepers, and impossibly tiny dogs shivering in the handbags of heavily made-up, anorexic-looking women. It is almost a cliché and certainly comical, but with these Bully dogs their owners were usually the kind who sport face and neck tattoos, violent inbred types who stalk the council projects with tempers that simmer away, always just one step away from boiling point. One flick of the switch or a wrong look and things were bound to spill over and break loose. Anger, violence, cheap beer and street drugs - a lethal concoction, then mix in those vicious dogs. Crazy.

The world was a mad place these days, no doubt about it. Everyone doing bad things to each other. No wonder Ian's dreams were so heavy and anguished. Why, the other day he'd been walking in the park to get some fresh air and be around that lovely greenery, just minding his own business, when he passed these kids, barely teenagers, all puffing away on vapes. Getting good and saturated before school. As he was strolling past, keeping his own judgments to himself, this one kid started giving him the hairy eyeball, staring him down like this was the OK Corral or something. He could almost hear his skinny voice poking at him like a spear.

'Go on, old man, just look at me the wrong way and I swear I'll fucking pull out that machete from my backpack and hack you to death. Right here in this serene public park. FUCKIN' TRY ME!'

What had gone wrong with the youth of today? Every kid on edge, endlessly plugged into the internet and social media, blasé about knife crimes, scouring porn and snuff sites, cyberbullying the weaker kids, and everyone immune to the subtle empathic feelings that used to make us human.

Ian Keswick had always been naturally melancholic; a glass half empty kinda guy. On any given day he had to work hard to see the good things in life. But lately, it did seem that things were on a definite downward swing. Every time he turned on the TV or checked his news app, modern life was becoming more and more desperate and twisted. The pandemic and economic crisis had only seemed to ramp things up. Every second person seemed to have a mental health issue, and everyone else was busy being ripped off, scammed or threatened with violence. Recently he'd been the victim of a phone scam, himself. Someone called him up to tell him he was wanted by HMRC for tax fraud. It didn't seem like any kind of joke. He knew there had been those few part time jobs he'd done, for cash, working under the table that he'd never claimed. How did they know? The woman on the phone explained just how serious a crime this was, but in her broken-English accent - which could have been the first clue, assured him that if he paid the £375 right now, over the phone, he could forego court proceedings. Court proceedings? Jesus, this *was* serious stuff. Once things went to court, she said, things almost never went in the accused's favour. £375 you say? Do you take credit cards, PayPal?

Bully dogs, scammers, and psychotic neighbours be damned - Ian decided that what he needed right now was a break. A complete getaway. Preferably someplace warm. Sit by a beach for a week, just staring into the ocean. Drink beers, eat seafood. That was it, of course -

somewhere on the Mediterranean. There was nothing else like it to return you to chill out-land and there were always cheap flights going all manner of places south from Southampton, plus, if you avoided the tourist hotspots, you could eat and drink for cheap - this was beginning to be a no-brainer. Ian opened up Google and quickly found a good deal for a sweet place in the south of France.

With everything booked, and not wanting to pay extra for baggage, he made sure to pack light, just a carry-on bag with a few changes of clothes and a rucksack with a few books, his iPad, phone and his toiletries all dispensed into small containers, and a new pack of condoms, for . . . well, you never know, do you? And then before he knew it, he was stepping off the plane into sunshine and wafting temperatures and being shuttled toward his hotel in the beautiful city of Adge, France. His hotel room wasn't too bad, a little on the small side, but there was a double bed and a clean bathroom. After all, what else did he need, he intended on spending most of his time down at the beach anyway. After a quick shower to freshen up he ventured down to the seafront to take in the views and find somewhere to have a celebratory drink and grab a bite to eat. Le Grande Bistro was right on the beach, with breathtaking views of the ocean and a menu which looked reasonable and varied enough. Ian was seated at a small table and presented with a menu. Before his first beer arrived, he could already feel his blood pressure dropping and knew the week ahead was going to be just what he needed to clear his head and rejuvenate himself. No psychopaths, no need to watch out for email scammers, and no aggressive pets - while the French certainly loved their dogs, they were usually the little fussy types – Poodles or Berger Picards, no threat there. The view from the restaurant was perfect, the sun twinkling and dancing on the lapping waves as the daytime heat began to melt into evening cool. Ian was on his third beverage and had already polished off a plate of calamari and was just thinking about what he might do next when an oddly familiar looking man approached his table.

'Excuse me, but me and my wife over there couldn't help but notice you sitting here alone, and well, my wife said if he's not an Englishman then she'd eat her hat. Now admittedly, she does tend to exaggerate, and I don't think there is any fear she will be chewing on her sun bonnet any time soon, but the thing is, we are also Brits and thought you might like a little company this evening? Feel free, of course, to tell me to shove off and mind our own business. Are you English, by the way?' Ian's mouth hung open for a moment as he took in, and tried to make sense of, this slightly abrupt interaction.

'Yes, I'm from Eastleigh actually, near Southampton. You know you look very familiar, have we met before?'

'I don't think so - hi I'm Terrance Wiggins, but most people call me Terry. My wife is Cynthia, but she likes it when people call her Cyn. You know, as in the seven deadly Cyns,' said Terry, smiling and reaching out his hand, 'we were just about to order some desserts and another bottle of wine. I bet this is your first night here, am I right?' Ian took hold of Terry's hand and shook it, still trying to make out where he knew his face from.

'Yeah, just arrived this afternoon, in fact.'

'In which case, do you wanna join us for a drink? We can give you the low-down on all the city's hotspots, best restaurants, lay-of-the-land sort-of-thing.' Ian nodded, and with the beers coursing through his veins, a little friendly company in the cards, decided that this would be a fine idea.

'Sure, what the hell, that's kind of you.'

After more wine, brandies and banter about the decline of England and the general malaise of the Conservative government, Ian finally clocked where he thought he'd recognised Terry from.

'Got it,' said Ian, 'I hope you don't mind, Terry, and this may seem strange, but I swear you're a dead ringer for that guy who was head of the National Gas Board. Remember when it was all over the news a couple of years back? That guy who was investigated for embezzling millions of taxpayer's money, but in a tragic twist, he committed suicide before anything went to trial. Didn't an MP even resign over that?' Terry stared at him, a small smile creeping across his tanned face.

'I mean, obviously that couldn't have been you,' said Ian, 'but I swear it's as if you're a clone or something – weird, huh?' Cyn looked at Terry and then back at Ian.

'No, not weird at all,' smiled Cynthia, 'Terry gets confused with other people all the time don't ya, hon?'

'As a matter of fact,' said Terry, leaning into the table, 'I do remember that news story. They say he got away with millions. Worked out of the Gas Board's head office in Reading. Though it was never actually proven he did it, obviously.'

'Yeah, real sad case. Imagine killing yourself over something like that. By the way, where did you say you guys were from?' Terry looked at Cynthia with his eyebrows raised and they both burst out with a little giggle.

'Reading,' said Cynthia. Terry raised his glass in salute.

'Now, retirement in the south of France, what would you say that's worth, Cyn?'

'I dunno. . . a million, at least,' giggled Cynthia.

'Chi-ching,' said Terry, grinning like a Cheshire Cat.

'What – you are that guy!' stammered Ian, 'you mean, you faked your own suicide?'

'Now, I wouldn't go jumping to any such wild conclusions,' said Terry, sipping his brandy, 'purely coincidental, ain't that right, babe? Reading is a big town, lots of people move to the south of France. How's your wine, by the way – top up?' Ian reached his glass forward and Terry poured in a healthy amount.

'But while we are getting all comfortable-like,

getting to know each other, there is something else Cyn and I wanted to put to you.' Ian's slightly drunken mind was still reeling, trying to figure out the news story, but Terry seemed keen to press on.

'You see, we're what you might call, swingers,' said Terry, taking hold of Cynthia's hand.

'Swingers?' said Ian, unsure.

'We get a kick out of changing sex partners,' picked up Cynthia, 'I mean, don't get me wrong I love Ter to pieces, but variety is the spice of life – ain't that right, babe?' Ian stared back at them without a single comprehensible thought in his head.

'Why, Adge is known to be the swinging capital of Europe, tens-of-thousands come here every year to engage in swapping partners and experimenting.'

'And here is the thing,' continued Terry, 'why would a single chap, like yourself, come to Adge, if not to get a little swinging action?' Ian swallowed his wine and thought back to the package of condoms he had judiciously packed. But swinging? Seriously?

'Terry's taken a real shine to you,' said Cynthia, 'the minute he saw you arrive.'

'Terry has?'

'Here, lemme explain,' said Terry. 'Thing is, not only do we swap partners, but lately we've also begun to experiment with same sex hookups.'

'Same sex?'

'Sure, you know, bisexual, omni-sexual, call it what you like. It's all just fun in the end. We like to spice up the old dishes with a few new exotic flavours.'

'Flavours . . .?'

'Why sure - why settle for plain old fish and chips when there is a whole smorgasbord of seafood delights to tempt the senses.' Terry swept his arm through the air as if to invoke a whole banquet of fishy delights.

'Oh, don't worry,' assured Cynthia, picking up on Ian's reticence, 'everyone we know is clean, respectful, everyone gets tested.'

'Tested?'

'C'mon Cyn, you might be putting him off. Thing is, we don't need to decide anything right here, right now. Tell you what, why don't we all get a cab back to ours, we got a real nice palatial pad, don't we hon?'

'It's really unbelievable what a million quid buys you in France,' laughed Cynthia.

'I got some real fine French wines, some of the best nose candy around, and a home entertainment set up, can't be beat. I don't think this party is done yet for the night. And we can simply see where things go from there. What do you say, Ian?'

Ian wasn't too sure what he made of all this swinging stuff, Terry and Cynthia seemed like nice enough folk, but perhaps it was the reassuring way that Cynthia, who was a fine looking woman for someone in her fifties, had put her hand on his inner thigh and given it a little squeeze, or perhaps the jet lag and wine had really caught up with him, but either way, Ian soon found himself lounging in the sunken 70's style living room of Ter and Cyn's opulent French villa.

'You like the Black-Eyed Peas, Ian?'

'The what?'

'The band. I love their music, those people are so talented with making beats, don't you think?'

'What people?'

'Let me tell you, we hooked up with this couple once – what were they called, hon?'

'Kofi and Jalisa,' said Cynthia.

'Right. Nicest folks ever, and you know it's true what they say.'

'What's true?' said Ian. Terry winked at him.

'Well, let's just say the smorgasbord that night was really something different, exotic and daring, and it turned me onto funk music something awful. You know I do believe that setting the right mood is really important.' With that, Terry punched a few buttons on the remote and seductive funky music began to drift out of hidden speakers. Terry pulled a little ornate box off a shelf and settled on the sofa and began to cut a few lines of coke on the glass coffee table.

'I'm going to get more comfortable,' said Cynthia, gliding across the floor before disappearing down the hallway.

'You know she may not look it, but once you've found her sweet spot, Cyn is like one of those energiser bunnies – she just keeps on giving.' Ian took a sip from his wine glass; it did seem like the red wine was the smoothest and most flavourful he'd ever tasted. Terry rolled up a hundred Euro note, dipped his head down and vacuumed up a couple lines of coke.

'Wow, this really is a wonder drug. Now I understand how Mick Jagger and all those rock 'n rollers kept going all of them years. Want a line?' Terry offered the rolled-up bill to Ian who tentatively accepted it. Terry was grinning widely nodding his head in time with the music and Ian could have sworn that Terry's shirt seemed to have come a little more unbuttoned. Ian put his nose to the table, sucked hard and was soon sniffling as the coke bit into his nasal passages. As he sat up, though, the euphoria was immediate; he felt a warm rush of well-being wash over him as the drugs and alcohol co-mingled in his bloodstream. Cynthia reappeared wearing a little see-through negligee number and took a seat next to Ian.

'Wow, you look great, hon,' said Terry, standing up, 'there's plenty of coke and wine for you both, I'm gonna hit the shower.' And with that Terry flicked a few buttons on another remote which dimmed the lights, flickered on some fake candles, and then tugging his shirt out of his jeans, Terry swaggered off down the hallway.

'I must say that man has a decent rack of balls,' said Cynthia, nonchalantly, 'but I've been wondering all night what someone else's are like.' With that Cynthia took hold of Ian's hand, placed it on her breast and began making cooing sounds, like a dove in heat.

Ian looked down and the floor seemed to be moving. Shifting all by itself. Then he noticed it wasn't the floor itself, but what was on it wriggling around. Snakes. The floor was covered with them. Big slothful constrictor types, medium sized wrigglers, and little ones that squirmed in and around all the others. Ian hated snakes. Always had. He tried to scream but couldn't make a sound leave his mouth. He tried to lift his feet to run, but his feet were leaden and besides, he discovered his body was tied tightly against a massive tree stump. He was captured. Was this some type of snake torture? Snakes were beginning to crawl up the stump and across his feet and legs. He was helpless. And frightened beyond belief. There was only one thing for it – he had to use his mind powers to imagine them gone. Ian closed his eyes and tried to ignore the sensations of the reptiles as they moved over his lower extremities, and focused instead, on mentally opening a door across the way. Breathe just breathe, he thought to himself. The door eased itself open and then Ian began making a trail of snake bait for them all to follow. Then slowly but surely, it began to work. One by one the snakes started to slither off in the direction of the open door until finally there were none left. Ian mentally slammed the door shut and inhaled a breath of relief. That had been exhausting. He looked down again and noticed he was naked. Why wasn't he wearing any clothes? He admired his genitals for a moment. A neat little package that could curl and uncurl whenever enticed to do so. He felt a faceless body reach round him and take hold of his penis. It began to uncurl and stretch itself like a snake waking up to feeling the first rays of warming sunlight glance its skin. Then suddenly he found himself perched on a precipice. The drop below him was steep as a canyon wall, all sharp and jagged boulders, and as he clung to the sheer rock face, he could feel the wind rustling at him, pushing him towards an almost certain demise. His fingernails scraped at the rock wall behind him trying to find any purchase at all. Then the rocks beneath his feet fell away and there was a sudden sensation of falling. Falling and falling, down and down . . .

At that moment Ian opened his eyes. Where he was, wasn't immediately clear. He moved his left arm slightly and felt the slight brush of a breast against his hand. It was soft and warm, and the nipple was a slightly erect. That felt nice. The aroma of musky skin filled his nostrils as he became aware of the female form laid in front of him. Cynthia. Then he became aware of another sensation, the warmth of another body behind him. An arm draped over his waist, skin and flesh pushed up against his back. A penis softly curled up against his buttocks. That felt nice. Terry. For a moment or two Ian basked in these strange and new sensory observations. Until finally his brain began to engage, and he realised he was sandwiched between two naked people, both spooning him, or being spooned by him. What had happened? His brain ached as he tried to recall the previous night's shenanigans. Plenty of booze and cocaine, that he remembered, the rest was a blur.

Ian Keswick ran his passport against the screen reader at Southampton airport. Home again. The week had flown by. As good as it was to go away, it was always great to be back home. And what a week it had been. Everything he'd wanted to experience and a whole lot more he never expected. That was gonna be one for the memory files for sure. Now as he stood on the platform at Southampton Airport train station waiting for the next one to whisk him the short distance up to Eastleigh, he noticed a group of teenagers staring into their ubiquitous phones. What were they always doing buried in those digital devices? Liking friend's posts on Instagram, ordering vape refills, sexting some girl they secretly liked, or looking shamelessly at swinger sites, watching the sordid things these people got up to? Ian heard his phone buzz. It was a text. From Cynthia. There were no words to the text other than 'a decent rack' and then just a picture attached. It was hard to make it out what the image was at first, until after squinting a little, Ian could make out what appeared to be a man's scrotum. His scrotum. From the angle in the picture, to Ian at least, it didn't look unimpressive. A decent rack of balls, indeed.

Curtain Call

While she slept her breath was like a rusty old squeeze box. More of a wheeze than a breath. Raspy, shallow and inconsistent. It annoyed me the same way it did when she scraped her plate clean. A noise that was so ordinary, yet so damn irritating. The needless chink chink of metal blade hitting porcelain. Why did she need to chase every crumb of food, every morsel around her plate? It's always the little inconsequential things that seem to be able to make or break you. Her irritating ways would just gnaw away at what was left of my patience; ignite that simmering hatred to make me want to stop it once and for all. It was in those moments that I felt like I wanted to kill her. It wouldn't be hard. She was more than helpless. Just a frail old lady in the final throes of her life, just wheezing her way towards death. Who would suspect anything? All it would take would be a pillow placed over her face. Hold it firmly and steady for several minutes. There would be no struggle, there couldn't be much fight left in the old bird. Would be doing her a favour really, putting her out of her misery, an end to the struggle for each breath. And what a dénouement - the death of Lady Macbeth, revisited and re-staged. I can see her now in full dress-rehearsal: blood-stained hands, sleepwalking, the final soliloquy spoken in poetic turns to the hushed, enraptured audience. Mother's finest hour. Stratford '66. Two standing ovations.

What thou art promised: yet do I fear thy nature;
It is too full o' the milk of human kindness
To catch the nearest way: thou wouldst be great;
Art not without ambition, but without.
The illness should attend it:
what thou wouldst highly
That wouldst thou holily; wouldst not play false

Or perhaps one day she would just fail to wake up. Isn't that how it always happens? Death by natural causes, or just old age? That is, unless she fell over. She'd already done that twice in the past six months. Unsteady and wobbly, lacking balance, she had fallen and bruised her arm and broken an ankle, but was otherwise, still alive. Such a tough old bird. But what if the next time she fell over, she hit her head hard against the kitchen counter. She would end up on the floor, unconscious, bleeding to death. Poor Lady Macbeth. It would only take a day or two before the unanswered phone calls would signal a cry for help. An investigation. By then too late, as the paramedics would arrive to find another expired old lady fallen over in a crumpled heap, on the cold linoleum. Light and lifeless as a feather. So typical. Silly so and so for thinking she could manage on her own, but then again, she'd always been hard-headed They'd never think to check if she'd stopped breathing first, would they? What would be the point? No, this would look routine, another unfortunate fall, the death of our aged ones. Happens every day. They'd never suspect I'd suffocated her first then thrown her down, broken her head open, to make it look like an accident. Easy.

I remember the first time Mother made me feel really stupid - it was my first proper report card from school. I was so proud to bring it home, show her the result of all my hard work, the 'A' I got in art class rising like a Phoenix above the row of undistinguished 'C's. Ms. Bryant had said my painting showed real promise, albeit a little dark and sinister for a ten-year-old boy, but she saw some sort of promise in me. In my art. A glint of something else.

'You should keep drawing Daniel, you're good at it.' Encouragement like that didn't come by too often. I wasn't the sharpest knife, I'll admit that, but I was methodical if nothing else. I did try hard, applied myself and I didn't quite recognise it then, but I seemed to possess an innate talent for imagining the abstract in things. That wouldn't properly develop in my art until much later. No, even as a kid, I knew I would have to work doubly hard for any scrap of success life would toss my way. There would be no cakewalk for Daniel

Hutt. Not like some of those other kids I knew - Gary Barns, Parker Jones and Mike Williamson. The trio of distinction-grabbing hombres who easily scored top marks in everything. They had it made. With their comfortable middle-class lives, good genes, athleticism and regular families, they hardly even had to try. They had a guaranteed meal ticket to whatever future they desired. Strange that they befriended me. Me, from the wrong side of the tracks who lived in an apartment over a butcher's shop instead of a suburban split-level rancher. Me, with a weird actress mother, who kept odd hours, worked weekends, and spoke in strange turns of phrase, all artistic and eccentric. Me, without a real father, just some torrid-affair-drunken-sperm-donor-director, twenty years Mother's senior, who left his procreative mark in life and forgot I even existed. No, I was the fourth wheel in an otherwise much-admired circle of friends. The odd one out. The others embracing me like one of their own, perhaps their proximity to a less-than, an unfortunate one, somehow made their lot in life seem better.

Despite being a single mom, mother still somehow managed to maintain all the pretense of glamour, albeit on a shoestring budget. Theatre work was always up and down, not steady like the other kids' parents' jobs; one un-fixed income doesn't provide much security with a second hungry mouth to feed. But Mother lived her theatrical life to the hilt, dining at swank restaurants off freebies from her agent friends. I would hear her talking about these great soirée evenings: Vichyssoise, Beef Wellington and poached salmon all washed down with a good bottle of French wine. Brandys to finish, naturally. Her fellow thespians with their late-night drinking parties, script readings, discussions about staging, costumes, and artistic intent, reciting famous lines - their thunderous voices echoing down our narrow apartment hallway. In many ways, Mother was oblivious to being a parent. Disdainful, in fact, of being a mother. She loathed being burdened with a little kid. She never said it out loud, but it was there - in her manners, her behavior, the lack of love she seemed able to show or give. I was there, always needing things - books for school, new shoes, like a sodden anchor strung around her neck weighing her gay life down. Sadly, I wasn't even one of those precocious children who could hold their own in adult conversation and charm the socks off a living room full of drunken impresarios. 'Sing us your song again Danny - the one from Billy Elliot'. There were never any enchanting comebacks, or youthful insight and naiveté. Unfortunately, having an ordinary kid didn't fit Mother's image at all. Her friends and associates, their conversations always on the edge, full of innuendo and witty banter, rarely even acknowledged my existence. They were all too wrapped up in themselves and their self-centered egos. Actors, directors, artistes, all. It was amusing to observe these people who thought of themselves in such high regard, an entire shelf above the rest of life's walking stiffs, strutting their egotistical stuff, when they were really as fragile as the next bad review. Even as a little kid I knew they were of a different ilk. But, oh, how those of the theatrical bent held such a special insight into the human condition. The ability to distill the essence of life, capture it, replay it, and then project it for the world to see. Mother would often say, 'what higher art form could there be than acting, darling?'

How they all lived for it. The smell of the grease paint, the lure of the footlights, and that most special feeling one got when that line of perspiration rolled down your back as you waited, bloodied dagger in hand, tarnished crown slightly askew on your head, in full Titus Andronicus pose, for the audience to fully appreciate the depths of your brilliant performance. At the end of the show would come the obligatory after-show drinks, back slapping, congratulations, and peacock strutting and preening. Fawning indifference, yet unabashedly desperate for the attention to shine down, a single follow spot, on the star of the show. And then there was the singing - ah God, how camp, how rousing, how . . . musical. On those late-night drunken evenings, when everyone would stumble back to ours, I can still remember being awakened by the booming voices of Lear, Ophelia, and Othello. After the wine was all well and truly drained and the brandy was flowing, someone would inevitably tinkle the ivories of the old upright Mother kept in the parlor and all would gather round like a flock of venerable magpies to join in with spirited renditions of their favorite show tunes. Songs from all the biggest hits: Gilbert and Sullivan, Les Mis, Cats, Phantom. Harmonies and stage gesturing intuitively coming on thick and strong. Mother's disheveled Persian throw rugs, strewn around the place, splashed by errant brandy as snifter-clutching hands instinctively reached out to emphasise the very emotion of the lyrics. Then some sensitive soul with a momentary sober insight asking if we might not be waking-up the sleeping lad?

'Don't worry darling, he's a heavy sleeper, and in any case, he can have the morning off school tomorrow.'

Then Mother would needlessly add, 'school's not his forte darling - unfortunately, he's not the brightest spark'. Mother's disappointment rising to the surface, expressed with an unabashed honesty through the fortitude of alcohol.

I grew up feeling, and knowing, that I was nothing special. A liability. Unlovable. Even as a young child I felt I was all alone in a Godless universe. I showed mother my report card that day and bit my lower lip, hoping for the impossible. Some platitudes of acceptance, a pat on the head, acknowledgment or acceptance. All mother did was laugh. I can still hear it clear as day, as piercing as a car alarm. Shrill and ugly, like a crow mockingly showing its disapproval. She tossed the carefully hand-written report card onto the table. Discarded. I remember crying myself to sleep that night. A strange feeling inside my stomach, a mixture of hatred and anger mixed up with a child's longing, a desperate need to be loved. Something a young boy couldn't really understand, never mind put into words.

As we became teenagers, Parker Jones blossomed into a young lady of some repute. She was beautiful and smart but had a sharp acidic tongue - you wouldn't want to cross Parker Jones. We'd been a group of friends for several years - Mike, Parker, Gary and I. Getting through school together, putting up with the endless homework, exams, boring classes, and decrepit teachers. Besides my predilection for art, I also played French horn in the school band and even tried my hand at athletics. I went out for the gymnastics club, but it never progressed very far as I just didn't have the coordination or strength to move beyond a handspring and some very basic tumbling on the gym's sour-smelling mats. So, I tried my luck at track and field. Running. I discovered I was quite good at cross country as this required nothing more than pure stamina. As a teenager I was rather gangly and had long spindly legs, which probably helped. If there was one thing I excelled at, it was going the distance. Never a sprinter, by any means, which took more strategy and focus, but putting your head down and going the distance suited me in every way. Maybe it was the psychological freedom of it all. Focusing on something far off, a destination unknown. Or perhaps running away from something, leaving everything behind, watching it get smaller and smaller the further you ran. But what did it really matter, running away or towards, once you were in that zone there was nothing to it, just you and miles of unforgiving asphalt. After five minutes or so your heart rate and breath would steady to a regular pulse, and with the wind in your face it was easy to block everything else out except for that one single goal of putting one foot in front of the other. Distance running became my thing.

Gary and Mike both played football, of course, and Mike played center forward for the Triple A hockey team. Parker and I would watch the games, cheer them on. They were natural athletes those two. Team leader material. But they never flaunted their prowess, there was no arrogance about their talents, they just loved what they did, and they did it well. I personally believe it is all down to genes. Natural selection. Some have it and some do not. Parker was captain of the debating team, her sharp mind and biting comebacks serving her particularly well. She also played clarinet in the school band. She sat two rows in front of me and I used to sit and watch the way her auburn hair danced on her shoulders as each breath produced another string of cheerful notes. Her green eyes were deep pools of alluring exotica. The window to a beautiful unfathomable soul. How I dreamed of dancing in those eyes.

I always felt that high school was such a weird unnatural environment. A place that imitates life in an absurdly surreal way. Young brains that are poked and prodded and stretched to the max. Learning about love, death and despair through Shakespearean sonnets, Greek poetry and dystopian novels. The physical world, examined and dissected by periodic tables and quantum formulas, as photosynthesis and osmolality keep the very fabric of life around us ebbing and flowing on a cellular level. Meanwhile, practical life skills are passed down and learnt in home economic and metal work classes: how to weld a joint, bake bread, and iron a shirt - invaluable life lessons. Finally, the development and expression of self was encouraged through art, theatre classes and music. Discover who you are, what you're good at, and who you might become. And all through these educational trials and tribulations, hormones were doing their thing, awakening physiology to the ripening changes taking place in growing youthful bodies. Then, just as the seasons arrive and one day summer is suddenly there in full bloom, we all became adolescents. Teenagers. With all the awkwardness and drama that brings. For athletic, valedictorian types like Mike and Gary the transition didn't seem too bad. Their shoulders filled out, they started to get stubble in all the right places, and their voices dropped, seemingly overnight. However, for me things were a little different. A late bloomer with acne and a painful awkwardness that only increased, adolescence was more like being dropped into someone else's skin. One I found hard to recognise and even harder to like.

It didn't take long, of course, before I began to

notice those other strange creatures - girls. Funny thing was it seemed that during summer holiday that year all the girls had metamorphosed into young women seemingly overnight. I remember it so well; the start of grade nine. School began to resemble a hothouse full of strange and marvelous blooms. Orchids, magnolias, roses and wildflowers. It seemed like every sweet and glorious variety was present. All the boys could do was look upon it all dumbstruck and dumbfounded by what had happened before their very eyes. One day we were all just kids sharing a playground, the next thing we knew there were young women everywhere you looked. Sitting next to you, shuffling in clusters down the hallways, primping and preening themselves in pairs in front of bathroom mirrors. And then there were those breasts and sweet-smelling hair, clothes that clung to new-found curves and those eye-liner eyes. What dark pools of unknown seductions lay inside them? It was because of this that I began to paint in earnest. I was filled up with the sights and intoxications of these new and wondrous creatures, the beauty that was unfolding all around me. I painted feverishly and pretentiously called my first collection of paintings 'Fleur de la Femme'. It was my attempt to imitate some of the early surrealists I was so enraptured with - Kandinsky, Rothko and Pollack. I used wild brush strokes and vivid splashes of colour. Splattering and moving paint around in rhythm to the dancing thoughts in my mind. Each canvas was a different girl's portrait, blooming on the stem of a different flower. I even titled them preposterous Latin names such as Andrea Helianthus, Ellen Narcissus Jonquilla, and Parker Rose Perpetua - the queen of all garden blooms, the Rose. It was the height of pretension, I know that now, but there I was, full of that youthful naiveté. These initial attempts at abstraction were really just mawkish, amateurish, and overtly sentimental but, perhaps, all part of some sort of necessary journey. For that first remarkable pubescent year of high school, it was all I could do to try to make sense of being a teenager.

Parker dated all of us at one point or another. It was almost like a game – dating and going out, something inevitable, a rite of passage, playing at relationships and infatuations. For Parker it was like she wanted to try out each different type of guy to see what she preferred. First it was Mike, then Gary, and then finally during our graduation year, it was little old artistic me. I'm sure that for Parker I was like the crackerjack prize at the bottom of the box, nothing worthwhile or of value, but something that could be amusing, for a spell at least. However, that was the highlight of high school for me. Those three glorious months in senior year when Parker and I dated. I willingly gave my virginity to Parker, but it was obvious I wasn't her first. She seemed to know what to do and what she liked, whereas I was awkward, unsure and clumsy. She eased me through it all, making the best of my crude attempts at being a lover. But beyond this, what I liked the most was just talking with her. We talked about all kinds of different things as she had a curiosity about the world that nearly matched my own. She and I smoked pot a few times and got into some late-night tangential topics, exploring thoughts, sharing ideas and feelings which was new and exciting territory for me; it was the first time in my life I felt recognised and valued. I felt a momentary glint of liberation where I could start to envisage what life could be like. She could be sarcastic though and could turn on you unexpectedly; skewer you with her knife-blade tongue. Just when you had let down your guard or opened up, her derisive jaunts would cut you off at the knees. She had a mean streak in her that reminded me of mother - hard and cold-hearted. But no matter what Parker did to me, no matter how many times I was embarrassed, and even when she unceremoniously dumped me after those three wonderful months, I never stopped longing for her.

Longing.

That was another new encounter. I discovered that longing is different than love. Love is something mutual, something shared. Longing is a lonely road - a solitary wish unfulfilled.

After school we all went our separate ways. I went off to university to properly study art. Mother deemed this to be a practical use of my now burgeoning talents and seemed more than slightly relieved I had chosen a path down an artistic road. God knows how she would have coped if she'd reared an accountant, and besides, we would be free of each other. Finally, she was able to take on those roles she'd always dreamed of playing. Summer stock in New York, leading parts in Chekov and Ibsen in Toronto, and musicals in London's West End. I went to the university furthest away so I wouldn't have to return until summer break. Dalhousie was a fair enough choice. I showed up, got stuck in and learnt more than I ever thought I would about art, the masters, the form, colour theory and beyond. My horizons expanded exponentially. I practiced how to paint nudes, draw still life studies, photo collage, throw clay, and even dabbled in fiber art. I imbued myself with a tenacity that was even new for me, and it was here I really began to forge my own creative style, influenced by some of the greats of modern art, but I could sense something unique was emerging.

I found university with all those choices and experiences vastly different from the life I had previously known. I was finally off the leash, and like so many others before me, I took full advantage of the drinking, drugs, parties and girls. With the high school slate wiped clean there were plenty of chances for a guy like me to get lucky. I was in art school after all, and being slightly awkward actually had its own cachet - a sort of bohemian charm. There was a slew of sexual conquests in those first heady months of university. Pretty girls, punk rockers, artists, serious studious types, and a couple of needy neurotic ones to boot, but after only a few months of experimenting and experiencing I quickly became bored of the party scene. I was never really one to overdo things anyway, and I found casual sex unappealing and empty. I started running again everyday day, which gave me focus. Long early morning runs through the university grounds before anyone else was around; the crisp winter air pulled at my nostrils as I pushed my body towards a new destination, a new future. For the first time in my life, I began to sense there was a place I wanted to go.

I really loved the stimulation academia had to offer, the way you could just read and read and think about things in a different way. I'd never experienced that before. There were some rather boisterous evenings with classmates, naturally fueled by multiple jugs of beer at the pub, as we stretched out and challenged our previous ideals and let our expansive new thoughts take flight. It was here that I was introduced to the world of philosophy. The great existentialists, and it was Nietzsche who put the meaning of man's existence into a framework I could understand. Life is a struggle. Life isn't fair. The world we knew was a God-less universe. Yeah, I could relate to that, alright.

God is dead.
God remains dead.
And we have killed him.
How shall we comfort ourselves,
the murderers of all murderers?

Here was an angst I could understand, and even trust. I suffered great anxiety over the dark feelings of violence that would sometimes well up inside of me. The anger and hatred, the big hairy feelings that would surface unexpectedly and scare the shit out of me. Oftentimes I felt like I wanted to kill my own mother. Punish her for what she did or didn't do, for who she was and who she could never be. How could you have a child and not love it?

Love. I'd tasted of that now. I'd fallen in love, but love is complicated. To love someone and not have love returned is tragic. When I looked at life and love, the random nature to it all, I could easily believe there could be no God. The existentialists had nailed it. I decided that if God was dead and we had killed him, that made us all vigilantes. Guilty by association. Potential killers, all of us. But despite these dark and worrisome thoughts, I loved philosophy and such debates. After all, it tried to make sense of the senseless. Why this? Why that? Why anything? Existentialism - I became fascinated as it made sense of the world of art as well. Creativity had more meaning when you understood the context from which it sprang. Renaissance, post modernity and contemporary art. It was clear to see that all art was related to the thinking of the day, reflected the philosophy of the times. But more than this, I came to understand that art put up walls and then gleefully tore them down. There was as much structure as there was anarchy in the artistic process. A balance between rebellion and conformity; too much conformity and you have sold your soul, but too much chaos led to abstraction for abstraction's sake.

After graduating from university, I took some time off to reflect, grow, experience and make sense of all these wild ideas I had taken to so liberally. I was in no rush to start life properly, so instead I dabbled at being a bohemian artist for a couple of summers. I smoked dope, read literature, and spent some time wandering in Greece. I painted what I saw and otherwise lived a carefree day-to-day existence. I sold my paintings mostly to the tourists who arrived fresh off the boats from the mainland and wanted to take home a souvenir of their own Greek adventure. I made enough to support myself and it rounded out what was left of my travel savings. For the second time in my life, I found myself in a relationship. Vaia Katsaros - she was a local girl. We met on the Greek island of Zakynthos. She only spoke limited English, but she was down-to-earth, uncomplicated and impulsive. A completely different creature than Parker. We would spend most days swimming and sunbathing on the rocks above the beach, picking up simple food to eat from the market stalls in town. Bread, cheese, olives and usually a bottle of cheap retsina that tasted harsh and rough, but something I quickly became accustomed to. I found a small room to rent in the back of a local bakery. It was hot and the earthy smells and sounds of the early morning bakers would often arouse us from our sleep. The warmth of a naked women lying next to me was intoxicating. We would make love in the early morning hours as the workers busied themselves preparing the day's daily breads: *daktyla*, *pita*, and *tsoureki* all baked in the hot stone ovens. After that we'd fall back to sleep in each other's arms, exhausted and spent, a gauze of sleepiness casting its spell over us like a dreamy fishing net. When we'd finally emerge to greet the day, we'd breakfast ravenously on fresh pastries all washed down with strong Greek coffee, the knowing looks and glances of the shop keepers neither condoning nor extolling the youthful lovemaking they surely heard through the paper-thin walls. Summer rolled on as one continuous and delightful banquet of tactile delights: bathing in the translucent waters of the Mediterranean; the prickly sand that never seemed to be gone from between toes; the hot sun; the simple food; the wine; the whitewashed buildings; the orthodox churches; steep rocky hillsides; olive groves and lemon trees. I drank it all up. And above it all, the sweet soft skin of a girl, who willingly and without expectation, opened herself to me. It was a special, picture-perfect moment in time, but as with all things that are cast in the cauldron of perfection, it was too good to last. But for one long hazy summer, life seemed to practically stand still. Days folded into each other, and evenings stretched out into one glorious sunset after another, then as September surely arrived, Vaia left for Athens. Her own journey to further education beckoned and we both knew it was simply time to say goodbye. As breathless and beautiful as our time together had been, it was not love I felt for Vaia. Not even the same infatuation I had felt for Parker, but more a freedom, a growing and becoming - a taste of the sensuality of life itself. We said our farewells and promised to write, but I knew there was a finality in our parting that was as obvious as it was alright. I packed up my belongings and returned to university that autumn with the goal of becoming a schoolteacher. A one-year add-on in teacher college, then there I would be, a little more life under my belt and a few more wild oats sown, but ready to take my place in the world. Daniel Hutt - art teacher.

Mother was pleased enough that I'd appeared to land on my feet. The thought of me moving back home seemed as repulsive to her as it did to me. Besides, she was booked to play several roles in the Niagara-on-the-Lake summer Shakespearean festival, so she'd already sub-let her Queen Street apartment. She was busy doing what she loved. Basking in her treasured roles: Desdemona, Cleopatra, and Madame Thenardier in Les Misérables. A full-blown diva nowadays, she was at the top of her game, living it to the hilt. I visited her briefly on my way out west. She seemed older, tired, but still full of her acerbic words and caustic comebacks. An art teacher was not something to be sneered at, although mother could find fault with anything if she tried hard enough, so she took it in her stride, even accepting a gift of one of the paintings from my most recent series I'd titled, Eros. My homage to the beauty and freedom I'd experienced in Greece. An abstract of a woman reclining on sea swept rocks, a sparse grove of lemon trees on the hillside beyond. A swash of vibrant colours and swirls - the turquoise and sparking golds of the Mediterranean Sea, the reds and dusty browns of the rocky cliffs, all done in brush strokes that were thick and sensual. Even mother understood the new-found liberation in my latest paintings as it was clear I had drunk from the fountain of life. She held any congratulatory comments close to her chest, though, but I think I caught a glimpse of something in the crinkles that formed in the corners of her mouth as she examined the piece. Not a smile exactly, but I took it as an acknowledgment of sorts. She accepted my gift and hung it in the stairwell, a rather less distinctive place than the living room walls. That was reserved to showcase art by artists she admired, framed posters of productions she had starred in, or autographed photos of actors who'd tread the boards with her. But she kept the painting, none-the-less.

Then one day I heard from Parker. It was an ordinary day, and yet extraordinary in so many ways, as it always seems to be when something earth shattering occurs. She popped up on Facebook - connecting people again after a lifetime of naturally drifting apart, old school chums, girlfriends, workmates and the like. I have to admit technology really has changed life as we know it. The internet is a strange and wondrous place. Shortening the distance between space and time, reality and perversity. The touch of a button. Click. Upload and share. Click. Friend me? Click. Many times, these rekindled relationships would wither almost as soon as they reformed. Attention spans moving on to see the next throw-away video link. Click. What was there really left to say anyway? Curiosity satisfied, but little else to relate to for those lost friends of thirty years gone by. Just the occasional *like* to keep politely connected. Click. Of course, what the Internet revealed was not always in glorious Technicolor, some people seemed to have really aged, let it slip away. It was quite a shock to see the gargantuan physique of someone I used to run track and field with, who back then was as skinny as a bean pole, but now looked like a heart attack waiting to happen. While others had kept themselves trim and well-groomed. The gym dogs. Those constant dieters. Those ten thousand steppers, racking up merits on some phone app or Fitbit. People with God-given genes, good hairlines, and excellent metabolism. Parker was one of those. She looked great, it was almost a given. Thirty years had been kind to her, ripened her, rounded her out, but in a good way.

I got the friend request on a Sunday night, and it didn't take me long to decide on my response. And then there she was - Parker. It only took a few brief email exchanges, a look throughout each other's home pages before curiosity got the better of us and we decided to meet up for drinks and a proper catch up. We arranged to meet at a downtown wine bar, something nice but not too fancy. She was in town on business and had decided to stay over for the weekend just so we could hook up. I found myself feeling nervous as the time approached to get ready and had a couple of stiff drinks just to pluck up the courage. I must have tried on four different shirts and three jackets to feel comfortable, make a good impression and hit the right note. After all, thirty years was a long time, an enormous divide in a relationship that had really, in the grand scheme of things, been as fleeting as it had been intense. So, what was the right note to hit anyway? Successful bachelor? Chilled out art teacher? Retro dude with a slight bohemian air? I finally decided on my much lived-in leather bomber jacket, a favourite fedora, and an old Clash t-shirt. I figured a decent pair of brogues would round things out nicely, balancing it all with a final note of respectability. An old rebel with a cause. I judiciously decided that being comfortable and relaxed trumped the need to be cool, besides, I figured there was no sense pretending to be someone I was not. I was a teacher, after all, normal and average stuff.

Parker's hair was cut shorter these days, more manageable and befitting of her age, but she still had that sly smile and twinkle in her eyes. I noticed she'd never had that one errant tooth fixed, the one that gave her smile yards of personality. However, she appeared to have taken up smoking as the smell of a freshly finished cigarette wafted and mingled with her otherwise expensive perfume as we both leaned in for the obligatory kiss. She had opted to wear something more business-like. A sharp cut skirt, an apricot-coloured blouse and delicate Celtic embroidered scarf she had draped meticulously over her shoulder. Or maybe, unlike myself, it was entirely possible she hadn't even considered her appearance, instead she had probably come straight from some high-powered business meeting. Parker wheeling and dealing, holding court and lauding cost improvement plans over her male colleagues demanding steady incremental increases in profits, management strategies for cornering the market share, and KPIs that must be met. I'd seen in her Facebook profile that Parker had her own PR firm. Big clients that were based all over, which meant she did a lot of traveling. She lived in New York but often made trips to the West Coast - Seattle and Vancouver. I'd been teaching art at Capilano College, a small community school in North Vancouver, a steady gig I'd had for the past fifteen years. Mother had finally settled in Vancouver as well, and now that her acting days were well and truly behind her, and with the inherent decline of being an eighty-something-year-old, she needed constant care and attention. So, in recent years, and despite our obvious dislike for one another, I'd become her de facto caregiver.

Parker and I settled down in a corner booth of the trendy Yaletown wine bar and had soon ordered drinks to smooth the nerves for the much anticipated catch-up. I decided to open things up.

'So, Parker, how great is this, and look at you, you look as beautiful as ever after all these years. God, I can't believe it's really been thirty years. So, tell me everything.' Parker leaned back in her chair, cradled her wine glass, and tilted her head slightly.

'Why don't we start with you, Dan, I'm sure your life has been much more fascinating than mine. I mean, I'm an open book, what you see is what you get, always has been, but you . . . you were always the dark horse.' Parker took a long sip of wine, flicked off her heels under the table, settled in and focused those deep green eyes towards me.

'Well, I'm not too sure about that, but okay, let's see . . . I never married, I guess I just didn't meet the right girl. You could say it's been a pretty standard bachelor life for me.' I instinctively smoothed the wrinkles of the t-shirt I was wearing.

'What about your career?' said Parker, sipping her wine.

'Career? I've been an art teacher for years now. It's a decent enough job - good benefits, the holidays are great, which gives me time to travel and soak up different cultures. And you know, churning out another crop of artistic hopefuls year after year isn't too bad.' I stared off into the distance and could almost imagine myself back in high school. Latest art project under my arm, waiting for Parker to come to her locker so I could walk her home from school.

'Just like someone I used to know,' smiled Parker.

'Yeah, I guess. These young kids, all the ones who don't fit in, you know, the artistic types - I can relate to them. Some of these kids are pretty fragile. College isn't an easy ride for everyone.'

'You always were the one to fight the good fight.' I shrugged a little and continued.

'What else? I have a summer place in Greece. Nothing too flashy, just a beach shack really, I try to make it over once a year, but that's harder to manage these days. It's getting complicated, what with mother on her own.'

'Greece, huh? Well now, that makes sense. Nice to see you're still painting, too - you were always so talented.'

'How do you know I still paint?'

'I have one of your pieces.'

'Really?'

'Yes, I bought it online. You had a show a few years ago, some sort of career retrospective. You've done some interesting work over the years, Dan, I'm impressed.' I looked over at Parker, she was as confident and composed as ever. A smile breaking on those tight, thin lips.

'So, you've been stalking me for a while then?' I laughed and took a healthy sip of wine.

'I don't think they call it stalking, curiosity maybe. Besides, I'm shrewd enough to spot a good art investment when I see one. Art teacher makes good. The world loves an underdog, Dan.'

I laughed, 'I don't think my stuff will ever be worth very much.'

'You never know with art, do you? I've become quite an aficionado over the years. I can't paint, but I can afford to collect.' Parker untied the scarf from her neck revealing more of her low-cut blouse, the tanned cleavage of her small but still pert breasts peeking out.

'You titled your show Eros. Very sensual. If I had to guess I'd say you must have had a muse or two in that barren bachelor life of yours.' I found myself blushing like a teenager; Parker still had that ability. Just like old times.

'So, Park, tell me a little about you. Looks like you never met the right fella. Divorced now I gather?'

'Men,' laughed Parker, 'can't live with them, can't kill them either. Thrice darling, marriage and divorce, just like a swinging door. But that's just tedious talk, I don't want to bore you with stories of lawyers, settlements, and recriminations from the past, I'd rather you tell me more about your paintings. What is it you look for in a good muse?'

After a few more drinks, Parker and I were more relaxed and soon found ourselves laughing and joking, it was almost like no time had passed. We caught up and reminisced about the good old days of school, the coming of age, of our mutual friends and friendships. She seemed to know just about everything about everyone. People I'd pretty much forgotten about. Where they were now, what they were doing. What became of

Gary and Mike? Parker, of course, knew it all. Every sordid, vivid detail. After we graduated Mike went to law school, became a corporate lawyer, specialising in environmental law. Protecting big businesses and their assets from small scale do-gooders looking to sue their corporate asses. Annoying environmental watchdogs biting at the heels of the big players. It was Mike's job to cut them off at the pass, negotiate this way and that, creating roadblocks and dead ends wherever he could and throwing restraining orders at anything to buy time. It sounded like a heartless job, but one that undoubtedly paid big bucks. Big business taking care of big business, I guess someone had to do it. Mike always had that easygoing charm about him, that firm 'look you in the eye' handshake, so he was always going to end up being a player. The likeable quarterback with the perfectly, predictably successful life. A beautiful wife, a million-dollar family, a sleek Mercedes in the driveway of his Rosedale Home. Gary, meanwhile, was a different kettle of fish. He wound up in politics. Becoming an MP in the sprawling, suburban riding of Mississauga. He also had big ambitions and an eye on the Liberal leadership. He was being groomed, had backers, people with money and clout, but it seems his personal life got in the way. His affair with his PA, a young Asian woman who had a taste for cocaine and nightclubbing, fell out of the bag. Incriminating photos of the two on a Younge Street corner, glassy eyed at 3:00 a.m. hailing a cab, made the tabloid rounds. His wife filed for divorce, and his family life ended in a shambles. He also got caught with his fingers in the political pie, cutting special deals and incentives for his business associates. He was nailed to the wall. Stupid, really. But greed and stupidity sometimes make good bedfellows, whatever the case, his political life lay in ruins. He filed for bankruptcy. It was the final straw. So, one night he calmly and assuredly went out to the garage with a bottle of Glen Fiddich, a hose from the exhaust of his Volvo pumping life-stealing toxins into the cream and tan leather interior, while he sat listening to another vacant round of handpicked banality on Spotify. A playlist to die to. It didn't take long before he was just another statistic. Brutal and sad.

Parker and I finished two bottles of really good wine, and we wolfed down several plates of West Coast oysters. Then, heady with the alcohol and the humid night air, we took a taxi back to mine. I live in a first-floor apartment of a majestic old house in Kitsilano, near Jericho Beach. It is literally steps away from the water's edge and the views of the mountains across the inlet to North Vancouver are stunning. I often sit out on my veranda at night, nursing a scotch just listening to the waves lap against the shore, the city lights twinkling on Grouse and Seymour. I have a spacious back bedroom that I have transformed into my art studio and Parker was keen to see some more of my paintings. Who was I to deny her? If she liked Eros, there was plenty more where that came from. We stumbled out of the cab onto the sidewalk, and Parker instinctively took hold of my arm as I rummaged around for keys.

'Nice place. Suits you.'

'It does me well enough.' I felt Parker tighten her grip on my arm and lean heavily into me, either unsteady from the wine, or else she was feeling something entirely different.

When I woke up the next morning and looked around, Parker was gone. We had drained a good portion of the Scotch I'd been saving, and with defenses down, we both surrendered to our animalistic desires Thirty years ago, we'd made it on the rec room floor of her parents' house, panties and jeans down around our ankles trying not to creak the floors and wake anyone up. And here we were again, screwing on the floor of my living room like two reckless and horny teenagers. It was all over in a matter of minutes. I can't speak for Parker, but I certainly hadn't expected to rekindle any kind of physical relationship, but I guess these things just kind of happen. But there was nothing at stake, no one to hurt, after all we were both consenting, unattached adults. A slight awkward embarrassment might be the only consequence. It was better than what I remembered; our love making now on equal-footing and delivered with an abandon that only comes with middle age. After it was done, we simply fell into a drunken, satisfied reverie. Spooning one another, arms sloppily slung over each other's bodies - it was nice to feel the warmth of someone next to me, and a body that was strangely still familiar. With Parker gone, I stumbled out of bed and made my way to the kitchen to make coffee and check my phone for messages. My usual routine. I found Parker's business card on the kitchen counter near an empty water glass.

Parker Katherine Jones – CEO
Parker Jones PR and consultancy
New York and beyond

On the back of it she had simply written one word – *lunch?*

We met up at Earl's restaurant, the one at English Bay, and had a table with a view. Along the sea front the city was buzzing with all sorts of laid-back weekend activities: couples strolling; people rollerblading; tourists snapping pictures; pods of gay men posing for each other; kayakers cutting through the smooth Pacific water on their way to Granville Island; and the sun worshippers laid out, oiled and nearly naked, soaking up every ray the sun had to offer. It was a decidedly chill Vancouver scene. The West Coast contentment was palpable - one of the reasons I loved living here. Parker looked different today. Gone was the business suit, and in place she wore a pair of tight-fitting jeans, long black boots and a low-cut cashmere sweater. Her makeup was softened and less dramatic and she wore simple amber earrings that caught the afternoon light. She seemed bathed in a warm glow that spread around her like a halo. We ordered Bloody Caesars and shared a plate of calamari. We made small talk about how nice Vancouver was and how great it was to see each other again. All surface stuff. We were both adult enough to steer clear of the previous evening's amorous adventures. Chalk it up to experience. Alcohol mainly.

'Dan, I have something to tell you.' Parker, put down her glass, uncrossed her legs, straightened herself up and leaned her chin on her hand.

'Do you remember our last year of high school?'

I nodded, 'of course I do, that's when we . . .'

'Do you remember I left school towards the end of term and finished up the year through distance studies?'

'Yeah, that's when you broke off with me. You had mono or something, right? I don't think we ever saw each other after that.'

'That's just it. I wasn't sick.'

'What do you mean?'

'I was pregnant, and I had the baby.'

'You what?'

'A girl. I had her and then gave her up for adoption.' I tried to look into Parker's eyes, but she was gazing off towards the horizon.

'So, that's some news. Wow! Well, what does that mean?'

'Well, what it means is . . . she could be yours, Dan.' The weight of Parker's confession felled me like a slab of concrete hitting the floor.

'Are you telling me I have a daughter?' Parker looked up squarely into my face and just stared.

'Holy shit, Park, I can't believe this. You're not messing with me, are you?' I said, starting to sound more than a little unraveled.

Parker shook her head, 'not this time Dan.'

'Well, Jesus, Parker, that's some news to drop after thirty years. Wait a sec, what do you mean by I *could* be the father?'

Parker shrugged a little, 'well, there was someone else.'

'Who?'

'Does it really matter?'

'Oh great, a double whammy. You tell me I might be the father but not for sure! What the fuck Park?'

'I understand how you might feel, but there's more to this than meets the eye.' My mind was reeling as wild thoughts crashed into one another. I tried desperately to retain my composure.

'Go on.'

'Megan has cerebral palsy. It's pretty severe. Spastic quadriplegia - the worst kind. She's barely able to move, do anything.'

'What? My God!'

'I didn't know myself - gave her up for adoption at birth. I only connected with her again six years ago. It was her call. It's always the kids who choose to . . . it's complicated Dan, please try to understand.'

'So why this, why now?'

'She lives in a care home in Burnaby, but lately things have gotten worse. I don't think she has long to live, and she asked me about her father.'

'But . . . you're not sure.... you said you don't know who.' Parker opened her purse and pulled out a picture of a young woman. She was sitting in a wheelchair, her hands, like twisted branches, withered twig-like fingers, one curled in her lap, one reaching upward into the air grasping at something. Her head rested against two padded supports, and I could see straight away she had Parker's auburn hair, her sly smile and thin lips, but her blue piercing eyes were just like . . . I knew right away she was my own flesh and blood. I just stared at Parker.

'Dan, I know this is a lot to take in. Believe me, I've wrestled with this over and over again. I just thought you might want to know.' Parker reached over and squeezed her hand around mine.

It was a cold and blustery autumn day. The leaves had almost escaped from the trees and only a few reluctant stragglers remained. I made my way toward the gates of Mountain Shadow Cemetery. I surveyed the long rows of gravestones, gothic statues, markers and other religious icons. The sun had given up trying to break through and the Vancouver clouds covered everything in a grey sadness. The narrow well-preserved paths cut sharp lines across row upon row of tombs that divided it all into neatly drawn cemetery grids. In my hands were two bouquets of flowers. I walked a few hundred yards, crisscrossing along the steep and narrow paths until I arrived at my first destination. Edwina Hutt. Mother. Like everything in her life her death had been orchestrated to the minutiae, marked by skill, precision and a flare for the theatrical. She had scripted it herself years before it happened, the details of which were neatly written in her last will and testament. She had left implicit instructions for how her dénouement was to be played out, as she had once followed stage directions herself. The type of service, the venue, the flowers, the music, the eulogy, the exact lines of Macbeth she wished to be recited. A collection of props, mementos and old photographs, handpicked, showing her finest thespian moments with the most famous and notorious of her acting friends and collaborators, on show for the faithful hoards to appreciate. It was Mother's curtain call. As if there could be any question of her place in dramaturgical history; Edwina Hutt, the finest Lady Macbeth that Stratford ever knew. For years she ruled the roost, was on top of her game, queen of the stage, a critic's darling. Her acting was simply magnificent. In every role she found the smallest nuance, the slightest detail, the merest wrinkle of human emotion to unravel, emulate and share with her rapt audiences. She never misstepped. She never missed a beat or forgot her cues. She commanded the stage like the veteran she was and could bring a tear to the stoniest of hearts. Her portrayal of love in all its forms was breathtaking and palpable, yet it remained the one thing she seemed incapable of giving her only son. For the record, I didn't kill her. I wrestled with those dark thoughts repeatedly, but I wouldn't have had it in me to act on any of them. Mother simply contracted pneumonia went into hospital and never came out again. So very ordinary, so very quick, and so very final. On her gravestone, the eulogy spoken by Macbeth.

Tomorrow, and tomorrow, and tomorrow,
Creeps in this petty pace from day to day
To the last syllable of recorded time,
And all our yesterdays have lighted fools
The way to dusty death.

The second bouquet, I laid on another grave. I never had enough time to really come to know Megan. We did meet and forged a bond of sorts. My arrival fulfilled her wish to meet her birth father before she died, which, as it turned out, wasn't long. Parker was right; she didn't have much time - a month or so. I sat with her, awkwardly and curiously at first, strange and unnerved to be in the presence of my own flesh and blood, my very own daughter. Her body, a twisted useless adversary, racked with years of pain. To look into her eyes was like looking into my own soul. I was happy I could at least provide her with whatever small dignity she hoped to get from meeting me. Her birth father; the missing link. Her service was simple, just her immediate family, her case workers, a handful of her close friends, Parker and me. As her adoptive mother spoke at the funeral, there was a solemn recognition that she was out of her suffering now. A tender regard for a life that had been lived as best as it could have, given the circumstances. Everyone was unanimous about one thing; she was a tenacious girl that never complained. Hers was simply a life that never grew wings and got to fly. But instead, Megan made the most of all the small things. She loved to read and would immerse herself in all sorts of literature. Books that could take her out of herself and her surroundings. Like me, she loved art and learnt to paint herself. She did simple water colours, painting with a small brush held between her teeth. Her brush strokes were light and delicate. Intentional. She had an innate sense of light and shade. Painting allowed her access to the outside world, places and scenes she only could imagine herself in. A life devoid of limitations.

She had a way that reached people too and made a connection. A gentleness, a kindness about her. In her last six months she worked tirelessly on a website and blog, to raise money and awareness for others living with CP. She journaled about her own journey and focused on the good things, the successes she'd had and the opportunities her condition had brought to her. She posted daily and was determined to do so until she was unable to do so anymore. It was amazing. She wrote with such clarity and such joy. I was really moved. To think that someone could be so positive in the face of a life filled with such adversity was remarkable. I felt a surprising, unexpected parental pride well up inside. She donated and auctioned off most of her paintings on her website and encouraged other fellow disease-ravaged travelers to follow their dreams in whichever small way they could. It was her parting gift to the world.

My mother and daughter both dead and buried in the space of a few months. My only flesh and blood, gone. It was a lot to take in. I decided I needed to make a dramatic sea change. So, I quit my job, sold off everything and moved to Greece. A wanted to taste freedom once more. I didn't want to squander whatever time I had left on this earth in some meaningless, frivolous way. I wanted to paint. I wanted to bathe in the sea, drink wine, buy fresh bread every day, and taste the fruits life has to offer. I returned to my beloved Greek island and settled myself into a simple day-to-day existence. My rekindled relationship with Parker had already retreated once again into the background of social media. A few polite remarks on postings, a few likes and so on. She was busy with her life, and I was reinventing mine.

I found comfort in the little things. The slightest detail. The shafts of sunshine that playfully dappled the stone walls of my humble abode. The morning dew, cool and refreshing on my bare feet as I walked to get my morning coffee. A simple meal. A single thought that brings momentary pleasure. Memories are all we get to keep. But memories can calcify, and fade and some memories aren't pleasurable at all. In the end all we really have is the present. This very moment. Tomorrow is never assured, and yesterday is gone. As for love, I'd learnt many things from it. Love is subjective. Love can be all-encompassing, giving, taking, ignoring, fleeting and comforting. Real or abstract. Sensual, sweet or

sometimes simply absent. While love might choose us or
not choose us, we all get to choose our loving behavior.
I decided it was time for me to work on forgiveness.
Forgive my mother. There was no use in holding onto
negatives in my life anymore.

I rinsed off my paint brush, satisfied with another
good day's painting. The Mediterranean looked beautiful
today. Sparkling and dancing in the reflected light of the
late afternoon sunshine - always my favorite time of
day. I poured myself a little wine and wandered out to
the beach. The sun was gently sinking into the horizon,
daubing the vista with the most magnificent and breathtaking colours. I picked up Mother's dog-eared copy of
Macbeth and turned to the page where I had left off. In
my mind I could almost hear the voices of mother and
her fellow actors, fortified with brandy, inspired by the
poetry of the words themselves, trying to find the beat,
feeling out the phrasings, looking for the nuance
between the lines. Hoping to shed some light on the
human drama that is unfolding all around us. So that we
can understand it, and in doing so, understand ourselves.

Life's but a walking shadow,
a poor player that struts and frets his hour upon the
stage and then is heard of no more.

Purgatory Street

She stood quietly in front of the gravestone, a small bunch of flowers in her little hand, waiting for her mammy to give the word.

'Go on then, wean,' said the woman finally, 'lay them nicely and don't forget to say a wee prayer for Gran while you do it.' Aisling knelt down, brushed some dead leaves off the little statue of Jesus and then put the small bouquet into the cracked plastic container that was sitting next to the headstone. It was another typically unforgiving November day in Belfast, the kind where the wind cuts straight through your coat and into your bones. Rain clouds were gathering too, but for the moment there was just the bitterness of the wind. After placing the flowers, the girl crossed herself, just like she'd watched the adults do on the times when they managed to drag themselves to church or were feeling particularly guilty about something, then she returned to stand next to her mammy.

'They look nice,' Aisling said, and quickly took hold of her mam's hand.

'Aye, they do. Did you say a prayer, then?' Aisling nodded.

'What did you say?' She looked up at her and shrugged.

'Well?'

'I asked God to help me mam.' Orla chuckled and stroked the hair off her daughter's forehead.

'Oh, your mammy's alright,' she said, 'I'm going to ask God to make sure Gran is happy where she went. Do you think God would do that for us?' Aisling smiled and felt her mammy squeeze her hand a little. Orla closed her eyes for a moment and they both just stood together in silence. Then Orla began to softly hum a tune, quiet at first, then louder and more assured as she felt the words rise up within her and the song begin to resonate.

Them that's got shall get
Them that's not shall lose
So the Bible said
And it still is news . . .

The girl didn't look at her mammy, she was used to her singing all those old Billie Holiday songs, so she just kept her eyes down towards the ground watching them pretty flowers swaying in the wind. They had picked them from a neighbour's garden earlier that day when Mrs. Doherty had gone down to the shops to get her usual morning paper and maybe some bread and milk. She felt bad stealing from her because Mrs. Doherty was nice, sometimes giving her sweeties when she got home from school, or sometimes when the ice cream van came round the streets blaring its cheery music, she even bought her an ice lolly. She hoped she wouldn't notice the flowers were gone. They were the last ones of the year and Mrs. Doherty always liked to keep a few in a vase on her windowsill. But her mammy didn't think twice about taking other people's things. Someone's milk bottles from off their front step, or down the pub when she'd nick a drink off someone's table when they'd nipped to the jacks, or even when they were at the supermarket, how she put extra things into her shopping bag without scanning them first. She was always doing that. She'd use the money she saved to buy things she really wanted like packets of fags or bottles of gin. The things that were harder to pinch. Orla finished the final refrains of the song, letting the words get taken up by the wind and echo across the cemetery.

Mamma may have
Papa may have
But God bless the child
That's got his own
That's got his own . . .

Aisling had heard her sing this song many times before. She liked it. It was the one about a child and how God was looking out for him. Even though it had God in the words, it still sounded sad though, least the way her mammy sang it. But a lot of the music in the church they sometimes went to sounded like that too. Maybe that's how God wanted things to be, sad all the time? The story of Jesus wasn't a very happy one either, in fact, it was pretty terrible and downright scary. Jesus being stabbed by those men and then put to death in such a horrid way. Nails in his hands and feet. Sometimes, when she was saying a prayer at bedtime and thinking about God and Jesus, those stories would give her nightmares. She wished her mam would sing happy songs sometimes, but she never did, especially when she was on one of her benders. Those times when Aisling got home from school to find her passed out on the settee, sleeping things off. Or the times when Jimmy would be round and the two of them would be smoking, drinking and laughing. But then the laughing always changed to shouting and then to screaming and then to things being broken. Then Jimmy would slam the front door, take off in his beaten-up van and her mammy would sit in the kitchen wiping at her eyes and sniffing up some sort of white stuff off the kitchen table. After that she would be calmer and nicer and make her toast with strawberry jam. Orla slid a little flask from out of her coat pocket and took a swig. She lit a cigarette and blew a plume of smoke into the cold autumn air.

'Anything else you want to say to your granny?' Aisling looked up. She shook her head.

'She would have loved you, ya know,' said Orla, 'if she'd gotten to know you. She always had a soft spot for weans.' She ruffled Aisling's hair and took another hit from her flask.

'She sure loved God, though,' said Orla, looking up towards the sky, 'I hope she's got everything she needs from that fucker now. Especially forgiveness. Aye, that's what we all need.' Orla held her flask up to the sky, 'you hearing me, God? How's about a little forgiveness for me and the wean, eh?' Orla dropped her cigarette onto the ground without bothering to stamp it out. She put the flask back inside her coat and turned to Aisling.

'Hey, how about some chips? And maybe a fried sausage, huh? That'll warm us up.' Aisling's face opened into a smile as she nodded her head.

'C'mon, wean, let's get us to the chippy.'

'Feck me, what am I, dead or something? And this place, what is it, purgatory?' Eileen Sullivan stared at the man in front of her with a resigned look on her face. Gabriel Mortimer put down his file, removed his spectacles and gave a slight smile.

'You know purgatory isn't a name we really like to use to describe this. It comes with so much negativity. I mean it's not the connotation that God intended, but I can see how from your perspective it still has some real negative baggage.'

'Negative baggage?' said Eileen.

'Yes, I think that's the appropriate term. Thing is, this isn't about your sins or being appraised at all. To be clear, we are not here to judge you, Eileen, just here to assist.'

'Assist? Assist with what?'

'Well, with lots of things - your reflection, the review and future choices, what happens next, basically.'

'Aye, so I am dead, then?'

'Well, that's another curious thing,' said the case worker, 'I mean, of course from your perspective you have passed over from your earthly life, but you're not finished just yet, because, well, here we are talking. Dead, but not dead – bit odd, don't you think?' Eileen furrowed her brow a little trying to let it all sink in.

'Feck me. So, is there a heaven, and am I going there next or what?' Gabriel shook his head slightly.

'Perhaps, I'm not doing so well at explaining things. You know, maybe you'd like a cup of tea? Then maybe I can start again in a way you'll be able to understand. Do you take milk?' Eileen nodded. Gabriel Mortimer returned and set down a cup of tea next to her along with a little plate of digestives.

'I thought a biscuit might be in order, digestives were a favourite of yours, weren't they?' said Gabriel, tapping the file with a pen. Eileen nodded and took a good drink of tea.

'Aye, now that's a proper cup of tea. You know I was quite fond of gingernuts as well. That in your file, Mr. Mortimer?'

'Of course you were, and it's been duly noted,' said Gabriel, 'but perhaps we can continue. So, here we are, you're finished with your last earthly life, and not in purgatory - as we've already established, but rather somewhere in-between things. Is that making more sense now?' Eileen nodded.

'Now, your file here tells me that you had the one daughter, Orla, is that about right?'

'Well, if that's what your file tells you Mr. Mortimer, then I think you've pretty much nailed it.'

'Good,' said the caseworker, 'you know I think we might be getting the hang of this, the wonders of a cup of tea, huh?'

'Feck me, tea?' said Eileen, looking into her cup.

'Shall we continue? As already mentioned, there is no judging to be done, but what we do encourage is for you to reflect on how you thought things went in your last life. You know, lessons learned, things you'd do differently next time around, that sort of thing.'

'You saying I have to do this all over again?'

'Well, that will be up to you, entirely.'

'Well, thank the feckin' Lord. Oh . . . is it blasphemous to say that here?'

'No, it's quite alright,' chuckled Gabriel, 'now regarding your daughter it might be helpful if we could talk through what happened.'

'What, and live through all that again?'

'I think it would be helpful, yes.' Eileen put her cup down on her saucer and set her face like she did when she was thinking hard about something then took a breath.

'Truth be told that child was a bastard hard birth - by Jesus, didn't I just know it. And I knew even then, as only a mother can, that every step of her blessed life was going to be exactly the same. Full of trouble, full of heartache, and such a torture for a single mam. You see my husband was murdered when she was only four – he was shot by the bastard British Army, he was.'

Gabriel nodded and patted his file folder, 'I know.'

'Aye and that's exactly how it turned out Mr. Mortimer - a torture. For sixteen long years, it was like the troubles at home every single blessed day. A battleground between me and her.'

Gabriel flipped open his file, took up a pen and said, 'you're doing really well, Eileen, but perhaps we could jump right to when things really started to go wrong between the two of you.' Eileen picked up her teacup, took a drink and then stared off into the middle-distance.

'I used to clean houses. I took in people's ironing too, whatever I could do to make ends-meet for me and her. It wasn't easy going being a single mam. I worked my fingers to the bone, I did. She didn't care about none of that. Took everything for granted, as they do. Then when she was hitting the puberty she fell in with the wrong crowd, all them young'uns from over in Shankill and Falls Roads. They was nothing but trouble that lot. She took up smoking and drinking and God-knows what else, cavorting about with all the lads. She plain refused to go to confession. She wasn't having anything to do with church by then. She told me she'd decided that God was nothing but a prick. How could he let them take her da away from her like he did. Then one day, when I got home early from work, she was already there, home from school. Aye, that's when it really kicked off, Mr. Mortimer.'

Eileen turned the key in the front door and found it was already open. Had she forgotten to lock it this morning? She put down her bucket and cleaning supplies in the hallway as she always did, took off her coat and walked through the front room towards the kitchen. She could smell smoke and when she pushed open the kitchen door her teenage daughter was sitting at the kitchen table puffing on a fag and there were a couple of empty cans of Strongbow nearby.

'Jesus, you almost scared the life out of me! What are you doing home already? And what the feck do you think you're doing smoking and drinking in here?' Orla dropped her cigarette butt into one of the empty cans.

'This letter is for you, it's from school.' Eileen walked over, picked it up, and began reading.

'You've been expelled?' said Eileen. Orla shrugged.

'What for, what have you been up to now?'

'Maybe you want to sit down, Ma.' Eileen took her time to properly read the letter and digest the words, then tossed it onto the table and looked up at her daughter.

'You're pregnant?' Orla shrugged.

'Jesus . . . how could you do something like this?'

'Oh, don't be so dramatic. It's just a kid. I'm not going back to school, and if you're thinking anything differently, to let ye know, I *am* keeping the baby.'

'Well, that's a right fecking mess you've made of your life, not to mention mine.'

'Yours?' Orla laughed and snapped open another can of Strongbow, 'you don't need to worry about anything Ma, I can look after myself.'

'Aye, can ye now? Is that what you're doing right now, drinking and all?'

'Well, you can call it a celebration if you want?' sneered Orla, 'farewell to all that school tosser bullshite. I'm gonna be a mammy now.

'Aye well, you know that drinking is no good for the baby. Smoking neither.' Orla shrugged.

'Listen Ma, I'll stay out of your face if you stay out of mine – alright. Ye ain't no saint yourself, now are ye.'

'I can't believe my ears. Is this how my own daughter talks to her mammy like she's got a right to?'

'Aye, leave it the feck out why don't ya.' Eileen pulled out a chair and plonked herself down like a stone.

'And what, pray tell, do ye intend to do next? And how on earth will ye manage with a wean?' Orla's phone buzzed, she read the text.

'That's Danny. Says he'll be right round. He's taking me out for the night.'

'Danny, as in Danny Gallagher from down the road? Is *he* the one! The father of the bastard?'

'You watch your mouth, old lady, or so help me.'

'Threats now and all. What next – Jesus Christ help us out here!'

'That's it – call on your useless saviour why don't you. Fat lot of good any of that'll do you.'

'Let me tell you something young lady, God will never forsake us,' said Eileen, 'ye need to remember that.'

'Well, he did fuckin' forsake me da, now, didn't he? Where was he when the bastards were shooting bullets into his back?' Eileen stared at her daughter, speechless. There was a knock on the door.

'That'll be Danny. Don't try to stop me, Ma. And don't bother praying to your stupid God neither. We'll be alright, you'll see.' Orla stood up, getting herself set to leave.

'Orla please, wait a minute. I'm still your mammy now. Why don't you stay and let's talk about this proper. Ye need your mammy; ye need a plan.'

'I've got one. And it doesn't include cleaning other people's jacks neither.' Orla downed the rest of her cider, pulled on her coat and walked towards the hallway.

'Orla – wait!' cried Eileen.

'What is it, Ma?'

'I want ye to know, I still loves ya. I'll always be here for ya. And God does as well, that's all I wanted to say.'

'Don't wait up for me, Ma.' And with that Orla turned and was gone.

Orla and Aisling were walking home from Wilde's fish and chip shop, ravenously enjoying their take-away - a spam fritter for Aisling and a battered sausage for Orla, both with a heaping of chips and extra scraps. The rain was getting threateningly close, and a few spits had already landed on the pavement nearby. As they walked along familiar back streets, all the while plucking salty treats out of their chip shop paper packages, Aisling noticed they'd taken a slightly different route home this time around.

'Are we going past your old house, Mammy?'

'Aye, we are. You've never seen inside wean, but it's where your mammy and granny lived right up until the accident.'

'I wish I'd met Granny.'

'Aye, so do I.'

Number 91 Albert Street was much the same terraced house as it had always been, except for one distinct difference – all the windows were boarded up and there were blackened sooty scars where the fire that had licked around its windows. The house had stood derelict for years, waiting for the council to finally decide on demolishment or, the more costly, refurbishment, but for now, at least, it just remained another eyesore and a painful reminder of the tragedy that had ended Eileen Sullivan's life.

As they got closer, Orla slowed down a little when she noticed another figure hurrying up towards the door of the old family home. Aunt Mary. Eileen's sister never forgot the anniversary of her sister's death, and here she was, a small bouquet of flowers in hand standing on the doorstep stoop.

'Well, if it isn't Aunty Mary,' said Orla.

'Is that you, Orla? Oh, and look, you've got wee Aisling with you. What a treasure.'

'How are you keeping, Mary?'

'Can't complain. Your Uncle Jock was asking after you. Wondering how ye was getting on. I'll let him know we spoke today.'

'Aye, give him our regards.'

'I was just paying my respects to your mammy. Always a sad day, this one, truth be told, I expect you've been doing the same.'

'Aye, we were at the cemetery for a wee visit, we're on our way home now. Thought I'd get the wean a few chips on our way and stop by the old house. Lots of memories in there.'

'This place was home to our family for years,' said Mary, looking at the house. 'When we were just girls, me and your mammy had the front bedroom. I remember we shared the same bed and used to whisper stories to each other before we fell asleep. Every night it was the same. Our ma used to be banging on the door – 'get ye to sleep now!' she'd yell, and we'd have to bury our faces in our pillows so she couldn't hear all the giggling.' Mary looked wistful as she recalled the memory. 'Didn't that eventually become your room?' Orla looked up at the second story boarded over window.

'Aye, it did an' all.'

'Now look at it,' said Mary, 'nothing but a derelict eyesore and a sodding shame.'

'See that room up there,' said Orla to Aisling, pointing to it, 'that was the room Aunt Mary and your granny shared, and then it was your mammy's too.'

'Who lives there now?' said Aisling.

'Nobody. Except for maybe a few mice, I expect.'

'Funny isn't it, how things can change just like that,' said Mary, 'one minute everything is fine, everything remains as it always has, then bang - it's all gone in the blink of an eye.'

'Ma used to say that was how life was, just one small cruelty after another,' said Orla.

'Well, God rest her soul, now,' said Mary, crossing herself, 'and God help all of us who are left behind too.'

'Aye to that,' said Orla, 'aye to that.'

The three stood silent for a bit just taking in the moment together. Off in the distance was the deep rumble of thunder.

'Well, here comes the rain,' said Orla, 'we best be off home before we get a soaking. Stop by for a cup of tea, Mary, whenever ye like, it's been far too long since we've seen you.'

'Aye, I will, which reminds me, it's been a while since Aisling's had any pocket money from us, here let me see what change I've got.' Mary dug into her purse and found a couple of pounds and pressed them into Aisling's hand.

'There you go wean – get yourself some sweeties and the like.'

Gabriel Mortimer closed his file folder and smiled at Eileen.

'Well, that was quite an emotional story, would you like another cup of tea?'

'Aye, another cup would be most welcome.' Gabriel quickly returned with two cups and some more biscuits and placed them down in front of Eileen.

'The one thing we haven't touched on are your feelings surrounding, well, you know, the fire and how that all came about.' Eileen picked up her cup and took a sip.

'Aye the fire. After I got over the news about Orla's pregnancy, we managed to find a truce between the two of us. It was no good me banging on at her about what a mistake it all was, after all, she was my own flesh and blood, as was the wean on its way, too. What's a mammy to do? You love your children whatever, don't ye?'

'Love is a gift, one of the greatest gifts God has given to us,' said Gabriel, nodding.

'So, I figured what she really needed was her mammy's help. We could do this thing together, her and I, raise that child.'

'But you never did get to meet Aisling, the fire - sorry to bring that up again - the fire happened, didn't it?'

'Aye, it did. I'd gone to bed that night, after taking me sleeping pill. I have trouble getting off to sleep, you see, so I needs a wee bit of help sometimes. Anyhow, Orla was as big as a house by this point and getting close to giving birth and wouldn't you know it, that good-for-nothing Danny Gallagher was getting cold feet. He said to Orla he didn't believe he was the daddy and therefore was giving his notice. Just like that, can you believe it? Cowardly little shit he was. I knew all along it was too good to be true, he wouldn't stick around, and we were going to have to do this ourselves, but these things have to play themselves out now, don't they?'

'So, what happened?' said Gabriel.

'I'd told Orla time and time again that smoking and drink were bad for the child. She did finally come around to listen to some sense, mind you, but that night - the night that bastard Gallagher let her down, she came home full of it all. And who can blame her?'

'She'd been drinking?'

'Aye, and God-knows what else, when Orla went off the rails she really went off. I did my best to listen through her tears, I tried not to be judgmental, but by God, what I would have done to that little shit if he'd shown his face round ours.'

'So, you went to bed. Did you wake up before . . .?'

'Aye, like I said, I took my little sleeping pill and went straight to sleep. There was nothing else to say or do about things. I left Orla downstairs on her own, smoking, having her drinks and stewing things over. I knew she'd just need some time to get through it all. Well, the next thing I knew I was hearing voices; shouts and screams, it was almost like I was in some sort of dream. I could smell smoke, feel an almighty heat all around, and then everything just went black. And then the next thing I knew, I was waking up – and I was here.'

'God does take care when the inevitable happens, Eileen. There is no need for any unnecessary suffering. He leads everyone gently through that door.' Eileen looked up at Gabriel.

'I never lost my faith in God, Mr. Mortimer, never.'

Gabriel Mortimer spent the rest of his time with Eileen Sullivan helping her decide on her next incarnation. There were many different options available to her such as returning to an earthly life to build on the lessons she had learnt from her previous incarnation. But in the end, Eileen decided on a different manifestation, something she felt she was well suited for.

'Hello, my name is Eileen Sullivan and I'm here to welcome you and help you along on your journey. Now despite what you may think, this isn't quite what it looks like. Aye, I like to call it Purgatory Street. You can think of it as a road that goes from here to there, takes you from your last life to the next stop on your journey. And I should point out, there won't be no judging here. No sins to atone for, none of that, least not on my watch.' Eileen laughed a little to help put her client at ease.

'Now, can I offer ye a wee spot of tea before we dive in and get started proper?'

The Great Dawn of Perfection

The two by two, sat side by side,
enraptured by the view,
each cell intuitively aware,
yet oblivious too.
no need for understanding,
just beingness now,
alive in the moment,
breathe in and breathe out.

An unhurried evolution,
as rocks and stones,
had surely,
would surely be, and had been,
tossed by endless waves,
in time's faithful hands,
to finally evolve,
into perfect single grains of sand.

But back then, before,
in another era,
the world had stretched
its awkward arms.
through chaos and wars,
through progress' charms,
technology and science,
and artifice's distortions,
into a raging birth,
of epic proportions.

The scars of progress
were plain in view,
for those with eyes,
and those who knew.
Giant monoliths,
of concrete and steel,
ascended from the earth.
and up and up,
to the heavens they flew.
each one bigger,
more fireproofed.
totemic symbols,
that shadowed the ground,
believing their own fabled truths.

Then clustered together,
like desperate orphans,
that multiplied and mutated.
unstoppable viruses,

of promised lands,
all gold and golden gated.
while the shanty towns,
of disease and decay,
the hospitals where the prosperous lay,
dead or dying anyway.

And eager minnow businessmen,
took orders from billionaire sharks,
who financed it all through deceit and greed,
and turned base metals into dark.
then there it shimmered.
and there it swayed.
in all its glory days.
revealed and revered,
on a bedrock of sand,
the modern world they had made.

And leaders sat,
in ivory towers,
devising plans and solutions.
promising change,
delivering peace
with nuclear fission.
and oh - how they took,
and took and took,
in tweets they said that taking was good.
all in the name of Allah and God,
Jim Beam and Eurovision.
and all they gave back,

was their tainted blood.

But blood from a stone,
water into wine,
everything that was possible was.
politicians sneered,
and the scientists made note,
the excuse papers wrote,
just because.

But down below,
the skyscraper cathedrals.
amidst the tangled webs,
of asphalt,
steel girders,
superhighways,
and navigation flightpaths.
alongside railway tracks,
cracked oil-spilling pipelines,
under moss and detritus,
where mould and dampness thrive,
we gathered and grew,
but mostly bided our time.

And then it happened,
as sure as it was writ.
the gleaming towers,
were the first things hit.
Symbolism in the simplest of memes.
the grass that took root,

by the offerings of chance,
finding purchase,
in the in-between.
amidst the cracks of the crushed heaps
of concrete and steel,
the vines and creepers too,
were quick to replenish and start anew,
a green revolution,
strident and keen.

Then the fires raged for decades,
some say it was millennia.
a cleansing cremation,
of gas and oil,
rubbish and plastic,
belching toxic pink smoke,
burning bigger holes in the stratosphere.
while gleefully,
the sun smiled - success.
the ozone,
no longer a barrier,
to its fearsome,
ultraviolet caress.

And the seas and oceans
took note and rose up,
and gurgled and laughed,
in murderous mirth.
as their waves began to reclaim,
what was theirs since birth,

drowning all,
in the depths,
from whence it had sprung.

And so,
here we sit and drink it all in.
an antennae that twitches,
in anticipation.
those tiny eyes,
that bask and wait,
for the dawn to reveal,
its glorious fate.

In time, some will return to the waters.
the oceans and streams,
slip out of our shells,
grow gills and fashion fins.
and learn to feed,
from the murky depths,
that over time,
have become rich again,
with nutrients new.
Others may grow limbs,
feathers beaks,
tails and claws,
learn to reproduce in the trees,
burrow in the sand,
walk on two legs or four.

But until that time,
that unhurried time,
we can simply bear witness,
and behold.
relishing in this moment still,
and watch the sun as it breaks,
on the distant vale and hill,
as the great dawn of perfection unfolds.

About the Author

Jude is a composer, musician, recording artist, and author. He has written and produced 20 albums of varied musical styles and genres with songs that include Americana, rock, pop, country, soul, gospel, blues, mariachi, Dixieland, and even a trilogy of spoken word & music albums. His songs have been licensed to numerous TV shows - *Baywatch*, *Cold Squad* and heard in feature films - *Return to Turtle Island*, *The Raffle* (with the soundtrack featuring Elton John and Dan Hill), and his first single, *Lifeline*, reached number 25 in the USA adult contemporary charts.

Between 2009 and 2012 Jude released the back-to-back critically acclaimed albums, *Circo de Teatro*, the sprawling double disc, *Outskirts of Eden*, and his most recent album, *Head Bone Gumbo*, all of which are distributed in the UK/Europe by Proper Records. In April 2011 both Circo and Eden received recognition at the BCIMA Awards winning Concept/Collaboration Album of the Year and Best Artwork/Graphics, respectively. All these albums have garnered rave reviews, receive radio airplay throughout Europe and North America, and have sparked comparisons to Tom Waits, Bob Dylan, and Lyle Lovett.

Jude has co-written two screenplay projects. *Drop Dead Scene* is about an imaginary LA rock band called Fetish and features an edgy 'soundtrack' album of original rock songs – *Neurotic Erotica*. Set in the post-plague future, *Slow Resurrection* follows the life of cowboy troubadour, Leland Frank and features the country soundtrack album *God's Big Radio* – a collection of traditional-sounding americana songs. This project evolved and toured as a multi-media theatrical production, featuring poetry, video, and live music.

In 2016 Jude released his first book of short stories – *Cripples & Creeps* and quickly followed this with a musical memoir – *Unspoken Heaven*. In 2019 he began work on his first novel, *Cybersoul*, which was originally conceived and written in the form of a stage musical.

The novels: *The Underwater Birds* and *A Writer's Prerogative* quickly followed and *Small Cruelties* is his second book of short stories. He lives with his wife in beautiful Cumbria, England. For more information and to listen to his recordings please visit:
www.judedavison.co.uk

A Writer's Prerogative

Revenge - what lengths would someone go to get retribution for perceived betrayal and hurts?

Midnight, Manhattan, and famous reclusive author Carson Crowe, sips his Scotch, stubs out a cigarette, and emails his final book manuscript to his agent . . . then kills himself.

Carefully orchestrating things himself, a week later seven family and friends gather to hear the author's final wishes. Speaking through a pre-recorded video, Crowe reads excerpts from his own bestsellers, the fictional character depictions singling out each person individually and the wrongs they have done him.

Crowe's fascinatingly deceptive stories include two astronauts on a daring space mission; a duplicitous medieval abbot; Satan overseeing her debauched underworld; and a poetry-loving murderer on a prison break.

In turn, each at the gathering finds themselves the target of Crowe's artfully revengeful skewering. But two questions remain - who will inherit his fortune and what is the meaning behind the strange packages the author has gifted to everyone?

The Underwater Birds

For some, running away to join the circus is a dream, but for others it's a last chance for redemption and survival. Traverse the harsh American landscape from the 1930s to the 1960s along with
Ringmaster, Sam O'Reilly, and his self-proclaimed, 'Greatest Show on Earth'.

Behind the mesmerising display of big-top daring tricks, animals, and clowns, are the people. Meet One-Eyed Pete and the tattooed Madeleine, the Midway act 'Beauty & the Beast'; Lee and Kwan, the singing Siamese Twins; Madame O and her mysteriously telling tarot; and Dalvinder Singh, who charms his King Cobra nightly into submission. Each one with a backstory of pain, heartache and skeletons locked away.

In 1962, as Sam lies dying, his circus family pay homage. Revelations unravel, fate unearths a secret, and life takes a twist. For some, everything changes, but for most, the show must go on.

Cybersoul

As the world descends into chaos, a young cyborg tightens the noose around his neck. How could life spiral down into such a black hole? The cyborg terrorist revolutionaries attacking the clones; the riot police retaliating with public hangings; executions being streamed live across the entire sector; and true love failing. The new world order brings a class struggle, social unrest, and injustice where an interracial love has no hope to survive.

Watching over these proceedings is a trio of guardian angels, the Soul Sisters, who are there to remind us that everything and everyone are connected through the universal energy of love.

'Without love, you ain't nothing but a Cybersoul!'

Originally written as an allegorical stage musical, *Cybersoul* was inspired by the U.S. black civil rights movement and soul music of the 1960s. Here, the songs inform each chapter and add a lyrical poetry to the story.

Cripples & Creeps
short stories and a poem

Among these energetic and highly entertaining stories: a suicide victim sits in a Spartan window-less waiting room eager to share his rage with God; a transgendered spy must remain in hiding and navigate the constrictions of a mental institute; a spurned lover has an unexpected liaison with his sexy voiced Satnav; and two old men discover an unlikely friendship as each faces their imminent demise on a hospital palliative ward.

Throughout these ten highly imaginative stories Cripples & Creeps reflects the struggles, epiphanies, desperation, loathing and simple joys of the everyday lives and not-so-everyday lives of people around us, ultimately revealing the layers of humanity in us all. The final story, Luck, ties the entire collection together in an unexpected and original way and reminds us of the fragility, serendipity, and sometimes seemingly random nature of the world we live in.

Uncertain Heaven
a musical memoir

From first picking up a guitar, to writing songs and discovering a connection to the universal source of creativity, Uncertain Heaven is a rock 'n roll memoir that tells the story of one man's creative path, a journey that becomes inextricably intertwined with a search for the meaning of our existence and mankind's relationship with God.

A story of record deals, songs heard by billions on syndicated television shows, the highs and lows of an indifferent music industry, the painful reality of playing 'music-by-the-yard' and the sheer joy of putting your finger up into the ethos and downloading a song - just like Keith Richards.

After years of following the muse wherever she leads, an existential crisis leads the author to peel back the mysteries of life itself, follow what surely seems meant to be, only to find himself standing on the precipice at his own potential demise.